The Elite

CORTNEY BARDIN

ISBN: 978-1-4669-2635-6 (sc)
ISBN: 978-1-4669-2636-3 (hc)
ISBN: 978-1-4669-2634-9 (e)

Library of Congress Control Number: 2012906623

Trafford rev. 04/11/2012

 www.trafford.com

North America & international
toll-free: 1 888 232 4444 (USA & Canada)
phone: 250 383 6864 ✦ fax: 812 355 4082

Dedication

To my mother and my family for always believing in me even when I was rejected. You really gave me the determination to do this.

To my friends who proof-read everything for me and the ones that always told me I'd do this one day.

Last, but not least, to Mr. Jason Cross for being a father to me when I didn't have one. You were always there to threaten a publisher that backed out at the last minute. If you could tell something was wrong, you were there for me to talk to.

Thank you.

CONTENTS

ONE

AUGUST 18TH

I bit my lip and turned my baseball cap backwards on my head. My long blond hair flowed passed my shoulders and I prepared to approach Spencer Kendal. He was eighteen at the time and I was only twelve. I just wanted him to accept me. I'd had a crush on him ever since I first saw him in fourth grade when he was a junior. He had come to our class for a presentation.

He was standing with a bunch of other guys. I hesitated a moment, but swallowed my doubts. I couldn't let his friends intimidate me. I'd be seeing a lot of them if everything worked out as I had planned.

I walked to him and smiled as he dismissed his friends. I was a good bit shorter than he was, but I didn't care. He knelt down to talk to me. His blond hair was cropped short and his blue eyes seemed to shine through me. He was healthy, muscle wise. He wasn't beefed up in a disgusting way, just enough to give him presence.

"Hi, Penelope." he said and my stomach filled with butterflies.

I was smiling uncontrollably. "You know I hate when people call me Penelope." I said.

He smiled and looked into my eyes. "What do you want?" he asked.

"You know what I want." I asked, trying my best to flirt. I knew I wasn't getting very far as he sighed.

1

"Pen, we're in two completely different worlds. I'm getting ready to graduate and go off to college. You're just too young." He sounded sincere.

I frowned. "Once I'm eighteen, it won't matter. Can't you just wait for me?" I asked.

Spencer chuckled. "I wish I could, but I have such a big world waiting." he said.

I took a deep breath. "I won't see you after this year." I said.

Spencer hesitated a moment. "Well, on your eighteenth birthday, I'll come see you." he said.

"Will you kiss me?" I asked.

Spencer smiled. "Yeah, I will." he said.

I wrapped my arms around his neck and he returned the short hug.

"You should get going, Penelope." he said.

I hesitated and swallowed hard. "What will I do until you get back? Guys don't like me." I said.

He smiled and we talked for a couple minutes about what I could do to fix that.

I shook my head, shaking off the memory. My eighteenth birthday was coming up very soon. However, I'd changed. I'm grown up now. I had started dying my hair brown and kept it shorter. It fell to my shoulders. I'd definitely gotten taller. I had started wearing girl clothes and discovered Mary Kay. My chest had filled out and my body had gotten curvy.

I still remembered Spencer though. The day he graduated was the day that I was forced to live with my aunt. My mother had died while giving birth to me. My father left me that day. He just never came back. My aunt didn't care much so I got emancipated from her this year when I proved that she was clinically insane. I had gotten my own job and apartment and using the money my mom had left for me to live. I had been doing just fine by myself. My apartment wasn't that great. I was fairly sure I had a few mice somewhere and mold in a couple of places, but it was what I could manage. I only worked at a little pizzeria a few blocks away.

I couldn't help, but let my mind flash to Spencer as my birthday crept closer. It was only two weeks away. I highly doubted he'd be back, though. He most likely forgot about me. I was such a tomboy. But, after Spencer told me that guys don't like tomboys, I started wearing girl clothes. Now, I'm one of the most attractive girls in the school.

It was mid-August; almost time to start school again.

I took a deep breath and turned on the news.

I had been seeing many reports of some serial killer going around and killing people off randomly. The only factor was that all of them were around my age. I had begun to board up my windows at night. I was terrified. I had no idea why he might want to kill me, but the victims had been random. I especially hated that no one had lived to tell the story of his attack.

My intercom by the door buzzed loudly before I heard the receptionist's voice. "Miss Crowder, a young man down here is asking to come up." she said.

I got up and pressed the button. "Who is it?"

"Jacob Maslin." she said.

I sighed. Jacob. I was going to school with him at the time. He was the quarterback of the football team and had led us to state championships three years in a row.

I pressed the button again. "Let him up." I said.

Two minutes later, two quick knocks rapped on my door. I opened it after making sure it was Jacob.

The black-haired, blue-eyed, beauty looked in at me. "Hey, Babe." he said and smiled. We'd called each other Babe since we were mistaken as a honeymoon couple by a hotel employee in our sophomore year. It had been during the class trip. Jacob had driven us separately just because I hated crowded buses.

"Hey, Jake." I said and stepped aside so he could enter. I closed the door behind him.

"I just wanted to let you know that Gene is throwing a party tonight because her parents are away." he said.

"I don't know." I said. I was a little shaky about going anywhere on an account that that serial killer is out there.

3

He walked up to me and put an arm around my waist, pulling me to his chest. "Oh, come on. We can dance and have a little fun." He paused a moment. "Remember fun?"

"What's that supposed to mean?" I asked.

"You don't want to go anywhere lately. You just stay home with your windows blocked with a book in your hand. We all miss you, Babe." he said as his hand moved from my waist to snaking up to back of my shirt.

"Stop it, Jake. I'll go if you get your hand out of my shirt." I said and smiled at him. He was just being typical Jake. He was such a good friend, but he had his own little way of showing that he cared.

"Thanks, Babe." he said and flashed his car keys. "Go get changed."

I was in sweatpants and a torn t-shirt. I was too lazy to change that morning. I sighed and went to my room. I changed into a pair of torn denim shorts and a tight tube top. I straightened my hair quickly and walked out to Jake. He whistled loudly.

"Stop it." I said, laughing, and we walked out to his Mustang.

On the ride there, I was putting on my make-up. I wanted to look good even if I didn't want to be there.

"You look fine, Penelope." Jake said.

I sighed and closed my eyeliner. "Don't call me that." I said.

"Why? It's your name." he said.

"It was my mother's name." I shoved my eyeliner back into my purse.

"Now, it's your name." he said as he took one of the turns.

"I would change it if I knew how and it didn't cost so much." I said and venom leaked in my words.

Jake shook his head. "Just because your mom's dead doesn't mean you have to change your name. You never met her. You can't say that you miss her or that you don't want to remember her."

I shook my head. I knew he would never know how I felt. I had to grow up with no female figure in my life. He always had his father.

Jake sighed. "Now you're mad." he said.

"No, I'm not." I said and pushed my hair out of my eyes. "I can't blame you for not knowing what it's like."

"What? You didn't even know her. How can it be like anything?" he asked.

"I'm a girl and I grew up without my mother!" I said.

"What does it matter? You had your aunt until you sent her to the insane asylum!" he shouted.

"I want my mother! I would give up my whole world just to have her." I said and shook my head. I bit my lip and I took in a deep breath through my nose. I was fighting the tears and Jake knew it.

"Oh, Babe. Don't do that. Don't cry." He sighed.

"I'm not crying." I said.

"You're going to though."

"No, I won't." I said and my voice cracked. I sighed. *Come on.* I thought to myself. *You're stronger than this.*

"I didn't mean anything by it. Come on. I'm sorry." he said.

I swallowed and wiped the make-up off my face with my sleeve. "I'm fine." I said.

"I'm sorry I brought it up." he said.

"It's not your fault." I promised. "Trust me, Babe." I said and smiled.

We got into the driveway and there were probably fifty cars there. It had to be packed inside. I sighed and got out of the car. Jake followed me.

He took my hand in his, startling me. He'd never held my hand before and we weren't a couple.

"What are you doing?" I asked.

"Just act like we're together for tonight, okay? I don't want anyone to come onto you if they get drunk. That could get bad." he said.

"What?" I asked. I didn't know there'd be alcohol. If I was going to drink, I would have stayed home.

"There are going to be some tough guys here and I don't want them hurting you." he said.

"Okay? When did you ever have to protect me before?" I asked.

"When crazy people are out there that could go around and pick off someone that they wanted to kill that night." Jake said. His voice was protective.

"Wow, Jake. You'd fight one of those guys for me?" I asked.

"Yes, I would. No one should be doing that." he said, his teeth clenched.

I smiled. I'd never seen him like that. I could get used to it. I could start to like it, actually.

I leaned on his shoulder. "Why do we have to *act* like we're together? Why can't we just be together?" I asked.

Jake smiled down at me. "If that's the way you want it, Babe." he said.

I smiled and laced his fingers in mine. *Take that, Spencer. I got over it. You're history.*

Once we were in the house, I smelled the alcohol. I nearly gagged. I hadn't drunk since I lived with my aunt. I wasn't sure how it would affect me anymore. I knew I wasn't getting out of here without drinking.

"Welcome!" Gene shouted as we walked into the house.

"Hey, Gene." Jake said and smiled.

"Jacob Maslin. My, goodness. I never thought you'd come to anything like this." she said and smiled at me. Her blond hair fell well passed her shoulders and her gray eyes shimmered in the light. My eyes fell to the red plastic cup in her hand.

"It's good to see you, too, Gene." Jake said and rolled his eyes.

We entered the house and I immediately saw all the men that were so much larger than me. They were already tipsy and messing around like a bunch of goons. I was afraid to know what they would do when they were really drunk.

"Come on, Babe." Jake said and pulled on my arm. I followed him. I didn't want to be left alone for a moment.

We walked out to the back yard where music was blasting my ears out and lights were flashing. We danced for a while and I started to get really thirsty.

We got out of the crowd and walked to the cooler. I opened it and all I could find was beer. I rolled my eyes and settled for what I had. I cracked one open and took a long swig. It tasted horrible, as beer usually does, but I couldn't change it. I needed something.

"Better?" Jake asked and took a swig of his.

I nodded and took another hearty sip. I knew I shouldn't be drinking and planning on driving home, but I wasn't thinking about it. I just couldn't get the thirst out of me.

"You were thirsty, weren't you?" he said and laughed as I gulped down the rest of the can. I tossed it into the garbage can and sighed.

"Guess so." I said and took a deep breath.

Within the next fifteen minutes, I'd drunk two more beers and I started to feel it. The alcohol was taking effect. It was fabulous. I was laughing and having a great time.

"Come on, Babe. Let's go into the house for a while." he said and laughed as I stumbled. He put an arm around me, holding me up. He was more sober than I was.

We went into one of the back rooms. I was still laughing as I closed the door and kissed his mouth hard.

I stopped when I felt something cold and hard against the side of my head and pulled away. I looked over and Jake had a gun pointed at my head. I swallowed hard and took deep breaths.

"What are you doing, Jake?" I asked.

"Back up. Put your back against the wall. Keep your hands where I can see them or I'll blow your brains out." he said roughly.

I did as told, beginning to sweat. "What are you doing?" I repeated as my voice cracked.

He pointed the gun at my chest. "Shut up, Penelope." he said.

My bottom lip quivered as he locked the door, but never took the gun's barrel away from me. "Please, don't." I said, silent tears rolling down my cheeks.

"Trust me, it won't hurt one bit. I'll make it quick. You're one of the lucky ones. You won't feel a thing. My other missions were harsh." he said and moved the gun barrel so it was just under my chin. "It was torture." he said and pressed the gun harder to my flesh. Fear boiled inside me. How could Jake do this? What had I done to anger him so much? "Drowning, stabbing." He brought his face just a little closer to mine. I felt his hot breath on my cheek. "Draining their blood."

I swallowed and took in a shaking breath.

"I was only told to kill you quickly." he said and pulled the trigger back just a little.

Then, the door busted down. Jake's attention flashed from me to whoever just busted down the door. I closed my eyes and curled into the fetal position on the floor. He fired the gun and I just hoped that he didn't hit whoever was there.

I felt a bullet graze my arm. I held my breath, figuring Jake would kidnap me once he killed whoever was at the door.

To my surprise, Jake wasn't there when I opened my eyes. He'd broken a window and left. The only one who was there was an older man. He had to be at least twenty.

His shaggy blond hair hung in his eyes and the blue of his eyes pierced me. He was better looking than I ever remembered. He held a gun in his hand and was panting.

He spoke only six words. "I told you I'd be back." he said.

I stood and ran to him. I wrapped my arms around him. "Spencer, oh, my God." I said and started crying.

He wrapped his arms around me to keep me from falling. "It's all right now, Pen. He ran off." he promised.

"No, it's not. He'll be back." I sobbed. "Dear God, He tried to kill me."

He hesitated a moment. "We have to get out of here." he said.

"I don't think I can." I said.

Spencer reached down and lifted my body to a cradle at his chest. "I've got you." he said and walked out of the bedroom. There was a crowd by the door.

Everyone clapped quietly as Spencer carried me out. I was shaking. I was so overwhelmed. I mean, I could have been killed and everyone could have just been listening in like there wasn't any danger.

An ambulance pulled into the driveway without its sirens on. The paramedics pulled out a stretcher.

"No, Spencer. Don't make me go with them, please." I said and gripped his shirt in my fists.

"You're in shock, Pen." he said.

"Then, you have to come with me." I said.

Spencer sighed and laid me down on the stretcher. My shaking had continued. My chest was starting to hurt too. I wasn't sure if it was because of being in shock or from my mental panic.

I grabbed Spencer's hand. "Don't leave me." I said and took in a shaking breath.

He smiled and pushed my hair off my sweating forehead. "Don't worry. I'm right here. I'm not going anywhere."

They loaded me into the ambulance and I never let go of Spencer's hand. I couldn't. I was too afraid.

When we got to the hospital, it wasn't any one that I remembered.

"It's the Witness Protection Program's." Spencer confirmed.

They put me into a room and started an IV to keep my shock from getting any worse.

After a few minutes, I'd calmed down a bit. Spencer was still by my side.

"What happens now?" I asked.

"Well, you're officially in the WPP. Once we set up a new identity for you, we'll have to make some minor changes in your appearance and set you up with an agent to guard you. Then, we send you on your way. That simple." he said.

"So, I'll just be given a guard that I have no idea who they are?" I asked.

Spencer smiled. "They've already assigned me to that because of the way you acted with the ambulance."

"I'm sorry, Spencer." I said and shook my head. "I was drunk and scared and . . . " I took a deep breath.

"You were drunk?" he asked.

"I probably still am, a little." I said and slid my hands down my face.

"Jesus, Pen. What were you thinking? You're seventeen." he said, his voice disappointed.

"Yeah, I am. A lot has happened since you left." I said.

"What happened?" Spencer asked. I could hear the concern in his voice. It wasn't overwhelming, but it was there.

"I got emancipated." I said.

"Why did you get emancipated?" he asked.

"My dad left and I had to live with my aunt. She always hit me no matter what I did. So, I proved that she was nuts and got emancipated." I said.

"I'm sorry to hear that." Spencer said.

"No, you're not." I said and shook my head. "Everyone who says that is lying."

Spencer raised an eyebrow. "Have you ever known me for being 'everyone'?" He put air quotes around the word.

"No." I said and smiled. "Everyone else doesn't want to be some sort of agent chasing down serial killers."

"No, they don't. Now you know why I couldn't stay after I graduated." he said and leaned back in his chair.

"Yeah." I said and sighed. "Thank you for busting down the door today."

He smiled. "It's my job."

"Yeah, I know." I said.

"You were close to him, weren't you?" Spencer asked.

"We've been friends for a long time."

"I'm sorry you had to find out that way." he said.

"I couldn't believe it." I said and smiled. "I should have known."

"You had no way to know, Pen."

"I should have. I took every precaution to protect myself and the one night I go out and have a little fun, I'm taken into the Witness Protection Program!" I said and sighed. It was too much to take in. My best friend had turned out to be the serial killer that I'd feared, I had gotten drunk and been stupid enough to fall into his game, and I was in the Witness Protection Program.

"If I could have gotten to you any quicker, I would have." he said.

"I know." I said.

He sighed. "Why don't you just go to sleep?" he said.

I smiled. "I'm gonna have a monster hangover when I wake up." I said.

When I fell asleep, it was peaceful. It was nothing like the real world.

TWO

AUGUST 19TH

My head was pounding as we drove. I closed my eyes and sighed. Spencer chuckled.

"I never thought I'd see the day when cute little Penelope would be hung over in my car." he said and chuckled.

"Shut up." I said and groaned. "Where are we going?"

"I told you that we have to set up a new identity for you." he said. "That happens in the sectional WPP building under-ground."

"Okay." I said.

We exited the freeway onto a dirt road path that was mainly hidden by trees and branches. From that, we went down a spiral ramp until we arrived at a small building.

When we stopped, Spencer got out first and I followed. We went into a building whose walls were completely mirrors. I looked like I'd been up for months.

We got into a room with a huge computer. The screen covered the entire wall and the key board was as touch screen and as big as the usual plasma screen television.

"Holy crap." I said.

A beautiful woman was standing by the computer. Her shoulder length light red-brown hair shined lightly. Spencer walked to her and hugged her. He kissed the top of her head.

"Thank God, Spence. You scared me. There was a huge report on the shooting!" she said and smiled.

"Well, I tell you not to worry. Maybe you should start listening." he said.

That's when I noticed the woman's wedding ring. My heart sank. I should have guessed as much.

"Come over here, Penelope." Spencer said. I did as told.

The woman started speaking as she slid her fingers across the touch screen. "We've already chosen your last and middle names. You get to choose your first name. You can obviously change your last and middle names if you'd like."

"Whatever you came up with is fine." I said.

"Any first names in mind?" she asked.

"I guess I've always liked the name Thea." I said and smiled at Spencer. I had been obsessed with that name.

The woman laughed. "I'm assuming you two know each other?" she asked.

"We went to school together, Amanda." Spencer said.

She raised an eyebrow. "She seems a bit young for you two going to school together." she said.

Spencer smiled. "In the school we used to go to, the fourth graders had lunch the same time as the juniors and fifth graders the same time as seniors. She was in both of my lunches with me and we saw each other outside pretty often." he said.

Amanda's smile widened. She looked to me.

"I had the biggest crush on you ever." I said and laughed. My head protested.

Amanda laughed. "So, you were the same romancer you are now?" she asked.

"No. She just had a thing for me." he said as she rearranged a bunch of stuff on a driver's license layout.

"Your license is done. Now, we have to go do your hair." she said. "This might take a while, Spence. Go do something to occupy yourself."

Spencer just smiled and looked at me. "Will you be all right?" he asked.

"I'll be fine." I said as I saw Amanda grab a gun out of the drawer and load it into her belt.

"Nothing's getting passed me, Spencer." she said.

Once she started, there was no stopping.

"What's your natural color?" she asked.

"Blond." I said.

"Well, let's welcome back the blond." she said and started mixing the color.

After about two hours, the color was set. It was my normal blond. I used to love it, but now I don't. I hated it.

"It needs to be longer." she said.

As she was tying on the extensions, she and I spoke.

"So, you knew Spencer when you were young?" she asked.

"We went to school together, but it wasn't much beyond that. When he graduated, he promised he would come back on my eighteenth birthday and kiss me." I said and smiled. It sounded so ridiculous now.

"I could picture Spencer saying that." she said. "I've only known him since he came here at eighteen. He was young and ready to be out there. That Spencer just wanted to go out and track down every single criminal and gun them down."

"I could picture that." I said and smiled. "How old were you when you met him?" I asked.

"I was only an intern. I was twenty." she said.

"Oh." I said and sighed.

"He's still as hot as ever, isn't he?" Amanda asked.

I smiled. I couldn't believe I was having this conversation with *her*.

"I like his long hair. It suits him." I said.

"I love it, too." she said.

She laid her left hand down on the counter for a moment. It was definitely a wedding ring. "I love your ring." I said and smiled, hoping to get some answers.

She smiled. "Thanks. Oliver has good taste." she said.

"Oliver?" I asked, excitement growing in me.

"He's my husband. We've been together since I was twelve. Married since I was twenty. Just before I met Spencer."

After another four hours of talking and tying extensions, she finished the last one and let me look. Now, my hair fell just beyond my breasts. I liked it long. I could play with it now.

"I love it." I said and smiled at my reflection.

"You can do the same with these that you do with your natural hair." she said.

"Good."

"Now, when you get to your new home, the closet should be filled with a new wardrobe." she said.

I rolled my eyes. *Great.*

She took the picture that would go on my driver's license and printed the license.

"He should be waiting for you." she said and smiled. "Get to know him. He's a great guy." she said.

"I will." I said and walked out to see Spencer waiting for me.

He smiled. "I remember your blond hair." he said and touched a single lock of it.

"Me, too. I hated it. My dad wouldn't let me dye it." I said and smiled.

"You told me that." he said.

"I know." I said and chuckled to myself.

We left to go to our new home. Oh, joy. I get to live with a man that is six years older than me. It just makes matters worse that I'm still attracted to him.

He handed me my license, passport, and my new birth certificate. "You are not Penelope Ann Crowder. Your name is Thea Marie Vogel. I'm just your older brother from a different father. My name hasn't changed." he said.

"Got it." I said and smiled.

"If you have suspicion about anyone, let me know. I can get a background check on them faster than you would think." he said.

"Okay." I said and pulled my hair over one shoulder.

We got to the house nearly three hours later and I went straight to the closet. I needed to get a shower and get changed.

"Thank you for everything." I said and smiled. "I know this must be a huge nuisance for you. I mean, you're babysitting a teenager." I looked at Spencer.

"Guarding and babysitting are two entirely different things, Thea." he said.

"Maybe, but I am still a child. Children can be a real nuisance." I said.

"It's not a nuisance. If it was, they wouldn't have put me with you. They would have found someone else." he said.

I paused for a second.

"How long have you guys known that Jake was the killer?" I asked.

Spencer sighed. "It may have been a week and a half. Every time we think we have him, he runs off too quickly. We thought for sure that we were going to catch him before he left your apartment, but he got through the holes in our plan."

"How long have you known he was after me?" I asked even though my breath was a bit shaky. I hated to think that someone was actually trying to kill me.

"Ever since we found the pattern in his attacks, we've known who he was going for next. When they told me it was you, I was after him as soon as I could." he said.

"You never intended to come back for my eighteenth birthday, did you?" I asked.

He smiled. "No. I figured you'd forgotten about it." he said and chuckled. "I didn't want to show up on your doorstep and you not remember me in the least. That would have been the most embarrassing thing I've ever done." he said and tossed his hair out of his eyes.

I smiled. "You do know that my life has sucked since you left, right? I've been looking forward to my eighteenth birthday ever since you told me that when I was twelve." I said.

He didn't break his gaze from mine. "I can still keep my promise."

"No, you can't, Spencer. I can't do that to you." I said and grabbed a pair of sweat pants and a t-shirt. "Now, if you'll excuse me, I need a shower." I said.

I sighed when I realized I had no idea where the bathroom was. I looked at Spencer. "Where's the bathroom?"

"Last door on the right." he said and smiled.

I walked down the hall to find the bathroom in the exact place he told me it was.

After I was done, I simply came back the way I went and found the washer. A hamper was sitting next to it. I tossed my clothes in and decided I'd do it later.

I tied my hair up in a ponytail and sat on the couch.

"So," I began as I looked at Spencer, who was sitting in the arm chair. "Is someone going to be joining us? Maybe there's girlfriend of yours?" I asked.

Spencer smiled. "I haven't had a girlfriend since I graduated." he said.

"You had a girlfriend when you graduated? Who?" I asked.

"Marcy Keller." he said and chuckled.

I groaned. "The slut." I said and covered my mouth. I looked at Spencer. "Sorry."

"No problem. I've heard worse." he said.

"I've said worse." I said.

"Trust me. I'm not the saint I used to be either."

"Are you a virgin?" I asked.

He chuckled. "Now, *that* is confidential." he said.

"Ha. You are." I said and laughed. But, I knew very well that he wasn't. No matter how much he wanted to set a good example, I highly—very highly—doubted that he was a virgin.

"That is none of your business, young lady." he said.

I just laughed harder at his usage of words. I couldn't help it. Only my father had ever called me "young lady". Spencer had no resemblance to my father so it was funny. I kind of had to laugh off the pain at the thought of my father as well.

I calmed and smiled. "Sorry. That was funny." I said.

He sighed. He stood and I noticed the gun in his belt.

"Do you carry that everywhere?" I asked.

"Now I do." he said. "So, I heard that you get into a lot of trouble in school now."

"I'm in a lot of fights and I back-mouth a lot." I said and sighed.

"You sure seemed like you weren't starting anything last night." he said.

"I was trying to lay low."

"Then, why were you drunk?" he asked.

"I don't know. I'm dumb." I said.

Spencer was quiet. Then, he walked from the room and spoke while he walked. "I forgot about something." he said. He returned in a matter of moments with a lighting shaped necklace.

"What's this for?" I asked.

"It's a tracking device." he said, his voice serious. "You need to wear it at all times."

I pulled it from his fingers. "Why? It's not like I'm going to run away." I said and looked at the necklace. The lightening shape was probably two inches long. It was silver. It would tuck neatly under my shirt.

Spencer shook his head. "I know you're not going to run away, but Jacob could come find you at any time. We want to be able to know where you are." he explained.

"No privacy. Got ya." I said and secured the clasp under my damp hair. It's not that I didn't like the necklace, because I did, but I hated when someone knew every step I took.

"We won't activate it unless we are worried, Thea." he said.

I simply shook my head. "Right." I said. Spencer was silent.

"So, do you want to talk? Get to know each other a bit?" he asked after a while.

"I don't care. What do you want to talk about?" I asked.

He hesitated a moment. "What about your dad?" he asked.

I took a deep breath. "Why would I want to talk about my father?" I asked.

"I figured you'd want to talk about it with someone. I mean, no one has ever tried to help you with it." He paused. "You've been alone."

"Yeah, I have. That's the way I've liked it." I said. I didn't want him in that part of my private life. My father is the touchiest memory I have. I just wanted to have it hidden in the deepest, darkest pits in my mind. I didn't want anyone to know. "That's also the way I'd like it to stay."

"If that's how you want it. I'm here to listen though. You can talk to me any time." he promised.

"Amanda set some rules too. I have to know where you are at all times and you can't get into trouble at school."

"Wow." I said and sighed. "You just take away all the fun, don't you?"

"We can't afford for you to draw attention. At least until we can catch Jacob." he said.

"I'm gonna miss him." I said and started remembering everything we did together.

"Thea, all the stuff you thought you knew about him . . . " he paused. "It was all staged. Not one word of what he ever told you was true. He wasn't who you thought."

"Then, who is he?" I asked.

"He's a cold-hearted, perverted criminal. He's twenty-six." He looked at me. "He's older than me."

I sighed. Why was I so naïve? All the evidence was right in front of me. Jacob had always been the tallest guy. He's always been the one that looked the most mature. I never thought about it.

"God, why hadn't I noticed?" I asked, my chest tightening. "I could have prevented this from happening." I said as my voice cracked.

Spencer looked back at me. "There was no way to prevent it, Thea. He knew who he was after for years now."

I took a deep breath. "I just made this all harder by getting close to him." I said.

"You did, but you couldn't have known. No one thinks they're going to be targeted by a serial killer." he said.

"No one should have to think about that." I said and bit my lip. "I'm going to bed." I said and stood up, walking back the hall.

"Thea?" Spencer said.

I looked around the corner at him. "Yes?" I asked.

He smiled. "I'm sorry this happened." he said.

"It wasn't your fault." I said.

"I could have caught him before he got to you." he said.

I shook my head. "Good night, Spencer." I said.

I sat in my bedroom, blankets up to my neck. I couldn't sleep. I knew I wouldn't be able to. I hated being here. I wanted to be in my own apartment with my same old bedroom with my same old bed.

I especially didn't want to be here with Spencer. It was the worst thing that could have happened. It was Spencer! This guy was six years older than me. I had a crush on him for years. He had promised me a kiss on my eighteenth birthday.

There was no way I'd survive this.

THREE

"You're taking martial arts classes." Spencer told me when I got out of bed. I had barely slept until around four that morning. It was only seven then. Three hours of sleep definitely wasn't enough.

"Why would I do that?" I asked.

"You'll need to know how to fight in case I'm not there one day. That way, you won't be defenseless." he explained.

"When do they start?" I asked.

"Whenever I feel like giving you a lesson." he said, turning the page in the newspaper.

I sighed. We sat in silence for a while.

"Are you hungry?" Spencer asked.

I shook my head. "Not really."

Spencer looked up from the paper. "You're lying." he said. I had been. I didn't want to bother him. He *was* being forced to babysit me, after all. He folded the paper and laid it on the table.

"So?" I asked and crossed my arms over my chest.

He chuckled. "Go get dressed. We'll go get something." he said.

I swallowed. "Spencer, I don't have money. All my money was in that apartment."

Spencer raised an eyebrow. "You think I'm broke? I'm getting paid a good amount to live with you." He smiled.

I bit my lip. "I'm sorry about that."

"If I didn't want the position, I wouldn't have accepted it. I'd rather you have me than some guy you don't know." He stood. "I mean, it's not like we're strangers. I want you to be comfortable when you're in the WPP."

"Don't you want a life?" I asked. "I mean, you're a man." I swallowed. "You have needs, too. What about a girlfriend?"

Spencer simply put his hands in his pockets and smiled. "To anyone I meet, you're my sister. I can still have a life. I can always have someone keep an eye on you when I'm gone, Thea."

"I never thought about that." I said.

"You could even just go in with Amanda and Oliver for a short amount of time. Amanda loves you. You're just like she was when she was seventeen." he said.

I went to get dressed after that. After I did, we went to a coffee house for breakfast. I just got a chocolate chip muffin and a coffee with two sugars and a cream. It was the way I'd drank it since I was thirteen.

The coffee house was somewhat full, but not enough to make the waiter very busy.

When a couple of boys walked in, I didn't think much of it. You could tell they were gay, but it didn't bother me. I'd never had a problem with homosexuality.

The shorter boy, obviously younger, was as cute as a small child. His dark hair was a little longer it the front where it came to a very short point. He didn't look gay, but the way the two were holding hands gave it away. He was thin, but had some muscle mass. He had to be seventeen or so. No older than eighteen though.

The other boy, definitely the older of the two, had shaggy dirty-blond hair and brown eyes that shined. He didn't look gay either. He had to be nineteen or older. He looked fully grown and had at least two or three inches on the younger boy. He was definitely the hotter of the two as well.

They took a seat at a circular table. There were only two chairs. They sat across from each other and held hands across the table as they waited for the waiter.

The waiter didn't smile at them. In fact, when he spoke, it was very soft.

"Go find somewhere else to go. You're not welcome here. We don't serve homos here." he said and left the table.

My hands clenched into fists as my temper flared. It seemed as if I was the only one in the coffee house that noticed his remark.

"Don't get involved, Thea. We can't afford the attention." Spencer said.

"I'm not going to let him treat them like that." I said through my teeth.

The younger boy went to the counter to talk to the waiter. He simply ignored him.

"Please. We're not trying to cause any trouble." the boy said. He had a higher pitched voice, but I wouldn't have guessed that he was gay from that.

"If you're not trying to cause trouble, then leave. I told you once. We don't serve you people." the waiter said, louder this time. Anger boiled in me as the boy headed back to his table silently. He looked disappointed and very hurt. I hoped to God he wouldn't cry. If he did, I'd be ready to explode.

I stood up. "That's not fair." I said to the waiter. Both of the boys looked at me. So did the waiter. Everyone else in the coffee house abandoned their conversations, giving me their full attention. I swallowed my fear and continued. "You can't refuse to serve them. They're as much of a human as you are. More of a man than you, that's for sure." I heard a few gasps from the other customers.

"They're gay!" the waiter shouted. "They are more of women than men!"

"At least they had the courage to come out and admit it. I can guarantee that you wouldn't admit it if you were gay." I said and walked over to the boys.

"It's not natural. Would you want your kids seeing this?" the waiter asked.

"If I had children, then, yes, I would. I'd want them to know that there are people that are different and I appreciate what they are and what they choose. We have to learn to live with different people. Besides, it's not your decision. What? Are you afraid of change? You coward." I shouted at him.

"If you want, we can go somewhere else." I said and smiled at them. They smiled back.

The younger boy looked at the older boy. He held out his hand. I shook it.

"I'm Josh and this is my boyfriend, Jayden." the younger boy said. He smiled. "We really appreciate that."

"Trust me, it was my pleasure." I said and looked to the waiter, making my voice louder, making sure to catch his attention. I turned back to Josh and Jayden. "I'm Thea, by the way."

"It's a pleasure to meet you, Thea." Jayden said. His voice wasn't as high-pitched as Josh's, but something about it made me think of him being gay. He seemed to have a feminine vibe coming from him.

"Why don't we just go somewhere else? We can talk freely somewhere else." I said and Jayden stood, pulling up Josh with him. "One second." I said and walked to Spencer. "You're not homophobic anymore, are you?" I asked in a very low tone.

"No, I'm not." Spencer said and laughed at the memories. He hadn't made his fear apparent to anyone, but he'd avoided gay people forever.

"Then, get your coffee and let's go." I said.

He did and his lips came to my ear. "That was amazing."

"Thank you." I said.

We started walking with Josh and Jayden and I learned a great deal about them. We didn't know that nearly everyone in the coffee house had left after we did.

Josh's parents were very accepting of him being gay and they were happy that he was happy. Jayden's parents weren't so accepting. They've been together for three years. Josh was seventeen and went to the school I was attending while Jayden was nineteen and in his freshman year in college. They had met when they were young children and had been best friends ever since they could remember.

"That's amazing." I said and smiled. "It must be nice to be so close to someone like that."

"Yes, it is." Josh said and smiled.

"So," Jayden began. "What's the deal between you two? You seem pretty close."

CORTNEY BARDIN

I hesitated. "This is Spencer. He's my brother." I said.

Spencer just smiled. He must have thought it was pretty funny that I went through with him being my brother. I guess he thought I was going to back out and say we were friends or something.

"I see." Josh said and studied both Spencer and I for a moment. "I don't see the resemblance."

"Uh . . ." I said. Spencer spoke before I remembered what we were supposed to be.

"We have different fathers." Spencer said.

Josh simply nodded. He was suspicious. *Wonderful.* I was just getting to know him and he's already suspicious of me.

"That makes sense, I suppose." Josh said.

We soon left Josh and Jayden to their business and resumed with ours by going home.

"You are the only American teenager I know that would defend gays. I mean, you didn't even mind when people stared at you." Spencer said and smiled.

"I'm not normal. What can I say?" I said and we both laughed.

Spencer just continued smiling as we walked back home. When we got home, Spencer made me change into a work-out outfit. I just put on a tank top and a pair of shorts. I pulled my hair into a ponytail and put on sneakers.

I went to the basement and Spencer was waiting for me. He hadn't bothered to change. I frowned.

"Why didn't you change?" I asked.

"Why should I? I'm not the one who's training. I already put in my year of that." he said.

"Well, to protect myself, all I need is a gun." I said.

"You won't always have a gun, Thea. You probably never will if I'm not with you."

"Why not? I can buy one." I said.

"That's not the point." Spencer said. "If you don't have a gun by chance, how will you protect yourself then?"

I swallowed and stayed silent.

"If it was Jacob, you'd freeze." Spencer was provoking me. He wanted me to break, to hit him. "You wouldn't know what to do. You two were really close."

24

I curled my fingers into fists and bit the inside of my lip.

"At least, that's what you thought."

My lip started to bleed as my anger grew and I bit harder.

"I mean, he was smart. He used you for his own gain. He got close to you so he could snap and you would have never expected him."

"Shut up." I said through my clenched teeth.

"You let him get close. You were suspicious from the very beginning, but you still let him close."

My nails were digging into my palm. Sweat beaded on my forehead. Everything about it just made me nervous and upset. I hated to be taunted and it was about something like this. I already blamed myself.

His lips came to my ear. "You were just too naïve." he whispered.

I couldn't stop myself. I pulled my elbow back and hit him in the stomach. I turned and punched him across the mouth. I grabbed his right wrist and twisted it behind him and pressed it to his back roughly so he was flat on his stomach on the floor.

"I told you to shut up." I said and released him. I swallowed back the tears that had come and wiped my bloody palms on my shorts. I took deep breaths and Spencer stood up. I made my way to a wall to lean my back against it.

"You know more than I thought." Spencer said, rubbing his wrist. I bit my lip again. "Are you all right, Thea?"

"No. You're right about everything. God, I was naïve and stupid to trust him. I was too suspicious about him to just let him waltz into my life like that." I said and a tear fell down my cheek. I wiped it away with the back of my hand.

Spencer sighed. "No, I wasn't, Thea. I was just trying to make you angry. I didn't mean it."

I took in a breath through my mouth and let it out of my nose. "Whether you meant it or not, it's true." I said.

"Come on, Thea. You know that I can't handle tears." Spencer said.

I laughed. "No, I didn't. If I had, I would have cried in fifth grade to get you to run away with me."

Spencer smiled. "I don't think I would have gone that far."

"I think you would have." I said and we both started laughing.

"God, I miss those days. Everything was easy and this job was only a dream to me. Plus, you were the funniest little tomboy I'd ever met." Spencer said.

"Was I really that bad?" I asked.

"You wore men's clothes, Thea. You were a hard-core tomboy." Spencer said and we were both laughing. It was so easy to laugh with him.

"Maybe, but I still got your attention. That was my main goal." I said.

"I think I noticed that, Thea." Spencer said, still laughing.

"Your friends always made fun of me after we talked. I always saw them laughing with you." I said.

"You didn't see me tell them to knock it off every single time." Spencer said. "I bet if I had waited for you, you'd still love me."

"I do love you, Bro." I said and tousled his hair.

"You know what I mean, Thea." He straightened his hair out with his hand.

"I don't think I would have. If I would have, my feelings wouldn't have changed over five years. Or, at least, they would have returned when I saw you." I said. "They never did. So, it was just a crush."

We went through a whole lesson on martial arts before I went upstairs to get a shower.

I cursed myself for being such an idiot. I should have told him. But, I was too much of a coward.

I got downstairs and Spencer was reading the newspaper. When he saw me, he read the headline out loud.

"'*Ode to the One Who Got Away.*'" Spencer said.

"Is it about the shooting?" I asked.

He nodded. "They're saying that you're the lucky one." Spencer said and continued reading.

I laughed. "When you read the newspaper, you look like an old man." I said.

Spencer smiled and ran a hand through his hair. "I'm one good-looking old man. I still have all my hair."

"No. I see a bald spot from here." I said and laughed.

"That's very funny, Thea." Spencer said and rolled his eyes.

"I think I'm pretty funny." I said and sat beside him.

"You would." he said.

"Be nice. You have to deal with me until Jacob's gone." I said and laughed.

"That could be very soon." Spencer said.

"Why?" I asked.

"They think they have him and his lackeys cornered. But, we can't be sure. We'll know the rest when they find out." Spencer said and sat down his paper.

I sighed. "You had my hopes up, Spence." I said.

Spencer smiled. "Don't worry. We'll get him." he said and put a hand on my shoulder. It sent a zap of energy through my entire body. I ignored it because I was almost sure that he didn't notice it.

"It's hard not to worry when he tried to kill me. He's still trying." I said and swallowed hard.

Spencer's smile faded. "No one is getting past me, Thea. I promise."

"I'm not only worried about me. I don't want you to get hurt trying to protect me, Spencer." I said.

"I doubt that will happen. Jacob is terrified of me. I've been after him on this case for a good while. I always seem to find him a moment too late, though." Spencer said and sighed. "I could gave had him last time."

"He got away, though." I said.

"He won't be out for long." Spencer promised.

"I hope not." I said.

I sat for a while and noticed how hungry I had become. "What do you want for dinner?" I asked. I'd become a pretty good cook over the years.

He raised an eyebrow. "*You're* going to cook?" he asked.

I smiled. "I've got some skill." I laughed. "What all do you have here that I can work with?"

"There probably isn't anything. Amanda isn't notorious for stocking up the cupboards." Spencer said.

"Then, I'm going to the store." I said.

Spencer sighed and got up. "Then, I have to come too."

"No, you don't, Spencer." I promised him.

"It's my job, Thea."

"You don't have to follow me when I'm going for five minutes and I'll be right back." I said and grabbed the keys.

"I'm not chancing it." Spencer said and took the keys from me.

"At least let me drive." I begged.

"No way. It's my car, so it's my rules." Spencer said and smiled playfully.

I sighed. "Jerk." I muttered.

Spencer's smile widened and he opened the door. "Come on."

I followed him and sat quietly in the passenger's seat.

While we were in the store, I saw a familiar face. He had gone to my school when I was twelve. He'd recognize me. His name was Weston Pickett. He had blond hair, a lip ring to the right of his lip, and a body that any man would die for.

We'd been best friends when we were twelve.

"Crap." I said.

"What?" Spencer asked.

"Don't do anything noticeable." I said and Weston looked at us. He smiled and walked to me.

"Penelope?" he asked, his smiled only widening.

Spencer looked at me. "Excuse us a moment." Spencer said to Weston and he pulled me aside. "Explain." he ordered.

"He went to our school when I was twelve. Weston isn't one to forget me." I said quietly.

"Why not?"

"I was his first kiss." I admitted.

"Jesus." Spencer said.

"What are we gonna do now that he knows who I am, Spencer?" I asked.

"Lie."

We walked over to Weston.

"Look, I'm not who you think I am, so, you may want to leave." I said.

Weston chuckled. "I'd recognize you anywhere." he said.

"My name isn't Penelope." I said as I crossed my arms over my chest.

"You always were a bad liar." he said.

I swallowed.

"So, what are you doing here?" Weston asked.

"I don't know what you mean. I just moved here from Iowa." I said.

"Sure you did." Weston said and laughed.

Spencer bit the inside of his lip.

Weston stepped closer to me. "Why exactly are you hiding, Penelope?"

I clenched my hands into fists. "My name's not Penelope." I said through my clenched teeth. "Why don't you just leave me alone?" I asked.

"Why should I?" he asked. He was smiling. "I haven't seen you in ages and I've had absolutely no connection to you." He was tormenting me. He wanted me to give in. He wanted me to admit it.

I gave Spencer my best "help me" look. He nodded.

"We have to get going, Thea." Spencer said and grabbed me by the arm.

Weston never took his gaze from me. He knew my identity as well as I did. I wasn't fooling him for a second. We'd been best friend for as long as I could remember and walking away was the absolute hardest thing I had to do to him.

"I'll do a background check on him. If he knows your old name, we'll need some way to keep his mouth shut if Jacob hasn't gotten to him." Spencer insisted as he walked us to his car. "In the meantime, don't talk to him. We can't chance anything."

"The only criminal record Weston has is shoplifting when he was eleven. Trust me; he's a nice guy." I said as I put on my sunglasses.

"You can't trust anyone. No matter how much you think you know them, it can all change once money is involved. Jacob could pay off Weston in a heartbeat." he said and pulled out of the parking lot.

"Weston's different. He'd never accept it." I said. I was growing even more insistent. He was the only thing left from my other life. I wanted to keep it.

"You can never guarantee that." Spencer said.

I shook my head. "Loosen up." I muttered.

Spencer looked angry. "Jacob almost *killed you*! How am I supposed to loosen up after that? That bullet was not even a foot from killing you!" Spencer yelled.

"That has absolutely nothing to do with Weston."

"It has everything to do with him! We don't know if he's working for Jacob. Jacob could have picked him off from the top list of people that knew you when you were young."

I sighed. "What you're all missing is that Jacob isn't the big man here! Someone hired him!"

Spencer looked at me and back at the road. "What?"

"Someone is telling him who to kill and how to do it." I said and took a deep breath.

"That's not possible. Everything is traced directly to Jacob and no further." he said.

"It's true. He told me before he tried to shoot me. He said that his other missions were harsh. *Missions*, Spencer! He's being sent to do these things!" I yelled.

Spencer shook his head. "How did we miss that?" he asked himself.

"I don't know." I said and sighed.

"Why didn't you tell me earlier?" he asked.

"I figured you knew."

"Well, I didn't."

"I'm sorry." I said.

"You didn't know." he said as he tried to calm himself down.

"I should have. I should have known everything. I should have known that something with Jacob wasn't right and I should have known that you didn't know that he wasn't acting alone."

Spencer sighed. "No, you shouldn't have. It's fine, Thea. We'll just have to change some things." he said and smiled at me. "We're always ready for stuff like this to happen."

"Does this mean I'll have to stay with you longer?" I asked.

"Yes. We're going to have to find the big guy. That's going to be worse than just finding Jacob." Spencer explained.

"It's not impossible, right?" I asked as my hope faded.

"No, but pretty damn close." he said and ran a hand through his hair.

I swallowed hard. "I'm sorry I'm causing so much trouble. I wouldn't have blamed you if you had just handed me over to Jacob the minute you knew it was me. All I ever was to you and your friends was a nuisance."

"To my friends you were, but I thought it was cute." he said.

"What was so cute about having your own twelve year old stalker?" I asked.

"You weren't a stalker." he said and chuckled at the memory. "I thought you were really nice. You were persistent, too. I've never seen a girl that would fight for what she wanted as much as you did. It was adorable."

I couldn't help, but laugh. No guy had ever called me adorable; whether that was my present or past self.

"What's so funny? I'm telling the truth." he asked and smiled.

"Just, coming from you, it's funny." I said as I tried my best to calm my laughter.

"It's funny that I cared about you, whether you thought so or not?" Spencer asked, suddenly serious.

I looked at him. "Cared about me? What do you mean by that?"

"I mean that, if your father had left before I did, I probably would have been the first to offer to take you in. Even if I was young, I cared, Thea." His voice was sober and he looked completely serious.

I couldn't believe he'd just said that. "You would have ruined everything you created for yourself over a twelve-year-old kid?" I asked.

"It wouldn't have ruined everything. I would have figured it out." he insisted.

"Spencer, if you're just saying this to make me feel better, stop. I can't take it." I said and took a deep breath.

"I don't tell lies, Thea." Spencer said and turned into the driveway.

I sighed. "You are lying. You're just trying to make me feel better for being such a lovesick puppy." I opened my door.

"No, Thea, I'm not. Have you ever known me for being a liar?" Spencer asked before I could get out of the car.

"No." I said.

"Then, why would I start lying now?" Spencer paused. "I'm being nothing but honest, Thea."

I bit my lip. "I'm overreacting. I'm sorry. I guess I'm just a little stressed out." I said and ran my fingers through my hair.

"You've been *a little* stressed out?" Spencer chuckled. "You've been through a lot these past couple days. I know you're stressed. I don't blame you for being so stressed. It's hard to have to completely change your life in a matter of a morning."

We got back into the house and I just made spaghetti with what I'd picked up from the store while we were there. That is, before we ran into Weston.

"Hallelujah! You actually cooked and didn't burn down the house." Spencer said playfully.

"I wouldn't be making fun of me if you want to eat." I said and smiled.

As we ate, I thought about my life before Spencer left. Mostly, I thought about my dad. I missed him more than I could ever explain. I was always his little girl and I meant everything to him. He'd always come home from work, take off his jacket, and kiss my forehead. It wasn't rare in any way for us to say that we loved each other. We always had an amazing time together. We had never fought.

But, one day, I got home from school and he never came back. My aunt had to come pick me up and I cried for a month straight. I couldn't believe he'd done that to his little girl. My aunt had to explain to me that he'd left and was never coming back. Of course, she wasn't even that nice about it.

I swallowed back my pain. I hated my father for leaving me at such a vulnerable age. I just wanted him back. We didn't even fight before he left. He just never came home. My father was the first man to break my heart.

I finished eating and just sat at the table.

"Are you okay, Thea?" Spencer's voice broke my haze.

I took a breath in through my nose. "I'm fine." I said.

"You don't look like it." he said. He sounded sincerely concerned.

"I'm fine." I repeated and left the room. I went to my bedroom and sat on my bed. My heart clenched in my chest and a single sob escaped me. I shouldn't have been crying over my dad, but it was just painful. He was a jerk that left his daughter for dead in a huge house. I hated him for doing that to me, but I couldn't help, but remember how much I had loved him. I just wanted to be daddy's little girl again. I missed him.

Before I knew it, I was crying into my pillow. I was muffling it so Spencer wouldn't be concerned.

I had to let it out. I had no other way. I'd never talked to anyone about it because no one wanted to hear it. I didn't want to talk to Spencer about it. He would never understand. He doesn't understand how hard and depressing losing both of your parents before you turn thirteen really was.

I just could never escape it. My mother was never coming back and all my information was gone so my father would never be able to find me if he really tried.

I calmed myself and washed my face. I was in the middle of drying it when Spencer knocked on my door. I opened it and smiled weakly at him. I couldn't manage anything more.

"Are you sure you're okay?" he asked, leaning against my doorframe.

"I'm fine, Spencer." I said and put more effort into my smile. It was hard, but I think I pulled it off.

He looked me in the eyes. I could see an oblivious sympathy clouding his eyes. "You can always talk to me. You know that, right?" he asked.

"I know, Spencer." I paused, fabricating my next lie. "But, there's nothing to talk about."

As I tried to close the door, Spencer put his hand on it so I couldn't.

"Weston's right. You suck at lying." Spencer said and smiled. "Now, tell me what's wrong."

I sighed. "Please, just drop it, okay? I don't want to talk about it." Unfortunately, my voice cracked. I cursed myself for even opening the door. I could have given myself more time.

"You're upset about something." he said.

"It doesn't matter." I said and actually closed the door this time. It wasn't long before he was knocking again.

"Come on, Thea. Let me in." he pleaded.

"No. Just let it go and leave me alone." I said and pulled my hair out of the pony-tail. It was only irritating me.

"All that's going to do is make you feel worse." he said.

"*Leave me alone.*" I repeated.

"I'm coming in."

He opened the door. I was sitting on my bed with my knees to my chest. My arms were wrapped around my legs, holding them there. My chin was propped on my knees.

"What are you gonna do now that you're in?" I asked.

He sat next to me. "Why won't you tell me?" he asked.

"I don't want you in the emotional part of my mind. I don't want you to know what goes on there." I said and looked out the window, away from him.

Spencer pulled my chin gently so I looked at him. "You can trust me. I promise." he said.

"You can't trust anyone; no matter how much you think you can." I said. I had used his own words against him and I could tell he hated it.

"It's a different story with me, Thea. You can tell me anything. I'm the one fighting for you, remember?" he said.

"I'm not going to tell you, Spencer." I assured him.

Spencer sighed. "Come on, Pen." he said, breaking out my old nickname.

"Don't call me that." I said and took in a deep breath.

"Then, tell me, or that's going to always be what I call you." he said and smiled at his own blackmail.

I was going to give in soon anyway. "It's my dad." I swallowed. "I just got to thinking about my life before you left and I couldn't help thinking about him. I just want to know why he left." My voice had cracked, but I couldn't have cared less.

Spencer's expression fell to sympathetic. "I'm sorry, Thea."

Spencer put an arm around my shoulders and pulled me to him. The same electric shocked me again. I leaned on his shoulder and my sobs shook me.

It was nice to have him comfort me and tell me that it would all be all right. But, I knew my father was never coming back. Neither of us could change that.

Once I calmed, he spoke. "Do you want to talk about what happened?"

"No." I said.

"It will make you feel better." he promised.

"I don't think so, Spencer." I said and pulled out of his arms. "Can I just go to bed?" I asked.

Spencer sighed. "Go ahead. If you want to talk, I'm here." he said.

"I know." I said and sighed. "I just want some time alone."

He stood and readied himself to leave the room.

"Wait, Spencer." I said and stood.

He turned and looked at me. I wrapped my arms around his neck and hugged him tightly. He returned it slowly.

"Thank you." I said.

"No problem." he said and I released him. I regretted it automatically. I felt so right in his arms. I didn't want to move from them. We fit together. I loved the feeling and I felt incomplete now.

"Goodnight." I said and he left the room.

FOUR

AUGUST 24ᵀᴴ

It was the first day of school. *Fabulous.* I never liked school in the first place, let alone being the new kid and having to lay low.

Spencer and I hadn't spoken about my father any more. I didn't want to talk about it and he respected that. He wanted to help, but he knew it wouldn't help if he forced me into it. It would just make things worse.

As I walked into the school, I went to the office to get my schedule.

The receptionist was young and beautiful. She smiled at me. "Thea, right?" she asked.

"That's me. Can I get my schedule?" I asked.

"Of course." she said.

I noticed a girl that was my age standing beside the counter. She had brunette hair that came to her waist and she was gorgeous. Her hazel eyes were so innocent looking. She was probably a little shorter than me, but she was far more beautiful.

"Thea, this is Colleen. She has all of your classes with you and will help you adjust." the receptionist said as she gestured to the girl.

Colleen smiled, revealing a perfectly straight, white set of teeth.

That's when the worst of it all happened. Weston walked in.

"Hey, Babe." he said to Colleen and kissed her lightly. Then, he turned to me. He gave me a free-hearted smile. "What was your name again?" he asked.

"Thea," I said and smiled. I had to at least act friendly.

"You two know each other?" Colleen asked.

"Nah, we just saw each other in the store and got acquainted." Weston said. "Could I talk to you out in the hall, Thea?"

I followed him and he closed the door.

"What are you doing, Penelope?" he asked. I put my hand over his mouth.

"Shut up, all right? I'll tell you." I said, afraid of him blowing my secret.

"Then, get talking." he said and I took my hand away. I hesitated. "You can trust me, Penelope. I can keep a secret."

I took a deep breath. "You're right. I used to be Penelope." I said.

"Why did you change your name and stuff, then?" he asked.

"You know that serial killer that's been going around?" I asked.

"Yes." Weston answered simply.

"Well, he came after me very recently. I got away though. I was taken into the Witness Protection Program." I said and sighed. My heart burned at the memory. I forced back my tears.

Weston looked sympathetic. "God, Penelope. I didn't know. Is there anything I can do?" he asked quietly.

"Stop calling me Penelope for starters. You can't tell a soul, not even Colleen or your parents or anyone!" I said and smiled.

"Don't worry. Your secret's safe." he said.

I laughed for a second. "You remember Spencer right?" I said.

"That guy you were obsessed with in fifth grade?" Weston asked.

I nodded. "He's my bodyguard." I said.

Weston burst out in laughter. "That is fate. You two were meant for each other." Weston said.

I smiled and he opened the door for me.

When we got back to Colleen, she looked at us expectantly.

"Don't worry about it, Babe." Weston said and kissed her head.

Colleen showed me to my first class. I sighed as I noticed all I had were academic classes. None of them were electives except Spanish II. Personally, I couldn't care less about Spanish. I just needed it for job opportunities.

I had Trigonometry with Josh, Weston, and Colleen. Josh hugged me when I saw him.

Colleen looked confused. "You know each other?" she asked.

Josh smiled. "Thea is the girl that I told you stood up for Jayden and me in the coffee shop." he said.

Colleen's smile widened even further. "Really?"

I smiled at her. "I just heard the waiter being a jerk so I told him to back off." I said.

"You called the guy a coward." Josh added and chuckled. "Jayden couldn't stop talking about it."

Weston just smiled and we all took our seats.

"So, how's your brother?" Josh asked and wagged his eyebrows.

"He's fine. He's a little irritable, but he always gets like that when he doesn't have a girlfriend." I said and smiled. I was getting good at this acting thing.

"Brother?" Weston muttered.

"You know my older brother, Spencer. He's the guy I was in the store with." I hinted.

He nodded. "I remember." Weston said.

Colleen smiled. "Is he cute?" she asked me. I laughed. I could have answered that, but I didn't want to look like I'd been checking out my brother.

"You do know that your boyfriend is right there, right?" I asked.

"Weston knows that I don't think about anyone, but him. It was just my curiosity." she insisted.

Josh answered her question for me. "Yes, Spencer is cute." Josh said.

I smiled. It was weird to hear a guy say that, but I didn't care. It was just Josh.

"But, I highly doubt he's even in our age range, Colleen." Josh said.

She looked at me. "How old is he?" she asked.

"He's twenty-three." I said.

"Oh." Colleen said and looked disappointed.

Weston wasn't even listening. He was off in his own little world.

"Are you and Spencer close?" Colleen asked.

"Yes, we're very close." I began. "We didn't even grow up together. I moved in with him when I was sixteen. We have different dads and my mom died while giving birth to me. So, my dad just left me with Spencer. Spencer hated the idea at first, but I convinced him."

"Wow. My brother would never do that for me." Colleen said.

"Spencer didn't have a choice. It was either that or let me live on the streets and that was something he wouldn't do. Even if he didn't know me until I was fourteen, it didn't change that I was his sister." I said and smiled.

"Is he gonna kick you out when you turn eighteen?" Josh asked.

"No. He wouldn't do that. He loves me too much." I said and chuckled as I thought of when Spencer and I were younger. He had told me in the car that he would have taken me in and I couldn't help, but wonder if he was telling the truth. I also couldn't help what would have become of us if he had. Somehow, I doubted it would have been how I imagined it.

Colleen smiled. "He seems like a good guy."

Throughout the day, I got to know Colleen, Josh, and Weston just a little better. Of course, Spencer would demand a background check so I had to get last names.

Spencer picked me up after school because God forbid I drive his car. I guess he was being protective, too. I loved his car, though. It had its own laptop coming out of the dashboard. He had all the perks of being a special agent.

"Got the check on Weston?" I asked.

"Nothing came up, but a couple of misdemeanors a couple years back. He's clear." Spencer said.

I smiled. "I told you."

Spencer smiled. "Don't be such a teenager." he said and I laughed.

"Have you had any luck with the guy above Jacob?" I asked.

"No. He can cover up his tracks well. Amanda has been working on it with Oliver on his tracks. Every time they think that they have something to work with, the tracks disappear." Spencer said.

I swallowed. "So, you told me that you found the pattern in Jacob's attacks, but what was the pattern?" I asked.

Spencer hesitated. "I—" He paused and took a deep breath. "I can't tell you."

I was frustrated already. "It is my life. You can't just leave me hanging here. I need to know."

"No, you don't. You can't. If you think it matters, try to break Amanda into telling you, but I can't. I don't have the authority and I was ordered not to let you know." Spencer sighed. "If I could tell you, I would. Whether any of us tell you or not, you'll figure it out."

I didn't want to push the subject. If I did, it may only hurt my chances of knowing.

I got home, did my homework, and made dinner.

While dinner was in the oven, I laid down. I was getting a major headache. I didn't know why and I honestly didn't care. I just wanted to sleep.

Spencer came back into the living room when he got out of his bedroom. He saw me lying on the couch and looked worried.

"Are you okay?" he asked.

"I just have a headache. It'll pass." I said and took in a sharp breath.

"You're really flushed too." he said.

I groaned. "I had better not be getting sick." I said.

He felt my forehead with the back of his hand. It didn't help that his touch made me feel warm inside as it was. I was starting to sweat. He felt my cheek and sighed.

"You definitely have a fever." Spencer said.

"Fabulous." I muttered and sat up. "Could you get me an Ibuprofen?" I asked.

"I'll be right back." he said and left the room.

Spencer handed me the Ibuprofen that I had sent him for. I swallowed the pills dry.

I put my hair up and told Spencer that dinner was ready.

Suddenly, everything was gone. My mind wasn't fuzzy, my fever was gone, and even my headache had subsided. It was really weird, but I wasn't going to question feeling better.

Spencer seemed to watch me very intently the rest of the night. He probably thought I would pass out or something.

I kept thinking that he was checking on me for a different reason. Maybe, it had something to do with why I'd been targeted by this serial killer in the first place. He needed to be sure that I wasn't putting the pieces together.

Every time that occurred to me, I just brushed it off. I figured that I was just being paranoid. A headache couldn't cause me to be targeted.

I figured that I shouldn't tell Spencer that I told Weston about my real identity. I quickly dismissed the idea. He'd just lecture me about how it was endangering my safety. Spencer would just yell at me and I couldn't take being yelled at right now.

"Weston goes to school with me." I said as we ate.

Spencer looked worried. "Has he been harassing you?"

"No. He gave up on Penelope. He just wants us to be friends." I lied. I'd never heard Weston say such a thing. Even when we broke up, he just assumed we were still friends.

Spencer nodded slowly. I hated lying to Spencer. I could never tell if I fooled him or not.

When I went to bed, I fell asleep once my head hit the pillow. I never even covered myself up.

Spencer was sitting in the main WPP building with Amanda. They were just having a casual conversation when the phone rang.

"That's probably Oliver." Amanda said and answered the phone.

Amanda was speaking in a different language. I assumed it was to keep the conversation private from possible eavesdroppers that would kill for some information. I couldn't understand a word. All I understood was that her tone was rushed and very frantic.

Amanda put the phone back on the receiver and looked at Spencer. "We have his next target. You'll have to hurry. We don't have much time." She tossed him a bullet-proof vest, a gun belt, and his loaded gun.

"I need a name, Amanda." Spencer said and put on the vest. He was rushing even more than she was. It was obvious that he cared even if he had no clue who the person was.

"Her name's Penelope Ann Crowder. She's seventeen and lives at this address." she said and handed him a small piece of paper.

Spencer took the paper and ran out of the building as quickly as possible. He jumped into his car and sped away. I was watching him as if I were a passenger in the front seat. He looked determined as he slammed on the gas again. I couldn't tell if he even noticed that he'd sped through three red lights.

He got to the apartment and Jacob's car was speeding away . . . with me in the front seat.

Spencer cursed and tried to follow Jacob. Unfortunately, he lost Jacob about halfway there. He somehow found the track and got to the house.

Gene almost didn't let him in when he said he was the police.

"Someone is going to die if you don't let me in!" Spencer shouted. He lost his patience and broke the lock. He was disgusted when he saw how drunk everyone was but, it wasn't his job to bust kids with drugs.

He heard my cries and busted down the door. A crowd automatically formed, but they all hit the ground when they heard Spencer's gun.

Jacob saw Spencer, took a couple of missing shots and hit the butt of his gun against the nearest window, escaping.

Spencer wasn't worried about that. He just wanted to make sure that I was okay. He knew I wasn't dead yet. Jacob would have been long gone already if I was.

I shot up in bed and took a deep breath. That had been the weirdest experience I'd ever had.

FIVE

I got up early and made my coffee before getting a shower and putting my hair up. I changed into black skinny jeans and a tight pink top with black writing. My black pumps worked well.

I blow dried my hair and straightened it.

As I walked out to the kitchen to get my coffee, Spencer smiled at me. "What are you so dressed up for?" he asked.

"I don't know." I said and sat my cup on the counter.

Spencer just chuckled and shook his head. "You are such a teenager." he said.

"No kidding." I said and smiled.

After my coffee, I brushed my teeth and put on my make-up. I didn't mention my dream to Spencer. I figured he would just think it was weird that I was dreaming about him. But, I wouldn't blame him. If I was his age and some teenager was having dreams about me, I'd be pretty freaked out.

The whole way to school, he was looking at me as if he expected something. I began to wonder if the dream was part of the reason I was targeted.

I shook my head. That wasn't possible. No one could know what was going to happen in my own mind.

Colleen was standing on the sidewalk. Her jaw dropped as she saw Spencer. She watched me as I got out of the car and closed the door.

"That's your brother?" she asked as he pulled away.

"Yeah, why?" I asked.

"He is so hot." she said. She shook her head though. "But, Josh is right. I don't see any resemblance between you two except your hair and your eyes."

"Well, we get it from our mom." I said and we walked into the school.

"I'd say. But, you guys definitely look close. He seems protective of you." Colleen pointed out.

"He is. He really wouldn't let anyone hurt me." I said and smiled. I knew it was true. But, it was his job. It wasn't because of the reason that I wished it was.

"That's nice for a brother to be like that. Well, until you get a boyfriend. Then, it's kind of a pain." Colleen said and smiled.

I nodded in agreement.

Josh smiled at us and Weston kissed Colleen.

"How's Jayden?" I asked and grabbed my books.

Josh smiled like a little school girl. "Perfect, as always." he said. I loved to see that spark in his eyes when he talked about Jayden. "What about your Hunk-of-Man brother?"

"He's fine." I said.

Josh smiled. "You always seem happier when you talk about him. It's weird." he said.

I had to think for a second. "Well, he's the only family I have. I'm just happy to have him."

Josh was still suspicious. I could tell.

Weston saved me from further accusations. "We should get to class. We wouldn't want to be late. It's only Thea's second day." He pulled Colleen by her hand and I followed. Josh came after me.

I was beginning to wonder if Josh could become a problem. I refused to believe it. Josh was a sweet guy. He was just a bit curious.

I looked at Weston thankfully. He just smiled. We got to my locker and Josh went over to the other side of the hall to talk to Colleen alone. I knew they were talking about me. I just listened closely.

"She's not who we think she is, Colleen. She's hiding something huge." Josh said.

"Don't be so judgmental, Josh. She fought for you and Jayden at the coffee shop. Why did you suddenly lose trust?" Colleen asked.

"You saw Spencer. Those two look nothing alike. Plus, you have to notice the way she acts when she talks about him." Josh said, trying desperately to gain Colleen's support.

"I'll admit it. It's a little weird to see the way she is when she talks about Spencer, but she's in a new place and all any of us are talking about is Spencer. It must be a little awkward." she said.

Josh just shook his head. "Fine. Get close to her. But, I'll guarantee that she is going to be something else than what she wants us to think."

"Don't be so paranoid." she said and returned to the group. We headed to first block as if nothing had ever happened.

Weston sat beside me in first block thanks to the new seating chart.

"You are such a bad liar, Thea." he said.

"I know. Josh is starting to notice." I said.

"He's a smart kid. He would have noticed even if you were a professional."

"This could completely wreck everything. If Josh finds something out, Jacob could find me. If Jacob finds me, I'm dead for sure." I said quickly, not taking time to breathe.

"Calm down, Thea. I'll talk to Josh. He'll listen to me. He's just very paranoid." Weston said.

"This is a life-and-death situation for me, Weston. Forgive me for being scared." I said. My voice was harsh.

"You think I don't know that?" His voice had been harsher than mine. It made me stiffen. He noticed and sighed. "I'm sorry. This is hard for you, I know. But, you have to make sure you move on in this new life. If you don't, Jacob will terrorize you forever." he said.

I looked at him. "You're right."

He was quiet a moment. "So, the romance is going nowhere?" he asked.

I raised an eyebrow. "What romance?" I asked

"You and Spencer." He smiled.

"There's nothing going on between us, Weston. He's just my body guard. I'm just some annoying kid to him." I said.

"Has he ever told you that?"

"No." I said, quiet.

"Then, it's not true. Us guys have no problem telling annoying girls that they're annoying." he said, laughing.

"Just because I was some psycho Spencer-stalker when I was a kid does not mean that there will be a Thea and Spencer, ever. He is just working to protect me. Nothing will ever come of it." I knew it was true, but I hated admitting it.

"Whatever you say, Thea." Weston said.

I fought through school until Spencer came to pick me up. He smiled slightly as I got in.

"What's wrong?" I asked.

"It's just Jacob. It's hard enough to keep up with him, let alone this guy above him." he said and pulled away from the curb.

"I'm sorry." I said. I felt guilty for being the reason he was so stressed out.

"You didn't do anything wrong, Thea." he said and smiled. "I honestly don't mind having you as a houseguest. You clean up after yourself very well and you don't need much supervision. I barely know you're there most of the time."

I was silent. That's exactly how I'd always wanted it to be. I didn't want to be a nuisance to him. In fact, I wanted to be something that he could get used to. It would be horrible if I was stuck with him and he hated me.

Maybe, I wanted more than to not be hated. I'd just never bring myself to say it to anyone.

"No problem." I said. "I've always had to keep my home clean. It's how I was raised."

"Well, I appreciate it." he said as he noticed the awkward vibes coming from me.

I wanted a moment before speaking. "I'm a bad liar." I said.

He raised an eyebrow. "What?"

"Josh is suspicious." I said.

"Don't worry. He won't find out anything out if you keep your mouth shut." Spencer said accusingly.

"He might. Plus, I haven't spilled so far. What makes you think I will?" I asked.

"I don't know." He looked at me. "You didn't tell anyone?"

"No." I said. I knew he could see right through me when he clenched his teeth.

"Who did you tell?" he asked. He was angry. I was going to get chewed out so bad later on.

"Don't be mad." I said.

"Tell me, right now." he said.

I swallowed, angry at myself for making him mad at me. "Weston."

The storm didn't come as quickly as I'd hoped. Spencer just pulled over and put his forehead against his palm. He closed his eyes. His breathing came slowly and deeply.

"Spencer?" I said quietly. "Don't be mad, please? I didn't want to."

He looked at me. "What happened then?" he asked. His voice was angry and not as quiet as I'd hoped. "You had better have one damn good explanation for this, Thea!" he shouted.

I took a deep breath. I hated to be yelled at by anyone. It always made my stomach get tight and I felt as if I would cry. When it was Spencer, it was a whole lot worse. "We were in the hall and he called me Penelope. I told him that I used to be Penelope and he just started acting like his old self. I told him and he's helping me keep everyone out of suspicion of me because of my lack of lying ability." I explained quickly and my voice died at the end.

Spencer was still breathing heavily, trying to calm himself. "That's what you choose not to lie about?" he asked.

I bit my lip. "I'm so sorry, Spencer. I know it was stupid." I took a deep breath. "I'm sorry that I'm such a stupid teenager."

Spencer sighed. "You're not stupid, Thea. You just aren't that aware of how much this could affect you later."

"I am, Spencer!" I shouted.

He pulled away from the curb. "We'll talk about this later. I'll have to find some way to clean up your mess." he said.

I sighed.

When we got home, I went to my room and worked on my homework. I didn't want to make Spencer even angrier. I hated seeing him angry, especially, when it was directed at me. I was very sure that I'd ruined every ounce of trust the Spencer had in me. We were finally getting somewhere and I ruined it.

I crossed my legs and ran my fingers through the lower part of my hair.

After a while, I grabbed some sweatpants and a t-shirt and headed into the bathroom for a shower. I had to head back out to my bedroom because I forgot my razor. I was only in my panties and my bra. I knelt down to get into the drawer with my razors and shaving gel.

I stood up and started to leave the room, but when I opened the door, I ran into Spencer's chest. I almost fell backwards from the force I had running into him. Spencer managed to catch me. His hand landed on the small of my back, holding me up. I hadn't noticed that I'd gripped his forearms in my hands as reflex. I looked up at his face. I noticed the heat rising up my neck to flush my cheeks. My heart pounded in my chest.

His gaze didn't avert from mine. He did let his hands fall and I released his forearms.

"I'm sorry, Spencer. I didn't see you there. I was just on my way to the shower." I said, trying to back away.

"It's fine, Thea. I was just gonna come in to try to apologize." He allowed his eyes to fall over me. I flushed again. I felt oddly exposed. "But, I can see that you're in the middle of something."

I smiled. "I'll talk to you when I get out of the shower." I walked passed him to the bathroom.

I got out of the shower and got changed. I thought about how I felt when Spencer had actually taken a second look at me. It was amazing. All of the possible emotion came barreling in all at once. It had been odd. I just never was embarrassed or scared. It was as if it hadn't been the first time he's seen me half naked.

I walked out to the living room and Spencer smiled at me. My heart jumped as I smiled back.

I sat on the couch. Spencer was on his laptop. I saw his e-mail account open and he was typing. I had no doubt that it was telling Amanda when a screw-up I was.

"What are you doing?" I asked.

He looked up at me. "Just e-mailing Amanda." he said. He closed the laptop and sat it beside the chair. He looked at me again. "Thea, I'm really sorry about the way I acted in the car. I shouldn't have lost my temper."

"It's fine, Spencer. I deserve it." I said. I pushed my wet side-bangs behind my ear just for them to fall into my face again.

"No, you don't, Thea. You're a teenager. I understand what you're thinking. I was a teenager too not too long ago." He smiled.

I sighed. "You were never a teenager in the Witness Protection Program, though. You will never understand how it is for me. I even suck at lying."

He didn't speak for a moment. When he did, it was quiet, but serious. "You're right. I never will understand that part of it."

I didn't reply to that. "If you ever get sick of me, Spencer, just leave. I'll be able to take care of myself." I said.

Spencer sighed. "How many times have I told you that I'm not leaving? You're not bothering me." he said.

I ran a hand through my hair. "I'm just trying to keep your options open." I said.

Spencer smiled. "I don't want my options open." He came over and sat with me. "I'm staying right here until you're finished with school."

My jaw dropped. "Are you talking about college, too?" I asked.

"I'll probably find somewhere closer to your campus. If we are still looking for Jacob by then, yes, I will. Even if we are done finding him and you just feel more comfortable with me closer, I won't mind. It's not like I have anyone around here that I'm attached to." he said, sounding sincere.

"No, Spencer. You can't. Once this whole mess with Jacob is over, you need to go get your own life. I'm already holding you back from that." I said. I was panicking. I knew what would happen if I spent more time than I had to with Spencer. This—what I was feeling around him—would intensify to a point where I couldn't ignore it.

"Thea, I'm in no hurry to settle down with anyone yet. I'm not in any hurry to date either. If someone comes along and is different, then I'll be ready. I'm just not going to go out with someone I don't know." he said.

I didn't speak.

"I guess if you trust Weston, I should too. I mean, you're the one who knows him." Spencer said.

It took me a moment, but I finally understood. "Whoa! You think I like Weston?" I asked.

"Isn't that why you really told him?" he asked, confused.

"No! He has a girlfriend!" I said and laughed. I couldn't believe Spencer had actually thought that.

Spencer smiled. "That would have been good to know." he said.

"I guess you're not as good at this as you thought." I said and smiled. "You shouldn't worry about me dating anyone. I've decided to give up on guys. They just cause trouble. Look at what Jacob got me into!" I laughed. "I give up."

Spencer laughed. "Good thinking, Thea. Guys your age are just looking for a quick hook-up. That's what causes the trouble."

"You got that right." I looked at him. "You do know that you were my age once, right?"

"How do you think I know so much about teenage guys? I was one of them. I had the same mind-set. I'm ashamed of it, but it's true." he said. He sounded ashamed. It was weird to hear.

"Don't be ashamed of it. It's over now." I said and smiled.

"It is over. I'm glad. Marcy was one of those girls. I thought she was hot and chickened out the moment it counted." he said and chuckled to himself.

"I don't want to know about Marcy and your sex life, Spencer. That's just gross." I said and laughed. I didn't want to think of the old Spencer and Marcy Keller together. It was one of my most horrible dreams come to life: my Spencer with someone that I couldn't stand.

"Nothing happened, Thea. That's the point. I never showed up. That's why she broke up with me. She called me a coward." he said.

"Jeez." I said. I was surprised by that. I never expected for Spencer to say that he chickened out. "I'm proud of you, Spence. That must have taken courage." I said.

He chuckled. "If you think that's courage."

"It is." I said.

Spencer looked up to my face. "You have such a good set of morals, you know?"

"My dad was a good guy. What can I say? He taught me well, I guess." I said.

"He did." Spencer said. "So, what did your dad do for a living?"

"He was a chemist for a huge lab in Harrisburg. He never told me what he ever did. He never even told me the lab's name." I took a breath. "He was very secretive about everything he did. He always told me it was just to protect me." I sighed.

"It sounds like he really cared about you." Spencer said.

I knew he wanted me to talk to him about everything I felt when my dad left and to just let it out. But, I wouldn't. I didn't want him to know about any of that. My emotions were my own and no one else's. I'm the only one in my personal mind.

"I thought he did." I stood up and stretched. "Now, I'm not so sure that he ever really did."

"Thea, I'm sure he cared a lot about you." Spencer said.

I looked at him. "You know what the worst thing about this whole situation really is?" I asked.

"What?" he asked. He was just happy to have me talking.

"We can never really guarantee that he ever did. We can't say that he wasn't in it for the tax reductions or that he only felt bad for me because my mom was dead. Once a better opportunity came to make more money, he was gone." I said.

"Thea," he said. "Don't make yourself think that."

I sighed. "What exactly am I supposed to think, Spencer? I'm twelve years old and my father seems to have jumped off the face of the earth. What explanation would you have?"

"I don't know, but you can't make yourself think it's your fault. That's the mindset you'll always have if you think like that." he said.

"Maybe it's true. Maybe I just frustrated him for the last time." I said and bit my lip. I could feel the tightness rising in my throat and tried to fight it back. "I'm done talking about my dad. I don't ever want to talk about him again, ever."

I went up to my bedroom and stayed there. I fell asleep sooner than usual.

S I X

AUGUST 26ᵀᴴ

W eston had talked to Josh and Josh agreed to give me a chance. I worked with Weston that morning on my lying abilities. There was no denying that I still sucked.

We were walking through the hall before lunch and Josh was laughing at something Colleen had said when a junior bumped into his shoulder. I thought his name was Peter. Josh apologized hurriedly.

"Fag." the junior muttered.

I hated that word.

Anger rose in my belly. I clenched my teeth and tried to fight the anger, but I couldn't let anyone mess with Josh. Even if he could blow everything, he was the first person I met here.

I spun to grab the Peter's arm. He was a muscle-bound boy. He spun around to look at me.

"What did you call him?" I asked through my teeth. His friends and mine had stopped. Josh looked humiliated. I hated seeing his innocent face twisted like that.

"I called him a fag." he said without the slightest bit of hesitation.

"That's a mean word." I said.

He crossed his arms across his chest. "What are you going to do about it, Mom?"

I slapped him across the mouth. The crowd reacted. They all gasped and my hand stung. I took in a deep breath, feeling a lot better.

He threw a hand up and hit me across the face, causing me to fall to the floor in shock. The whole crowd gasped and I took in a deep breath and tasted the blood in my cheek.

I had no idea he was going to come after me again.

He grabbed my hand and yanked me to my feet. He threw his fist into my stomach, but I tightened my abs just in time to block it. He punched me in the face again.

Anger and adrenaline burned in my veins. As his next attack came, I grabbed his fist the exact way that Spencer had instructed me. I threw my fist into his cheek and sent my knee into his stomach.

However, he got me on the ground again. He got onto his knees quickly and started throwing punches into my torso. I couldn't get a breath in when his fist made contact with my face again. It stung and shocked me. I wasn't ready for this.

His fist made the hardest contact with my rib on my left side.

Weston pulled the boy off of me as I heard a male's voice from around the corner. I hadn't noticed that my nails were digging into the flesh of my arms to keep myself from crying out in pain.

The teacher looked down at me. "Oh, my God." he said.

Weston helped me stand and I felt my injured rib immediately. I sucked in a quick breath. Even taking deep breaths hurt.

Josh looked concerned.

"I'm fine." I insisted. I stood straight up and my rib protested.

Josh helped me down to the office where they had already called Spencer. They were suspending the junior, but they weren't taking any disciplinary actions toward me.

"I'm so sorry, Thea. I feel so responsible." Josh said. His voice was sympathetic.

"How would you be responsible? I hate that word so much. I couldn't stop myself. I froze up on everything Spencer taught me." I said and sighed. It hurt.

"It was because of me." he said.

"Don't worry about it, Josh." I said and he opened the office door.

I sat down and I had to sit up straight because slouching hurt. I was waiting for Spencer to pick me up. The teacher claimed that he believed I had a concussion, but I was absolutely sure I didn't. The only serious injury I had was my rib. It was probably just cracked.

Spencer came into the school soon after and I was breathing as lightly as possible. It hurt just to breathe.

I was holding my left side when Spencer came into the office.

"I'm so sorry!" I nearly shouted. "I have a horrible temper." I said and bit my lip against the pain.

"Calm down, Thea. We'll talk when we get home." he said. He didn't seem angry as he helped me stand.

We got into the car and he still didn't seem angry. "Why aren't you mad?" I asked.

"Should I be? They said that the only hitting you did was in self-defense." he said.

"I started the fight. The kid called Josh a fag and I lost it. I just hate that word so much and I just wanted Josh to trust me. I slapped him and he got angry and started hitting me." I said and took deep breaths.

"Don't worry about it." he said. Sometimes, I swore Spencer was just like me in the temper department. When it came to understanding, he was close.

"They said that they thought you had a concussion. Do you think so?" he asked.

"No. I never hit my head." I said. My voice was soft. I was getting used to the pain when I breathe, but it hurt really badly when I spoke.

"Okay." He looked at me. "Then, where does it hurt?" he asked.

"I'm fine, Spencer. I'm not some little girl. I'm a big girl and I can take care of myself." I said. He pulled the car into park and I got out of the car and tried not to make a sound as I stood. I made my way into the house and Spencer took my bag from me.

I walked up to the bathroom and tried my best to cover up my bruises. It didn't work very well, so I just washed the make-up off. I pulled up my shirt to see the purple-red bruise on my rib. It was dark and seemed to pool under my skin. It was really disturbing to look at. I sucked in a breath and tried to ignore the pain. I pulled down my shirt and went back downstairs.

"Did you eat yet?" Spencer asked. He had startled me and I gasped. I put my hand to my side and took in another higher-pitched gasp as pain flashed in my chest.

Spencer put a hand on my back and I looked up at him. He looked genuinely concerned.

"I'm fine." I lied. I walked away from him to stand by the couch.

He followed me. "What's wrong, Thea? Obviously, it's worse than I figured." he said.

"I'm just bruised up." I said.

He shook his head. "You're not going to tell me?" he asked.

"I don't see why I have to." I said and crossed my arms over my chest.

"I need to know how bad it is so I can help you if we need to get out of here." Spencer said.

I sighed. "I got punched in the rib. That's it."

"Let me see."

He pulled up the hem of my shirt to see the injured rib. The bruise was worsening. He sighed. "It's not broken, but it looks pretty nasty."

"I'm going to have to forge a doctor's note because I highly doubt you're going to let me take you." he said, standing.

"You're right." I said and smiled. "Why would I need a doctor's note?"

"You won't be able to do gym class for a while." he said.

"No. You are not taking gym from me too. That's my favorite class." I complained.

"It hurts when you breathe. If you are breathing heavily, it's gonna hurt even worse." he said. He looked at me.

"When will my rib be healed up?" I asked.

"Probably a good month or two." he said.

I sighed. "Great." I said.

Spencer smiled and chuckled. "You are so impatient."

"Well, I've never been patient." I said.

"That's not good. Men like patience. Remember? I told you that a long time ago." he said.

I did remember. I remembered him telling me that when I was twelve. "I remember." I said.

He smiled. "I remember that day like it was yesterday."

"Me too." I said, laughing to myself. I had been so naïve. I was twelve and had actually expected an eighteen-year-old guy to come back for me.

SEVEN

AUGUST 27TH

I woke up in the morning, expecting my rib to still hurt when I breathed. But, I sat up and it didn't hurt near as badly. I took a deep breath and it hurt a little more, but not near as badly as the previous day. I just got up and got ready for school.

I got downstairs and Spencer looked at me. "How you feeling?" he asked.

"Better." I smiled. "A whole lot better."

Spencer's eyebrows pulled together. "What?"

"It doesn't hurt near like it did yesterday. I thought you said it would be a couple weeks before it felt any better?" I said and grabbed my bag.

"I did. That's true. Come here a second." he said.

I did as told. I didn't protest as he pulled up the hem of my shirt again. He felt over where the bruise had been. It sent goose bumps up my back. The energy flowed from his fingertips to my skin again. It seemed to electrify me.

"That's impossible." he said, baffled.

"What?" I asked, his tone scaring me.

I looked at my rib and there was no bruise. "What the—" I paused. I'd never seen a gruesome bruise like that heal in that short of time.

"I don't know." he said.

"Does this have something to do with why Jacob targeted me?" I asked, my voice shaking.

"I'm not sure." he said and pulled back down the hem of my shirt. "I'll have to call Amanda later on. She knows more about this than I do."

I bit my lip. I hated this. I hated knowing that I'd been targeted for something that I may never know about.

"Why won't you tell me wants going on?" I asked. My throat was contracting. "It's happening to me! Shouldn't I know about it?"

Spencer wiped a hand down his face. "If I could tell you, Thea, I would. I don't have the authority to tell you anything right now."

I bit my lip. "This is so frustrating. I just want to know. You know what's going on with me and I just want to know what to be ready for." I said.

Spencer looked down to me. "I'm sorry. I know you have every right to want to know what's going on. I wish I could tell you. Honestly."

I sighed. "Can we leave?" I asked. I was quiet.

"Yeah." he said and grabbed his keys.

I was in the car quickly. My hair was going all different directions so I put it into a pony-tail.

As Spencer stopped at the school, he spoke. "I'll talk to Amanda. If she thinks it's time to tell you, I'll have her talk to you, okay?"

I nodded and got out of the car. I didn't bother with my usual goodbye. I was too frustrated.

I met up with Colleen at my locker. I smiled at her.

"How are you feeling after your beat down?" she asked.

"I feel fine." I smiled, unloading my bag.

She raised an eyebrow. "You seem stressed."

"I am." I said. "You can see right through people."

"What's wrong?" she asked.

"It's just Spencer. He gets on my nerves sometimes." I said and put my books into my bag.

Colleen sighed. "What? Does he have a totally horrible girlfriend or something?" She was laughing.

"No." I answered and thanked God for that.

Josh came up and nearly tackled me. I hugged him tightly.

"I'm so glad you're okay!" he shouted. I could tell that he really was starting to like me. He wasn't very suspicious anymore either.

"Don't worry. Just a couple bruises." I said and smiled.

"Good! I mean, that's not good, but it is good that you're not too badly hurt." he said and flushed.

"I know what you mean, Josh." I said and laughed.

"Jayden was so worried about you! He was worse than me!" he said.

I really did like Josh. I liked Jayden, too. They were nice people.

"Tell him that I said that I'm more durable than that." I said.

Josh hugged me again.

Weston came down the hall and I smiled at him over Josh's shoulder. He smiled back.

Colleen noticed. However, she didn't say a word. She just ignored it.

I got through my classes without the pain in my rib intensifying. If anything, it lessened. I sort of figured that it had to do with why I had been targeted. I wanted to know why I had been.

I grabbed my bag out of my locker and walked out to Spencer's car. He looked about as stressed out as I felt.

I got into the car and closed the door lightly. I didn't say anything. Spencer looked at me. I smiled to let him know that I knew he was there.

"Amanda told me that she doesn't think it's time to tell you yet." Spencer said.

I sighed. I didn't want him to feel like I thought it was his fault when I knew that it wasn't.

"When does she think it will be time to tell me?" I asked calmly.

He pulled away from the curb. "A little while after your birthday." he said.

I nodded. I was frustrated, but he didn't need me to blame him. I just pushed the frustration away for a while. It wouldn't do me any good.

It was the last Friday night of my childhood. I'd soon know why I was almost killed by my ex best friend.

I ran my hand through my hair. I was stressed out and confused.

"I'm sorry, Thea. I wish I could tell you. I really do." Spencer said.

I shook my head. "It doesn't matter." I said quietly. "I guess I'll find out eventually."

Spencer looked at me and then focused back on the road. "It's not that simple, Thea. Amanda thinks that you should find out for yourself. It will become very obvious soon enough, but it will be scary to figure it out alone. Things are going to change in your life. That is, more than they already have."

I swallowed. "I'm already scared, Spencer."

He bit his lip. "What do you have to be scared of right now?" he asked.

I looked at him, but he didn't look at me. "What don't I have to be scared of? Jacob is still trying to kill me for reasons that I don't know. You guys won't tell me anything. I am terrified of what is going to happen and I'm afraid that Jacob will come bust down the door and kill us both." I said. My voice had broken and it was shaking. My eyes had welled up with fearful tears.

Spencer shook his head again. "Don't cry. I won't ever let him touch you." he said and looked at me as he stopped the car in the driveway. "He'll be dead before he gets a shot at you." Spencer promised.

"After this all ends, I'm all alone. I don't have anywhere to go or anyone to run to. My mom is dead. My dad is anywhere, but where I can find him. My best friend turned out to be a psycho killer. All of my family is dead." I couldn't help, but start crying. "I can't make you stay with me. I can't let you pay for college for me, either." He didn't look away from me. "I just can't do that."

"You aren't making me do anything. I'm right here and nothing in this world could take me away. I'm always going to be here. After this is over and every day until you can manage to pry me away, I'll be right here. I'm not going to let you ever be left alone." he said.

My lip trembled. I was glad that Spencer was here for me, but I didn't want to have to count on his when I should have never gone through this.

"Thank you." I said and leaned on his shoulder. He didn't move away from me. I thought it was a good sign.

"No problem, Thea." Spencer said. My heart leapt as he put his arm around my shoulders. It was kind of an awkward half-hug, but I liked it. I was close to him and the ever-present electric pull between us grew. It was like pushing two magnets together. We couldn't help, but attract each other. I wouldn't have stopped it if I could have. It made me feel as if a Penelope-and-Spencer could actually be possible.

Then, my rational mind returned. I pulled out of Spencer's arms as I remember what a large age difference there was and how irresponsible it was while Spencer was working to protect me.

"We should go inside. I have uh . . . homework." I said and opened the car door. I climbed out and went inside.

I went up to my bedroom to try to do my homework. I didn't want to be around Spencer. It was going to cause trouble. I had to keep my mind off of him as well.

I just couldn't focus. All I could think about was Spencer. I thought about the dream that I'd had about when he'd rescued me. A shiver surged through my body as I thought about the way his shirt had stretched over his nicely muscled chest and his abs. His abs hadn't been washboard and I liked that. They were just slightly defined. It made my stomach quiver. His chest had looked as if he'd put in some time at the gym. It was beautiful. Everything about him was. He was generous and caring and sensitive. It was what I'd always loved about him. He was one of those guys that are gorgeous on the outside and an amazing person on the inside. He'd give the shirt off his back for someone who needed it.

I started writing my English essay and I kept getting off subject. I kept trailing off about how Juliet and Romeo may have been irresponsible, but they did what they felt they had to. They couldn't deny the way they felt. I was supposed to be writing about how they reacted on lust . . . .

I crumpled the paper and threw it into the garbage. I ripped out another piece of paper and tried to write it again. Unfortunately, I trailed off again.

"Damn it!" I yelled and crumpled it before throwing it against the wall.

"Whoa there, Gunner." Spencer said. He was standing in the doorway. He was laughing and looked at me. "What was that all about?" he asked.

"It's nothing." I said and swallowed as my mouth went dry. I tried to pull myself out of the trance, but I looked right at his deep blue eyes. I cursed under my breath and looked away.

"It's obviously something." Spencer said and picked up the ball of paper. I jumped up and took it from him.

"No. It's just a dumb English assignment. I just can't seem to word it right." I said and tore up the paper. I didn't want to risk him putting the pieces together.

Spencer looked suspicious, but didn't say anything. He just jammed his fists in his pockets. "I may be able to help." Spencer said.

"That's not necessary, Spencer." I said. I just wanted him out of the room. I couldn't even think with him in the room let alone work.

Spencer shook his head. "You never let me help with anything." he said.

"I told you that I don't want to be a nuisance. If I let you help, I'll get dependent and I'll become that annoying twelve year old all over again." I said and smiled.

Spencer looked at me and his hair fell into his eyes. "You weren't annoying."

"I was so!" I argued.

"How would you know?" he asked.

"Your friends said it all of the time." I said and crossed my arms over my chest.

"You were annoying to them, not me. I couldn't possibly care less about what they think anyway. They're all either in jail or became total jerks just because they have good looks. I think Drew has had two wives." he said and laughed.

I started laughing. I couldn't help it. Spencer just made me so relaxed and bubbly. He made me so tense too. It was one of the best contradictions I'd ever experienced.

I grabbed my notebook and started writing again. He just watched me. "I can't concentrate when you're staring at me, Spence." I said and smiled.

"Then, let me help and I'll get out of your hair." he said. He sat on the end of my bed and propped his feet up beside me. I was sitting so I was leaning against the headboard and my knees were bent. My notebook was propped up on my thighs.

"I'm not going to let you help me. I'm fine." I said. I enjoyed his presence, but I couldn't concentrate with him there. My mind was too far off in fantasies with him near me.

He didn't move.

"You're seriously not going to leave?" I asked.

He shook his head.

"I can't think when you're in here watching me." I said.

He was still.

I sighed. "Get up here if you want to help." I said and scooted over so he could slide in next to me without the extra effort of sitting up. He did as implied. I read the assignment out loud and he smiled.

"That's what you're having trouble with? I had the exact same assignment my senior year." he said. He took the pencil out of my hand and his fingers brushed mine. The air was taken from my chest and I couldn't breathe. He jotted down a couple of notes about the play and had me interpret it.

I nodded and wrote the whole essay in ten minutes. I didn't realize how easy it was. I guess I was so wrapped up in everything that I couldn't think.

I closed my notebook and shoved it in my bag. I stood up and pulled my hair into a ponytail. Now that it was longer, it annoyed me to leave it hang.

"You never let your hair down." Spencer said.

"It's annoying. I can't leave it down. Why do you think I cut it all off?" I asked and smiled as I wrapped the ponytail thing around one more time.

"It's the only way to disguise you other than plastic surgery." he said.

"No one is getting anywhere close to my face with a knife." I said. We both laughed.

"I figured that's how you'd react." he said. He looked through my back pack as he spoke. "You have all your academic classes this semester. That must suck. You'll be loving life next semester, though." he said.

"I hope so. I hate having only academics. It's all homework all of the time." I said and sighed as I sat next to him. "Speaking of which, I have math homework to do." I said and slid my math binder out of my bag. I started to work on my trig homework and Spencer didn't move. I looked at him. "Is it interesting to watch me do my homework?" I asked and smiled.

"I have nothing better to do." he said. His smile had widened.

I finished my homework while I talked to Spencer about the stupidest things. It was funny to hear the things we started conversations about.

I finished my homework and my muscles were screaming for motion.

I looked at Spencer. "We should go work out." I said.

Spencer raised an eyebrow. "You want to work out?" he asked.

"Well, I'm too weak to do anything for myself. Like you said; I won't always have a gun to protect myself. I need to be strong enough to win in a fight." I said.

Spencer nodded.

I changed into a pair of athletic shorts and a t-shirt. I slid on sneakers and headed down to the basement where Spencer was waiting. Down there was a bunch of athletics machines. I smiled.

"So, this is what you do while I'm at school." I said.

"That's the only time I have to work out." he said.

"The rest of the time, you're watching me do my homework." I said and chuckled.

After the work out, I was sore and tired. I got a shower and used hot water to try to calm my muscles. I wasn't sure if I'd ever worked that hard in my life.

I walked out to the living room and I sat on the couch.

"Are you a little sore?" Spencer asked as he saw me wince.

"A little is a bit of an understatement." I said.

"It's good to be sore, Pen." he said.

My jaw tightened. I knew that he didn't notice that he'd called me Pen.

"You just called me Pen." I said quietly.

He sighed. "I'm sorry. It's a hard habit to break."

"I understand." I said.

"You'll always be little old Pen to me." he said.

You'll always be little. I thought and sighed. *You'll never be a grown-up like him.*

"Well, if you let it slip, we'll have more than a *little* problem." I said. I hadn't meant to snap at him, but it sounded like I did.

"I won't let that happen, Thea." he said.

"Good." I said. I tried to not sound totally depressed and hurt, but it was hard when I knew I was only little Pen. I'd never even be a little bit more than that.

"Are you okay?" he asked.

"Of course." I said and smiled at him. I couldn't help, but smile when his blue eyes locked with mine like this.

"You're sure? You seem a little upset." he said.

"No. I'm fine." I said.

"I see that you have returned to lying again." he said.

"I have not!" I shouted. "I'm fine, okay!" I yelled.

He put up his hands as if surrendering. "Whoa, okay, Thea. I was just kidding." he said.

I crossed my arms over my chest and swallowed.

Spencer didn't speak to me for a while.

"Look, Spence. I'm sorry I yelled." I said.

"It's all right, Thea. I know you're stressed out and everything else. I just wish when you're upset, you'd talk about it. Otherwise, it just eats away at you." he said.

"I'm not really a talker. I take care of my problems alone." I said. It was the truth. I'd never looked to anyone for help with my problems. I'd always been completely independent. I'd never asked for any help.

"Well, it's never too late to change." he said, smiling. "I'm here and I'm open to listen."

I swallowed. "Why do you always forgive me so quickly?" I asked. I had just noticed that he'd never stayed angry for very long. Whenever I had done something to anger him, he'd gotten over it in no time at all.

"I'm here to protect you, not be angry with you. Plus, you're a good kid and everyone gets upset and irritated. I know it's your way of letting it out and I try to stay calm and not react against you."

I smiled. "I appreciate that."

He smiled and took in a deep breath. "It's my job."

It's his job. That's all it is to him. I thought and my throat contracted. I clenched my teeth.

"Yes, it is." I said and swallowed. "I have to get to bed." I said and didn't waste any time getting to my bedroom.

No matter the amount of times I had denied it, I still had feelings for Spencer.

EIGHT

I woke up and blinked a couple of times. I was so tired because I hadn't slept. All I could think about was Spencer.

I got up and went downstairs. I couldn't lie there any longer. When I did, my mind was free to go wherever it wanted.

I didn't see Spencer anywhere.

"Spencer?" I called into the house.

Amanda came around the corner and smiled at me. "Good morning, Thea." she said.

"Hey, Amanda." I said. "Where's Spencer?"

"He's on a date. He figured that he shouldn't wake you. Apparently, you were a little on edge yesterday." she said and smiled.

"He's on a *date*?" I asked.

"Yes. This pretty little thing called and asked him to join her for lunch. They seemed like they knew each other." she explained.

I couldn't comprehend it. He'd told me that he wasn't interested in dating at the time. He'd told me that he wasn't going to go out of his way to fall in love.

"He told me that he wasn't dating." I said.

Amanda smiled. "It was sort of last minute. He was never big on the dating concept. I guess she convinced him."

"I guess so." I said and ran a hand through my hair.

Amanda tilted her head to the side. "Are you all right?" she asked.

I managed a smile at her. "I'm fine." I said and walked passed her to the fridge. I got out the milk and anything else I could eat. I was still really sore from the workout yesterday. I just wanted to eat and lounge around. It was Saturday so I could do whatever I felt like.

Amanda sat in the kitchen chair. Her long red-brown hair was tied up in a pony-tail and her side-bangs fell in her face. "You are really tense." she said.

"I'm a teenager in the Witness Protection Program. I'm going to be tense."

"Not like this. It seems like you're upset about something." she said. She thought for a moment and her jaw dropped. "You don't want Spencer to date, do you?" she asked.

She knew everything.

"No, I don't." I said.

She smiled. "You still like him?" she asked.

I bit my lip. "Please, don't tell him. I will . . . eventually." I said.

"It's your secret, not mine. I have no reason to tell him." she said.

I didn't look at her. "I wish I didn't, you know?" I said.

"Yeah, I do. My parents hated Oliver when I brought him home, but they got used to him. I had wished that I didn't like him like I did. I just couldn't change the feeling I had for him." She looked at me apologetically. "I know that your situation is so much different and is much more complicated. I know you can't control it. Spencer's a good guy, but he's very moral-oriented. This isn't something he'd even think about."

I swallowed. "I know." I did know that. He wasn't going to change for me. I wasn't that special.

"I'm sorry. I know it's hard to hear, but it's the truth." She smiled. "He's never been one to go against himself."

"Trust me, I know." I said and sat in the chair beside her.

Amanda and I only talked for another couple of minutes before it was one o'clock and Spencer was coming back. He opened the door and shook the water out of his hair.

Amanda got up to leave and hugged me tightly. "Good luck." she whispered.

"Thanks." I said and she left.

Spencer smiled at me. "Good morning." he said.

"It's the afternoon." I corrected him.

"It's not my fault that you slept until noon." he said.

I smiled. "Look who's on edge today. I was kidding." I said.

He raised an eyebrow. "I'm perfectly fine."

I looked at him. For some reason, I knew he was lying.

"Don't lie to me." I said sharply.

He looked surprised and—most of all—caught. However, he got a hold on his rebuttal. "You don't have a problem lying to me."

"I don't want to." I admitted.

"You still do." he said.

I sighed. "You're in such a bad mood." I said and stood. I didn't want to deal with him when he was in such a bad mood. I'd just make him angrier judging by my track record. "I'm going to get a shower."

Spencer smiled. "You should probably do your workout before you shower." he said.

"What workout?" I asked.

"You said that you wanted to get stronger. That's not going to happen over one workout." he said.

I scrunched up my face in disgust. "Is it gonna be as hard as yesterday?" I asked.

"Oh, yesterday was not hard. You're just too weak for what I normally do." he said and smiled widely.

"So, now I'm a dumb, *weak* blonde." I said. He shook his head as he laughed. "I mean, you had to help me with an 'easy' homework assignment and now you're calling me weak to my face."

"You wouldn't be weak if you'd workout more." he said.

"I'll go get changed." I said and headed upstairs. I got changed quickly and came back down to the basement. Spencer was waiting.

We got to talking about his date. It had been Marcy, trying to get back together. It hadn't ended well when she asked for money for her twin babies. I had gloated about how I knew it was gonna happen from the beginning.

I was actually doing a little better until we got to the bench press. He had me try to bench one hundred and I couldn't do anything, but a dead-lift. I tried to do reps, but I couldn't get it. It felt like someone was tearing my muscles into pieces.

"Come on, Thea. You were doing ninety-five just fine yesterday." Spencer coached.

"Well, I'm sore and just because I can do *ninety-five* just fine, doesn't mean I can do one hundred." I said.

"Push yourself a little, Thea. Why do you think not many people work out? It's hard and uncomfortable. That is, if you do it right." He smiled at me. "Just do two reps and I'll leave you alone." he promised.

I decided that there wasn't any amount of complaining or fighting that would get him off my back. I lifted the bar from the cradle and lifted one . . . two . . . three times. Then, my arms collapsed and the bar landed right on my chest. I groaned and Spencer lifted it off and set it in the cradle easily.

I rubbed the spot above my sports bra that was surely bruised. I sat up and sighed. "Ouch." I said.

"Are you okay?" he asked.

"Yeah, I'll live." I said and looked up to realize how close he was. I could feel his breath on my face. He smelled pretty amazing. I swallowed and my mouth went dry. I could barely breathe.

Spencer looked confused. "What's wrong?" he asked.

Goosebumps covered my skin as he spoke. I looked up into his eyes. My breath came out in a rush and my palms started to sweat. No one had ever had this effect on me.

My heart pounded in my chest as I stood. We were only inches apart. The rational part of my mind was screaming at me to push passed him and head to the shower. Another part overwhelmed it viciously.

I put my hands on the back of his neck and pulled him down to me. I kissed him lightly. Spark burned on my lips. I knew for a fact that he was kissing me back.

My heart seemed to skip a beat as I wrapped my arms around his neck. I got on my tip toes to reach him and my whole body screamed for this.

Kissing Spencer was special. It was different than anything I'd ever felt. It was better than anything. I knew it would be good, but I never would have expected this.

I pulled back before I wanted to because I felt Spencer's hesitation. I looked up at Spencer and turned to run out of the basement. I ran upstairs to the bathroom even as I heard him yelling for me. I closed the door and locked it. I started bawling my eyes out. I couldn't believe that I'd actually done that. My throat was tight with regret and humiliation. I hated myself for it.

I started the shower water. I just wanted to wash the whole day away. I wanted to make it so it had never happened.

I got to my bedroom and locked the door. I tied my hair up and lay on my bed, staring at the ceiling. I started crying again and thought about how stupid I was. I was stupid to even think of Spencer as anything more than someone to keep me from being killed.

A soft knock came on my door. "Thea," Spencer said.

"Leave me alone." I said and tried to keep my voice from cracking. As always, I was unsuccessful.

"We have to talk." he said calmly. I figured he'd be shouting at me. I hoped he wasn't angry. Even if I deserved to feel horrible, yelling would only make everything worse.

"No, we don't, Spencer. Please, just go away." I begged.

"Just let me in." he said and rattled the doorknob. I'd actually invested in a lock for my door. Even if I was at risk of being killed, I had a right to my privacy.

I didn't give him an answer. I just sat, playing with my sheets between the pads of my fingers.

"I'll break the lock right off the door, Thea. Just let me in." he said. He was still pretty calm. It made me think that he was saving the angry for once he got to me. I knew he wouldn't hit me, but yelling would have the same effect.

"Just break it then." I said.

I didn't think he'd actually do it. I wasn't sure how he even did it. He had the doorknob in his hand when he walked in, though. Spencer looked right at me and my throat got tight. I bit the inside of my lip to keep it from trembling. That would inevitably lead to crying. I didn't want to cry. Not over this and definitely not in front of him.

He just stood, looking at me.

I took a deep breath. "Just get on with it. Tell me how stupid I am."

He still didn't speak.

"Not talking at all isn't helping, Spencer." I said.

"I figured you'd have this big defense." he said.

"Well, I don't." I said and my voice broke. I cursed under my breath and swallowed back the rest of the tears.

Spencer didn't speak for a moment. "You have no reason? None at all?" he asked.

"No. I'm just stupid and hormone raged, I guess." I said. I wasn't looking at him. I was looking down at my sheets.

Spencer was looking at me, though. I could feel it. He was silent. I hated that.

"You're not stupid, Thea." Spencer said suddenly and quietly.

I got up and walked passed him. He grabbed me by the arm before I could pass. I turned to look at him.

"Let me go." I said.

"No. You're not running out again." he said and nearly dragged me to the bed. He sat next to me. "What made you to do it?" he asked as if having a casual conversation.

"Uh . . ." I said. "I don't know." I lied.

He looked at me expectantly. "You're not getting any better at lying, Thea. Just tell me, okay? I'm not going to judge you or get mad."

I bit the inside of my lip again. "That's part of the reason. I've never had someone treat me like so much of an equal before. My father even looked down on me. If I make you mad, you get over it so quickly." I hated telling him this. If I lied, he'd see straight through me, though.

Spencer took a deep breath. "That's just how I am, Thea."

"I don't know what to tell you, Spencer. I mean, I did it. I can't take it back. I feel like an idiot for it." I said.

Spencer didn't really react.

"I'm so sorry. I was just stupid. Can we just forget this ever happened?" I asked. "Please?"

Spencer nodded. "I think we can."

"Thank you, Spencer." I said and stood up. Spencer left me alone. I was thankful for that. I didn't want to be around him right now. It would just stress me out.

I stared at the ceiling silently. I didn't want to go downstairs because it would be so awkward. I still couldn't believe I'd done it. I'd actually kissed him. I tried to swallow back my disappointment at his reaction. He acted like he expected it.

Was I really that predictable?

I started thinking of the kiss. He had kissed me back. I knew it. He hadn't completely pushed me away.

That means, for him, there was something there for me too.

I smiled at that and started tossing a small tennis ball up into the air and catching it. It became very repetitive . . . and boring. So, I returned to staring at the ceiling.

I groaned and decided to check my e-mail. I went downstairs to do that. I borrowed Spencer's laptop and checked my old e-mail. An e-mail from Amanda was waiting for me. It was sent the day that we had moved me to the house with Spencer. It wished me luck and gave me all my necessary information.

I opened a reply to it and told Amanda about what a stupid idiot I had been and what I'd done. I asked her to not mention to Spencer that she knew. I just needed someone that understood.

I closed out of the window and turned off the laptop. I put it back where I had found it and sat at the kitchen table in silence. I didn't know what I could do. I'd really messed up. It was going to be super awkward between us now.

I wanted to punch something. I really did. I sighed and bit the inside of my lip. When Spencer came into the room, he looked at me, but I stared at the table. He cocked his head to one side. "Are you okay?" he asked.

"Yeah, I'm fine." I said.

He glared at me. "You really should stop saying when it's not true." he said.

I shrugged. "It doesn't matter. They're my problems, not yours." I said.

He sighed. "Are you really never going to talk to me when you have problems? Or am I always going to have to pry until you cry. I've done it twice. I can do it again."

I looked at him, but didn't say a word. I didn't want to tell him the truth, but I knew he'd see through any lie I could come up with. So I didn't say anything.

"Is this my fault?" he asked. "Will you need a different guard? I can arrange that if I need to, Thea."

"No, Spencer." I said quickly. "It's not you. You don't need to arrange anything. I'll be fine. It's just my problem and I'll get over it."

"What's going on, Thea?" he asked. He was quite obviously sincerely concerned.

I swallowed. "It's nothing. Can we just drop it?" I asked.

Spencer shook his head. "You are so defensive. I just wish you'd talk to me. I could actually help you whether you think so or not."

"You can't help me. I don't talk about my problems and I never will. It's just not what I do." I said.

He sat in the chair next to me and my heart leapt into my throat.

"We keep having this argument and we don't get anywhere. You know that I'm standing my ground." Spencer said, smiling at me. "I'm going to until you tell me."

I was silent for a while.

"If you don't tell me, I'll have to ask Amanda." he said and a cocky smile spread across his mouth.

"You read my messages?" I asked, appalled.

"No. I just saw who you were sending them to." he said.

"I remember closing out of the window, Spencer." I said.

"But, you never signed out of the account. I went to the site to check my own e-mail and you were still signed in. Your outbox was open and I happened to see it. There's nothing wrong with that." Spencer said and crossed his arms over his chest.

"That wasn't any of your business and it still isn't." I said.

"It is my business. In case you don't remember, I'm the one keeping you from being just another dead body. I'm keeping you safe

here and I can't let there be any gaps that Jacob can get through."
Spencer said. He was looking at me in an odd way and I knew that
he already knew.

I stood up and started to walk away. It was embarrassing. I
cursed myself silently and Spencer stood up. He caught me by the
wrist and I turned to him. His skin seemed to burn against mine.

"Just let me go, Spencer. You already know what's wrong so you
can stop doing whatever it is that you're doing." I said and tried to
pull my arm away from his grasp. He just wouldn't let go.

"Thea, it's okay, all right? You don't need to be upset about it."
Spencer said, trying to make it better.

I shook my head. "Please, just leave me alone." I said.

"Thea . . ." he said quietly.

My throat and my chest got tight and I felt tears trail on my
cheeks. I swear, I normally did not cry this much. "Do you just like
to see me cry?" I asked and didn't look up at him.

"Thea, I hate to see you cry, but it seems to be the only way you
vent." he said.

"I can cry by myself, Spencer!" I yelled and made a gallant yank
to break his grip from my wrist. I walked to my bedroom, but I no
longer had a lock. I just closed the door and sat in front of it so it
wouldn't open.

Spencer never came to knock on my door. I guessed that he
figured it was better to leave me alone.

I swallowed hard and tried to catch my breath. I hated this. It
was my fault that I'd messed up everything with Spencer.

I lay down in my bed and just watched out my window. I watched as
everyone was enjoying the nice day. It was sunny now and probably like
ninety degrees. I saw mothers with strollers walking down the sidewalk.
They were smiling and some of them were with their husbands—or
boyfriends. I didn't look to see who was married and who wasn't.

I even saw a father just walking with a little girl. I smiled as I
saw how happy the two of them were. They were both smiling and
they seemed so happy and content with their lives.

Tears trailed on my cheeks and I wiped them away. I couldn't
help, but think that my father had left because of me. It had to be
something I had done.

I walked to the bathroom to wash the moisture off my cheeks. Violently, frustration rose up in my belly. My throat grew tight and I clenched my jaw. I had the uncontrollable urge to punch something. I needed my anger out.

I looked into the mirror just to see my own face. It was the face of a screw-up. I punched it with all my might. I heard the audible crunch of bones before I felt it. I gasped and looked down at my fist. My knuckles were split open and bleeding. Pain burned in the right of my hand, more toward my thumb. I'd punched the wall with my left hand.

I managed to look at the mirror. I'd shattered it right in the center. Blood dotted the edges of some of the glass.

I wrapped my hand in toilet paper. I didn't want Spencer to see it. He'd freak out.

Just as I threw down the chunk of bloody toilet paper, Spencer stood in the doorway.

"I heard the mirror break and I wanted to see what—" He paused when he looked at me. "You punched the mirror?" He knelt in front of me and lifted my hand to see it.

"I'll be fine. I just need to wrap it and it will be fine." I said and tried to pull my hand away. Of course, the broken bone protested and I bit my lip.

"You broke your hand, Thea. I need to take you to get stitches and a brace or something." Spencer said and grabbed a dark colored towel from the cabinet. He wrapped it around my hand. "Let's go." he said. He grabbed my arm and yanked me along.

I got into the passenger's side and buckled my seatbelt.

"Why did you punch the mirror, Thea?" he asked.

"I was just frustrated. I just needed to punch something." I said and it wasn't a lie. I actually felt a lot better now.

"Why were you frustrated?" he asked.

"I just saw this little girl walking with her dad and it brought back that pain all over again." I said and swallowed hard. My chest got tight so I took a deep breath. I tried to push it all away, but tears welled up in my eyes again. I cursed and wiped them away with my sleeve.

Spencer sighed. "I'm sorry, Thea. If I could change it, I would." he said.

"It's over, Spencer. You couldn't change it if you wanted to." I said.

"I would if I could." he said.

I swallowed and looked at him. "I'm sorry I'm putting you through this. I know you have better things to worry about than me breaking my hand." I said.

"I'm just glad that you finally let it out." he said and smiled.

"See, I don't have to talk about it." I said. I kind of wanted to now though. I wouldn't give him the satisfaction, though.

"It would help." he said.

I nodded.

We arrived at the hospital and it took forever to get an x-ray and stitches. I got a brace that covered the top part of my hand and they splinted my index finger. The bone that is connected to my index finger is the one that I broke. They told me to keep the brace on for four to six weeks.

We got back to the car and I was laughing. "Only I would break my hand on a mirror." I said.

"Isn't that the truth." he said and laughed.

I looked at him. "Do you think this will heal as fast as my rib did?" I asked.

"Maybe. If we're lucky, we won't need to send you to school with it." he said.

"Let's hope so." I said.

We were silent the rest of the ride home. When we got home, we cleaned up the broken glass out of the bathroom. Spencer got the broken mirror off the wall and took it down to the garbage and took the garbage out.

I smiled at him when he got back. "I'm sorry." I said.

"It's fine, Thea. As long as you're not breaking people, I'm fine with it." he said and smiled.

"Thank you." I said. "You've been completely amazing ever since I met you and I'm so not used to it."

Spencer just smiled. "I don't see why I wouldn't be nice to you, Thea. You're definitely not as horrible as you come off on your record. You're actually a really good kid."

I smiled slightly. Again, he had to say 'kid'. "I'm pretty horrible, Spencer."

"No, you are not." he said.

"How am I not? I've already gotten into a fight, broken your mirror, blown my cover with a kid that I've known since I was twelve, and kissed—" I cut myself off. I was babbling and I didn't want to bring up the kiss.

Spencer looked at me.

"Sorry. I didn't mean to bring it up again." I said. Spencer just shrugged.

"It's not wrong to bring it up. I'm not going to yell at you for it." he said.

"You should. Maybe then I'd get it through my thick skull." I muttered.

"There isn't anything to get through your skull. You didn't do anything wrong." he said.

"You're twenty-three! That's illegal!" I shouted.

"That would be my fault, not yours."

"Why would it be your fault?" I was confused.

Spencer looked at me. "I kissed you back." he said.

"That doesn't matter. It didn't mean anything." I said.

Spencer shook his head. "You can stop denying it, Thea. You're not fooling anyone anymore." he said.

"I'm not denying anything. I'm saying that it meant absolutely nothing to you. Besides, I'm not telling anyone. I only told Amanda because she knew that I still had feelings for you before I even admitted it to myself." I said.

Spencer didn't say anything. I took that as a confirmation.

We got up the last bit of glass and I went to bed.

NINE

AUGUST 29ᵀᴴ

"Thea," Spencer's voice broke into my dreamless mind. He shook me gently. I groaned and looked at the clock. It was only eight o'clock.

"What?" I asked.

"Amanda is making us breakfast. Get up and get ready." he said. He was a bit on edge and I had no idea why.

I sat up and ran my hand through my hair. Spencer had left the room and I decided on a shower. I had to keep my left hand wrapped in a grocery bag and duct tape to keep the brace dry. I got a nicer shirt out and a pair of skinny jeans. I scrunched my hair so it fell in waves down my shoulders. I straightened my side bangs and went downstairs.

I met up with Spencer at the bottom of the stairs. I tried my best to not think about the kiss or the way he had confirmed that it had meant nothing to him.

"Are you ready to go?" he asked.

"Yeah, let's go."

"You're not wearing make-up, are you?" he asked.

I hadn't bothered with make-up. I didn't feel the need. I didn't have anyone to impress anyway. "No." I said.

He nodded. "You look nice." he said.

"Thanks." I said and smiled. I hoped to God that I wasn't blushing. I went to push my hair behind my ear with my left hand and sighed. "Are we sure this isn't healed yet?" I asked.

He shrugged. "There's only one way to find out." he said and started pulling the Velcro straps away from the base. He pulled it off and I cringed. It still hurt. It wasn't as bad as it had been, but it still hurt.

"Put it back on." I said.

He smiled. "It still hurts, huh?" he asked.

I nodded. He replaced it and laughed.

"Maybe you shouldn't punch the mirror next time." he said.

I glared at him. "Shut up, you jerk." I said. I was laughing too. That probably didn't help my defense.

As we headed toward Amanda's, the radio played. Spencer tapped his thumbs against the steering wheel to the beat. I smiled. I hummed along to the songs that I knew.

Amanda lived about an hour away so we had some time to relax. I had a bad feeling about this. I know that Spencer did too.

We arrived and Spencer went inside first.

A dark-haired man looked back to us. His hair was sort of sticking up, but it wasn't in an unattractive way. Nothing was unattractive about him. His eyes were an inky brown and his features were next to perfect. He'd definitely put in some man-hours at the gym. A body like that didn't come without work.

"Hey, Spencer." he said. His voice was next to perfect too. It was just the right pitch. He had to be Oliver, Amanda's husband.

Amanda walked in beside the man and smiled. "I didn't expect you both this early. The food will be done in a couple minutes." she said.

"There's no rush, Amanda." I said. Spencer walked inside so I did too. I followed him to a round table. Oliver sat down too.

It was such an awkward silence. "So," I began. "You must be Oliver." I said.

Oliver nodded. "You must be Thea." he said.

I nodded.

More awkward silence set in.

Then, Amanda came with food. She laid a plate in front of each of us. It consisted of a pile of scrambled eggs, two pieces of toast, and three pieces of bacon. She kissed Oliver quickly before sitting.

About ten minutes into the meal, Oliver left to shower. Amanda spoke. "I'm sure both of you are a little curious as to why I asked you to come here." she said.

We nodded.

"Well, Thea e-mailed me and told me about what had happened between the two of you." she said.

I swallowed hard. She was going to do this now?

"What exactly happened?" she asked.

I bit the inside of my lip and cursed silently. I took a deep breath and started to talk, but Spencer beat me to it. He told her what had happened in a nutshell.

Amanda nodded. "Well, you both need to be made aware that this can't affect any of the work we're going through. Also, there cannot be a relationship between the two of you. At this time, it's illegal anyway. But, even after Thea turns eighteen, there can't be a relationship. It's too much of a distraction." she explained.

"There's no need to worry about that, Amanda." Spencer said, unfazed.

My chest tightened and I swallowed.

"He's right." I said and took quiet, deep breaths.

She nodded slowly. "I don't want to do it, but I could change guards just as quickly as I assigned them."

"We understand." Spencer said.

"Good." she said.

On the way home, it was so awkward and quiet.

"I'm so sorry, Spencer. I didn't know she'd do that." I said and didn't look at him. I couldn't. I was so embarrassed.

"It's not your fault." he said.

I didn't argue with him even if I wanted to. I just wanted that day to have never happened.

I went home and started doing the laundry silently. I didn't want to talk to Spencer. The conversation with Amanda had been so awkward. I highly doubted I'd ever want to be in the same room with him ever again. I tossed a pile of laundry into the washer and turned on the washer.

I really just wanted to disappear.

I swallowed and just sat on the floor. I didn't want to deal with all of this. Maybe Jacob should have killed me.

My chest tightened at the thought of Spencer allowing Jacob to kill me. I didn't want to die. I was terrified of that. It would have been so much easier on Spencer, though. I've been doing nothing but causing trouble.

He'd also been nothing but nice to me.

I was silent and still for a long time. I guess Spencer thought I'd gone and jumped off a cliff. When came to check on me, he stood in the doorway and I didn't say a word. Spencer came and sat next to me on the floor.

"Are you all right?" he asked.

I nodded. "I'm just really embarrassed."

Spencer shook his head. "Don't be embarrassed. There's nothing to be embarrassed about." He looked at me. "But, what Amanda said was true."

I swallowed. "I know that. I knew it was wrong, but I wasn't really thinking when I kissed you."

"I didn't try to stop it either. I knew it was coming and I didn't do anything about it." he said.

"I was still the one that was stupid. I did the wrong thing and I wish you would stop taking the blame and punish me or something." I said.

"You want me to punish you?" he asked. His tone was a bit skeptical.

"Do something about it!" I shouted. "Punish me, or yell at me, or . . . something! I can't stand that you're being so nice to me about it when I know you don't feel the way that I do."

"I'm being nice to you because you actually acted on how you felt instead of bottling it up." Spencer said.

"What are you, a therapist?" I asked. He always talked about bottling up my emotions.

"No. I just know that it's not healthy to pack all of your emotions inside." he explained.

I took a deep breath. Maybe he was right, but I'd already come to this conclusion yesterday.

"Well, both times I let it out, it backfired in my face. It's not very good motivation to keep doing it." I crossed my arms over my chest.

"Neither completely backfired. I mean, you could be dead." he said.

I smiled. "I could be. I mean, I only completely humiliated myself and severely injured my hand, but I'm still alive."

He looked at me and didn't smile. "You did not completely humiliate yourself, Thea. It's very admirable that you can go after what you feel. You can express yourself and just go for it even if you know it's wrong."

"It *was* wrong. That's my point. It was stupid and wrong and it could have gotten you in so much trouble." I said and swallowed hard.

He chuckled. "All you're worried about is how much trouble I would have gotten into?"

"Of course I am. You have a job that you love and a great life. I just keep messing it up." I said.

"You are not messing it up." He sounded stern.

"I am, Spencer. I'm just some idiot teenager."

"Shut up, Thea." he said, catching my attention. I looked at him. "You are not an idiot and you are not messing up my life. If you were, I would have no problem telling you so." He smiled. "I've actually been having a really good time getting to know you again, even if you are stubborn."

Just as I was going to speak, we both heard the breaking of glass in the living room. Spencer was up the stairs with his gun up. I followed him. When we got upstairs, I immediately heard gunshots. They weren't from Spencer.

Spencer grunted and grabbed his shoulder. I gasped when I noticed that he was shot. He shot a couple of times at our attacker before he escaped through the window. Unfortunately, he missed his target.

Spencer cursed and loaded his gun back into his belt.

"Oh, my God, Spencer!" I shouted and ran over to him. He was bleeding heavily. "This is my fault! It should have been me!"

"Calm down, Thea. I'll be fine." he said and winced as he lifted his hand to examine the damage.

"He was after me. He shouldn't have shot you. It shouldn't have been you." I said, panicking.

"It shouldn't have been you either." he said. He was really good at handling pain.

"I'll go get a towel. Just hang tight." I said and ran upstairs. I came down with a couple dark red towels. "Let me help you." I said and moved his hand. I pressed a towel to his shoulder and thought about how it should have been me. I wished I could take away his pain. He didn't deserve this.

Then, I felt it. It was a tearing pain in my shoulder. I heard the bullet drop from Spencer's shoulder to the floor. I grabbed my shoulder and gasped. My hand was sticky with blood. I looked at Spencer and he wasn't bleeding. He looked as if he'd never been shot.

Spencer forced me to sit on the stair and pressed the other towel to my shoulder calmly. I whimpered and bit the inside of my lip.

"What the hell?" I shouted. It hurt to talk. I took a deep breath as I noticed how much it really did hurt.

"Calm down. I'll explain everything later." he said and started dialing a number into his cell phone. I recognized it as Amanda's. He told her that he was taking me to the hospital and to meet him there. He lifted me to his chest.

"I'm not going to a hospital. I don't even know how this happened!" I shouted. I tried to struggle out of his arms, but it hurt me more than it helped. I gritted my teeth and Spencer took me to his car. He put me in the passenger seat and buckled the seatbelt. He got into the other side and sped away from the house.

"I promise that I will explain everything once they get you all patched up." he said. My hand was lying on the console and his was on top of mine, holding it gently. It sent shock waves through my skin and heat climbed up my arm.

I took a deep breath when I realized that his action had made me forget how much pain I was in. "It really hurts." I said quietly.

"I know it does. Just hang in there. We'll be there in just a couple of minutes." he said. He sounded very calm, but I could hear the hidden concern. His thumb rubbed my hand softly.

"I don't understand. You were the one that was shot, not me." I said.

"It's hard to explain. Amanda will explain everything. I promise. Just don't stress about it now."

"Don't stress about it? Spencer, you were shot and I'm the one with the gaping hole in my shoulder!" I shouted.

"I know and I wish I could explain it better, but I don't understand all of this myself." he said and swallowed. "Amanda's the expert."

I looked at him. "This is why I was targeted?"

Spencer nodded. "This is what we've been waiting for."

We got to the hospital and they put me to sleep so they could check for other damage.

When I woke up, I heard the beeping of a heart monitor. I blinked hard and felt the tubing in my nose. I wrinkled my nose before deciding to reach up and try to pull it out. A hand caught mine.

"Don't even think about it." Spencer said.

I looked up at him and smiled. "Hey." I said. My arm was in a sling and bandaged heavily.

Spencer smiled. "Hey. How are you feeling?" he asked.

"I'm tired. I'm sore too." I couldn't move my shoulder. "Where's Amanda?"

"Out in the waiting room." he said.

"Get her in here. We need to talk." I said and sat up.

"Don't worry about that now. You should just get some rest. You've been through a lot." he said.

"No. I'm so sick of waiting! I'm going through it and I want to know!" I shouted.

He swallowed. "All right, I'll get her."

He returned with Amanda. She smiled. "How are you?" she asked.

"I want to know what's going on." I said simply.

She sighed and sat in Spencer's seat. He didn't seem to mind and leaned against the wall. "I figured you'd find out soon enough." Amanda said.

"Just tell me." I said.

Amanda took a breath and ran a hand through her hair. "Well, you are part of an accidental race called the Elite."

"Accidental?" I asked.

"You remember that your father was a chemist and biologist, correct?" she asked. I nodded slowly. "Well, in his lab, he and his colleagues were working on a combination of DNA that would create an enhanced psychic energy in the mind of the modified child. This would help with police searches and murders. This was before you were conceived.

"One day, all of the scientists were exposed to the DNA and it clung to them like a virus. It connected to their DNA and became part of them. When you were conceived, you were infected with your father's modified DNA. Therefore, you have very enhanced psychic energy. You were blessed with sympathy healing." she explained.

"What is that, exactly?" I asked. My voice was shaky because I was a bit overwhelmed and confused. I'd never been told any of this. I always thought psychics were crazy and liars. They only told people that they knew more than they did because it would attract attention and money.

"It is the ability to suffer someone's injury for them when you feel sorry or guilty for it. However, you heal extraordinarily fast. That's the bonus none of us knew about." she said.

"Anyway, after children began developing these abilities, a large group of people decided they needed to be killed. So, Jacob was the person appointed to go through with the murders before the children could become aware of their abilities, thus resulting in the serial killings.

"We aren't aware how many people now have this modified DNA after the original children had children of their own before they were located."

Spencer was watching me intently.

"Is this possibly why my dad left?" I asked. An entirely new fire ignited in my chest.

Amanda nodded. "He was aware of your abilities early on and let the agency know so they could keep the killers away from you. I can't imagine why he'd ever leave. He definitely loved you very much."

I took a deep breath. "Well, it doesn't matter. He's gone whether we know why or not."

About an hour later, Amanda left and Spencer took me home. I was so jacked up on pain killers that I slept the whole way home.

When I woke up, we were in a home, but not ours. Spencer was carrying me carefully.

"Where are we?" I asked.

"It's my parents' house. We're going to be staying here for a while. It's more secure." he said. We entered the house and it was larger than I thought it was. "No one is home. They'll be here in the morning."

He carried me to a large bedroom and laid me on the bed. He pulled the blankets up around me and smiled. "Get some rest."

"What about all of my stuff?" I asked.

"Oliver had it all moved here. Don't worry. Just sleep." he said and brushed my hair off my forehead.

I fell asleep quickly.

TEN

I woke up to Spencer moving me gently. He was taking off my arm brace.

"I'm sorry. I wanted to check everything before I got you up for school." he said. "Your shoulder is healed enough if you feel like going."

I sat up and started pulling off the bandages around my tank top. Spencer rewrapped it and helped me stand. It hurt a little so we decided I wasn't doing gym. I had to act like I was fine.

We got to school and Weston was alone at first.

"Where's Colleen?" I asked.

"She's home. She had the flu." he said and noticed my change in posture. "What's wrong?"

"My shoulder's just sore." I said.

He raised an eyebrow as if he didn't believe me. "What happened to it?"

"I can't talk about it." I said. I'd never been told to not tell, but I didn't really understand it.

"Spencer didn't hit you, did he?" he asked with his teeth clenched.

"No, he didn't." I said. "I'll explain later. But, I have to tell you something privately." I said and pulled him by his shirt down the hall. "I kissed Spencer."

His eyes widened. "What? When?" he asked.

"Saturday afternoon. We were working out and I looked up at him and . . ." I shivered. "It just happened."

"What happened, exactly?" he asked.

"I kissed him and he kissed me back. He found out that I still had feelings for him and it all got messed up." I explained. "Then, I told Amanda about it."

Weston shook his head. "That couldn't have ended well."

"No, it didn't. She told Spencer and me that we can never have a relationship." My voice had cracked.

Weston sighed. "I'm sorry, Pen."

Somehow, the nickname comforted me.

I hugged him tightly and he returned it. "Thank you for being here." I said.

"No problem. What are friends for?" he asked.

We released and he took my hand and scribbled something on my palm. It was a phone number.

"Call if you ever need me." he said.

That's when I saw Josh around the corner, right behind me. His face had gone white and I wasn't exactly sure what he'd heard.

So, Weston grabbed him. He had a hold of Josh's hood.

"What did you hear?" Weston asked.

Josh ignored the question. "So, how far does this *friends* thing go with you two? I mean, you two should probably talk to Colleen." Josh said.

Weston's grip tightened and he pulled Josh upward, off of his feet. Josh's legs dangled and kicked blindly.

"Nothing is going on!" Weston shouted.

"Then, what is up with all the touchy feely stuff? Giving away phone numbers?" Josh asked.

"It was a hug and we're friends. Besides, there is nothing wrong with me giving a friend my phone number!" Weston shouted. It was kind of frightening seeing him angry now. He could probably do some real damage.

"A hug can mean many different things." Josh muttered.

"You are so paranoid." Weston said.

"Then, what was the hug for?" Josh asked.

"I'm not getting along with Spencer well and I was upset." I said. My voice cracked when I noticed it was almost true.

Sympathy flashed in Josh's inky brown eyes. "I'm sorry, Thea. I didn't know." he said. Weston released him and he fell onto his butt on the floor. He grunted and stood up.

"It's fine." I said and started walking away. I headed to first block quickly and sat in my chair next to Weston.

"Are you okay?" he asked.

"I'll live." I said.

"I'm sorry." he said.

"It wasn't your fault." I said. "Maybe we should just keep our distance until Josh cools down."

"He's just paranoid, Thea."

"But, he might tell Colleen and that could ruin what you have with her. I would never let that happen because of me." I said.

The teacher called our attention.

Spencer picked me up after school and gave me his usual smile. "I unpacked all of your stuff. Now, you just have to meet my sisters." he said.

"You have sisters?" I asked.

"Yeah, four of them." he answered and smiled.

"Tell me about them." I said.

"Grace. She's twenty-four and pretty easy going. She doesn't judge. Brittany is twenty. She's a hair-stylist so she'll probably be at your hair all of the time. Miranda and Allison are twins and they're nineteen. Miranda is definitely persistent. Allison is just stubborn, but always seems to have the best intuition of all of us." he explained.

"They all live with your parents?" I asked.

"Grace and Brittany don't. They're both married. Miranda and Allison are just home for a couple of days from college." he explained. "They heard I was home and came back. They haven't seen me for a good while."

I swallowed. "What if none of them like me?" I asked.

"They'll all love you."

My stomach twisted into knots at the thought of meeting his family. It intimidated me greatly. I mean, these girls grew up with

CORTNEY BARDIN

Spencer. They knew him better than anyone. I swallowed as Spencer pulled into the driveway. The house was beautiful. It was on an estate. It was three stories high and white with navy blue shutters. It had a porch with white pillars holding up the roof that was level with the top of the first floor.

"Your parents much be rich." I said.

"Well, we've never really been *poor*." he said.

We stopped at the top at the driveway. I noticed the enormous line up of cars the whole way across the driveway. Spencer debated for a moment who to park behind.

"Whatever. Grace can complain that I parked behind her later." he said and swung his little car behind the black Corolla.

We got to the door and I swallowed hard. I fixed my hair quickly as Spencer unlocked the door and walked inside. I followed him hesitantly.

The inside was even more beautiful than I remembered it. The short hallways served as a laundry room where the washer and the drier were sitting. At the end of that hallway was a kitchen that looked completely white and spotless. We went through another door to get to the dining room. It had a huge glass crystal chandelier hanging several feet above the table. The ceiling had to be twenty feet up. The walls were painted a dark red with brown wood trimming. The table was a dark wood and only had chairs on the sides.

We left that room and entered a living room where five women were standing. The ceiling was high again and the furniture was all brown leather. There was a recliner, two loveseats, and two three-person couches. A huge plasma screen television hung above the mantel where pictures of all the children were. They were in golden frames with little name plates on them.

The women looked at me. They all resembled Spencer in the facial features. All of them had to same perfect nose, high cheekbones, and dashing blue eyes.

The oldest of the women smiled. She had to be his mother. "You must be Thea." she said. Her voice rang out like wind chimes on a breezy summer afternoon.

I smiled back. "Hi." I said shyly.

92

"I'm Mrs. Kendal, but you can call me Brenda." she said and held out a hand for me to shake. She was dressed in business-like and obviously expensive clothing. She had on khaki designer pants and a frilly blouse. She looked very fit for having a twenty-four-year-old child and four more after. She was thin and beautiful.

I shook her hand and smiled.

The other girls soon identified themselves. Grace was a tall and beautiful woman that worked in modeling for years. Brittany was another tall, blond, and gorgeous woman. Miranda was the one wearing the least make-up and the best outfit; sweatpants and a t-shirt. Allison was a more athletic looking girl, but it wasn't bulging or too obvious.

They all seemed to like me except Allison. She seemed to be tense around me.

"How old are you, anyway?" she asked.

"I'm seventeen. I'll be eighteen in two days." I said.

She looked disgusted. "You're living with Spencer and you're only a child?"

"Allison, that's enough." Spencer said sternly. "Excuse us." He took the top of my arm in his hand and took me to the dining room. "My family doesn't know about the whole WPP thing." he said.

My jaw dropped. "So, what do they think?"

"That we're . . ." he paused uncomfortably.

My eyes widened. "They think we're together?" I asked.

"Something like that." he said.

"Why didn't you just tell them the truth?" I asked.

"We're not allowed." he said.

"Why not? They're your sisters!" I shouted.

"I know. Amanda came up with it all. We don't have to prove anything to anyone, either. It's just going to be an act for a little while. Once we track down a place more stable, we can drop the whole thing." he said.

I nodded. "Is that why Allison obviously doesn't like me?" I asked.

"I'm guessing so. She did talk about your age." he said. He sighed. "Just go along with what I say, okay? No one will ask questions if we're careful."

"No problem." I said.

He laced his fingers with mine. I looked up at him.

"Is this okay?" he asked.

My breath caught in my chest and my body seemed to shoot up in temperature. "Yeah." I said.

He led me into the living room and I just smiled and hoped this could be routine. I mean, it wasn't every day that I could hold Spencer's hand and just be together.

We started getting asked a lot of questions. They were mostly from Allison.

"Why do you live with Spencer if you're still a minor?" she asked.

"Uh . . ." I said and looked to Spencer.

"Thea doesn't really like to talk about the issues she had with her father." Spencer said.

Allison looked a little suspicious of his answer, but didn't criticize it. "Do you guys have separate bedrooms?" she asked.

"Yes." I answered. I didn't want to hear the excuse Spencer thought of for this one.

She raised an eyebrow. "So, there's no sex?" she asked.

"Allison!" Brenda yelled.

"It's a question. It's still kind of illegal, Mom. Do you want your son, who was a cop, to be having sex with a minor? We don't know how he lost his job." she asked.

"Stop, Ally." Brenda said sharply.

"Oh. You just want to think he'll be a virgin forever, huh?" Allison asked.

Brenda sighed. "Just stop it, Allison!"

Allison rolled her eyes.

My hand had relaxed in Spencer's. I was comfortable with it. However, his body had tensed at the question.

"Are you still going to school, Thea?" Allison asked.

"Yes, of course." I said.

"Are you going to college?" she asked.

"That depends on if I can save enough money by then." I answered.

"Spencer could pay for it. I mean, he has a good amount of money." Allison said. "Or, are you just looking for a sugar daddy?"

"No, I am not!" I said. "I told him that he isn't paying for a cent of my college tuition."

"You're very defensive." Allison said.

"You're calling me a gold-digger. I'm going to get defensive." I said, trying to calm myself.

"That's sure what it seems like to me. I mean, you're not even comfortable being here. You're tense all over." she said.

"I'm not with familiar people other than Spencer. It kind of makes me nervous." I said. I was very calm. At least, I was trying to be.

She looked as if she was not even close to stopping the questioning.

"Allison, is this really necessary? Can't you just be happy that I'm happy?" Spencer asked.

"Not if you're dating a gold-digging-whore. I don't want you hurt, Spence. She most likely is not the little angel she's leading on to be." Allison said.

I bit back my comment because I didn't want to fight with her.

"Just knock it off, Ally. Thea isn't hurting anyone." Spencer said.

"Not now, but she will be." Allison countered.

"Allison, just knock it off." Spencer said loudly.

"I just got here and we're already fighting?" The male voice had come from the doorway. I looked up to see a man with buzzed blond hair and had that same striking resemblance to Spencer.

"I'm sorry, Dad. I didn't know you were home." Spencer said.

"You shouldn't be fighting anyway." Mr. Kendal said and looked at me. "Who is this pretty little lady?"

"Darling," Brenda began. "This is the girl Spencer was telling us about."

Mr. Kendal nodded. "Thea, correct?" he asked.

I smiled. "That's right."

"You don't look very old. How old are you, again?" he asked.

I swallowed and Allison answered for me. "She's seventeen." she said.

Mr. Kendal looked surprised. "You're only seventeen? Isn't that a bit young?" he asked.

"Now, you sound like Allison." Spencer said.

Mr. Kendal didn't say anything else.

When it was time to turn in for the night, I pulled Spencer aside. "Why are they even letting us stay with them?" I asked.

Spencer looked down at me. "They think I lost my job and need a place to stay for a while."

I shook my head. "Why do we always have to lie?" I asked. "I don't like it and I know you don't either."

"You're right. I hate it, but we have to do something. We're not allowed to tell them the truth, Thea. We both know it. If I could, I would." he said.

"What does it matter? They're your family and most of them are nice and happy to see you 'happy'." I said and put air quotes around the word.

"I'm sorry, all right? I hate this as much as you do." he said.

That's the problem. You hate it. I don't. I thought.

"Whatever." I said and noticed that I had no idea where I was sleeping. "Am I sleeping in the guest room?"

"No. Take my room. I'll go down to the guest room." he said. He grabbed a pair of gray sweatpants and left his bedroom.

Once I lay down, someone knocked on the door.

"Come in." I said and sat up.

The door opened and Allison turned on the light. I squinted against it.

"I'm sorry. I thought Spencer was in here." she said. She didn't sound very sorry, though.

"No. He's in the guest room. What do you need him for?" I asked.

"I just need to talk to him." she said.

"You're going to talk about me?" She looked at me. "It's very obvious that you don't like me, at all, Allison. Why? Just tell me why you don't like me."

Allison cocked her head to one side. The sloppy bun on her head flopped to the side. "Give me one reason why I should like you, Vogel." she said.

"I make your brother happy." I said simply. It was a lie, but I think I pulled it off.

"I don't believe you."

Never mind that. I didn't pull it off.

"Why not?" I asked.

She shook her head. "This isn't Spencer. He'd never date a girl with that much age difference to him. Not even if he thinks he'll be happy. You two have to be pretty in love for Spencer to even think about this. He's so tense, too. Around all of us, he's usually really relaxed. I mean, we're his family. I'm his sister! He shouldn't be this uncomfortable! Spencer never was until you came along! Now, his job is gone and he has to live with our parents. I don't find it coincidental." She was nearly shouting.

I didn't like to see Spencer like this either. I didn't understand why she couldn't see that.

"I'm sorry, Allison. I never wanted any of this to happen." I said.

"Shut up, Vogel!" she shouted. "I used to be the only one in this family that Spencer would talk to and now he's pushing me away. You have no idea how that feels. We both promised that a girl would never come between the two of us. He seems to just be a liar lately."

"Allison, I promise you that I never meant for this to happen!" I said.

She shook her head. "You're the one playing this game with him. If you didn't want it to happen, drop the game that your kid mind is playing. Spencer isn't your little toy! Drop the act and tell the truth to him!" she shouted.

"I'm not playing a game!" I shouted and my voice broke. I realized that I was already crying. I cursed to myself.

"Obviously, you two aren't even that serious if you've never slept in the same bed. Why isn't he in here?" she asked.

"I'm not ready for that yet, Allison." I said quietly, trying to keep my voice level.

"Are you finished, Allison?" Spencer asked from the open doorway. He was leaning against the frame. He was only in a pair of gray sweatpants and wasn't wearing a shirt. I swallowed when I realized he looked angry. No one had noticed him so we'd probably been arguing in front of him for a while.

Allison whipped her head around to see Spencer. "I didn't see you there, Spence." she said.

"Obviously." he said. He gestured toward the door. "Come out here with me for a minute."

Allison obeyed and Spencer closed the door. I didn't bother listening in the conversation. I didn't want to know. By the way Spencer had let the light on when he left told me that I was the next one to get a talking to.

I started crying when I realized that my being here could severely damage Spencer's relationship with his family. It could take a huge toll on the entire relationship.

Spencer opened the door slowly. He closed it once he got into the room. "Are you all right?" he asked.

"You should check into getting me a different guard." I said bluntly.

"What she says right now doesn't matter. We can explain everything to all of them once all of this is over. Don't let it bother you." he said.

"None of your family likes me, Spencer. They only do because I'm your 'girlfriend'." I said and used air quotes again.

"Once this is over, they'll love you. Allison won't be like this once she realizes that you're not out for my money." he said.

"I don't want to stay here, Spencer." I said as my voice cracked. "It's hurting your family and I don't want to do that."

"Pen, it's not hurting them. They'll be fine." he said.

"Allison sure seemed hurt. You're her brother! You heard what she said! This is all my fault and I will not be responsible for your family being torn apart." I said and wiped the wetness off of my cheeks on my sleeve. "I'll talk to Amanda if you want." I said.

"You're not going anywhere." he said assertively.

"I'm not going to do this, Spencer! I hate pretending to be what I'm not!" I said, getting angry.

"It's either this or you go out into the world and be murdered. I'm not willing to let that happen." he said.

"Why do you keep saying that? All this is to you is a job. Why should it matter if I'm dead?" I asked.

"It does, Penelope." he said. He always used my real name now in private. It didn't bother me. I missed it.

I took a deep breath. "Allison is really suspicious, isn't she?"

He nodded. "Her heart's in the right place. She just knows something is off." he said.

"How can we get her to calm down?" I asked.

"To get her to finally believe it, we'd probably have to play it up a little bit." he said and looked at me.

"You're going to be sleeping in here now, aren't you?" I asked.

"I'm afraid so." he said.

"I call the floor." I said and tossed my pillow onto the floor.

"I was going to take the floor." he said.

"Then, we'll alternate. I'll take the floor tonight, you have it tomorrow." I said and sat down.

He shook his head and turned off the light.

ELEVEN

AUGUST 31ST

When I got to school, Josh didn't say a word to me. Neither did anyone else. I understood Josh and Weston, but unless Josh had opened his mouth, I saw no reason for Colleen to be angry with me. I didn't say anything about it. I just moved through my day and hoped Spencer had taken what I'd said about getting me a new guard into consideration. I didn't understand my sympathy healing and being in a place where everyone hated me didn't help with me being stressed.

I ate lunch alone and waited out the remainder of the day in silence.

I got to Spencer's car and waited to arrive at a place that nobody wanted me.

We got back to the house and I resided in Spencer's bedroom to do my homework. I couldn't be down there with them when I knew that I wasn't welcomed in the least.

I went to get a shower and I heard them downstairs. I couldn't help, but listen when I heard my name.

"She's still a child, Spencer." Spencer's father said.

"I know that, Dad." Spencer said.

"The point is that you're not! No matter if she's eighteen tomorrow or not! She is only a kid. This isn't like you. You've always had such good morals. I've never had to have a conversation like this with you; ever." his father continued.

"It's not going to change anything. She's not going anywhere for a long time." Spencer said.

My breath caught in my chest.

"You understand that your sister thinks this girl is using you, correct?"

"Yes. I talked to her last night." Spencer said.

"Allison is never wrong when it comes to her feelings about people and their intentions." Mr. Kendal said.

"Thea is not doing that, Dad. We've got all of this figured out." Spencer said.

"Are you really going to push everyone away because of a teenage girl?"

After that, I'd heard enough.

I walked out of Spencer's bedroom window. I couldn't stay there with all of this. I was going to ruin the family Spencer had. No matter how much I envied him for having it, he couldn't lose it.

I just walked down the streets for a while. I didn't know where I was going, but I had to go somewhere.

After about an hour of walking, I came to an old jungle gym. I sat on the bridge and stared out into the field behind the playground. I just needed a little bit of a break from walking.

My cell phone started ringing and I looked at the Caller ID. I didn't answer it because I didn't want to talk to Spencer. I didn't want him to know where I was, either.

I could just picture Allison once she figured out I was gone. I could see her laughing and just telling Spencer to tell me good riddance.

As the sun set, I was still walking. I had walked for nearly three hours. I just wanted away from this place.

I was walking on the side of a road by then and getting tired quickly. I knew that if I was out here alone, I was most likely going to be tracked down by either Spencer or Jacob. Eventually, I'd have to give up.

I listened to the three messages that Spencer had left me on my voicemail. They were all just asking where I was and threatening for me to come back to the house before he came after me.

I closed my phone and turned it off so he couldn't track it. Even if the feature wasn't there, he'd find a way.

I wasn't dressed right for it to get cold, but it did. I just sat on the sidewalk against a building and wrapped my arms around my legs. I didn't help much, but it was my fault for leaving without thinking through it.

Even if I had wanted to go back to the house, I couldn't have found my way back anyway. I was about a four hour walking distance from the house and it was dark.

When headlights came up the road, I got back up and started walking. I could tell from the silhouette of the car that it was Spencer's. I just needed to keep walking.

The car slowed down beside me and Spencer rolled down the passenger window.

"What the hell are you doing?" Spencer asked, trying to stay calm.

"I told you that I couldn't stay with them. I can't let you ruin everything for me." I said and kept walking.

"Penelope Ann, you better get in this car right now." he said.

I didn't say anything. I just kept walking. I was shivering and my teeth were chattering together.

"Don't make me get out and force you, Pen. I don't want to do that." he said.

"So don't." I said and looked at him. "Just leave me alone."

Spencer stopped the car and got out. He stood in my path. He was wearing a leather jacket and jeans. He looked so warm compared to me.

I had to stop before I ran into him.

"Let me through." I said calmly.

He looked down at me. "You must be freezing." he said.

"Leave me alone." I repeated. "How did you find me anyway?"

"You never thought to take off that necklace." he said.

I reached up and touched the cold metal. I sighed. I should have known.

"Come on." he said and grabbed my arm.

I yanked away from him. "I'm not going back there, Spencer." I said.

"The hell you're not." he said.

"None of them like me. I'm so sick of being somewhere where everyone hates me." I said.

"They do not hate you." he said.

"Bull. You and your father were already fighting about me being there, Spencer. Allison really hates me." I said and my voice cracked. "I just want to go home."

Spencer wrapped his arms around me and I laid my head on his chest as sobs shook my body. I put my arms inside of his coat and he was so warm. I stayed there while I cried.

"I know you do, Pen. I'm sorry. This shouldn't have happened." he said. "Let's just take you back so you can get warmed up. You're freezing."

"I don't want to." I said.

"Well, you're going to." he said sternly.

"I won't." I said and looked up at him.

"Bet me."

"How much?" I asked.

He scooped me up into his arms and carried me. I didn't fight him. All I'd do is cause a scene.

Plus, he was holding me.

Spencer sat me in the front seat and the car was really warm. He buckled me in after he got in because my hands were shivering so bad that I couldn't even keep a hold on the buckle. I didn't understand why it was so cold.

When Spencer's hands closed over one of mine, trying to warm it up, I couldn't move and a warm shiver shot up my spine.

"What were you thinking? You could have gotten yourself killed, Pen." he said as he shrugged off his jacket and put it around me. I wrapped it around me tightly. It was so warm from his body heat and it smelled like him.

"I'm sorry. I just want this all to be over so we can get back to our lives and you can start telling the truth again." I said as my teeth clattered together.

"I think we all want that. Let's not get ourselves killed, though, okay? That includes running away when I have my back turned." he said. He cranked up the heat and started driving.

"How long of a drive is it?" I asked.

"It's about an hour. We'll be back before you know it." he said.

I leaned against the window and watched the dim street lights pass.

"I'm sorry. I didn't mean for you to come after me. I wish you wouldn't have." I said quietly.

"Well, I'm always going to. I told you before that I actually do care about what happens to you." he said and looked at me.

"You shouldn't. All I'm doing is tearing you away from all of your family. It's not fair that you care about me when I'm causing the damage that I am." I said.

"This was my idea, Pen. It wasn't yours. It's just very secure there. I mean, both of Grace's and Brittany's husbands are cops. Dad's retired, but he was a cop too. We have one amazing security system there." he said.

"I don't want your family to hate me because they all think I'm just using you. Even though we're not together, I don't want the reputation." I said.

"They don't hate you. Allison has good intuition and they all know it. They just don't want me hurt." he said.

"They do hate me, Spencer. Allison even told me that she doesn't like me." I said.

"That doesn't mean she hates you." he said.

I shook my head. "Don't be so optimistic." I said.

"Come on. How can they not like you, Pen? You're nice and beautiful and young and just a great person. I'm sure if we weren't in this situation, they'd love you." he said and looked at me. My heart pounded as his gaze connected with mine. He held it for a moment and then focused back on the road.

"Without this situation, I would have never met them, though." I said and leaned the back of my head against the window and pressed my back to the door.

"Maybe not." he said. He swallowed hard.

I just looked at him as my body started to warm up. "Is Allison still suspicious?" I asked.

"Very." he said and stopped at a red light. "I think it's getting worse instead of better. She knows something isn't right. She isn't going to give up until she finds what it is. Not even if we move out. She'll find out eventually."

I swallowed. "I'm sorry. I still just suck at lying. Plus, I'm really sick of it. I don't really try as hard when I don't want to lie." I said.

"There is no way to not lie. We're in too much of a fix to do anything right now. I mean, Amanda and Oliver are doing all they can, but we can't do anything, but wait. That's all we're allowed to do." he said.

"All we're *allowed* to do? When have I ever followed the rules, Spencer?" I asked and smiled.

"You're going to start. We cannot afford any danger to you other than what you just had." Spencer said.

"I'm sorry. I didn't know it would worry you." I said.

"You didn't know it would worry me?" he asked, laughing. "I've been trying to keep you safe because I actually give a rat's ass about what happens to you. How would I have not been worried?" he asked.

"I don't know. I just wasn't thinking about it. You were just fighting with your dad and I didn't want to be the stake that drove you all apart. I would never have been able to live with that." I said.

"You won't have to. You're not tearing us apart. We're all going to be fine for the time being." he said.

"It's only for the time being, but not forever. What are you going to do when it does start affecting all of you?" I asked.

"We'll figure it out, Pen." he said quietly.

"Not in time, we won't." I said.

"Yes, we will. Just relax. Get some sleep." he said.

"I don't want to sleep." I said.

"You're so stubborn." Spencer said.

"Shut up. You love it." I said and laughed.

He smiled and shook his head.

"So, that's not a no." I said.

Again, he didn't answer me.

"Can I ask you something?" I asked.

"Of course." he said.

"When I kissed you, you kissed me back. Why?" I asked.

"Instinct." he answered simply.

"No, it was more than that. You wouldn't have gone against what you thought was right for an instinct." I said. "No lies."

He didn't answer.

"You actually feel something for me, don't you?" I asked.

"That is none of my concern." Spencer said.

"Liar!" I shouted.

"Pen, just let it go." Spencer said. "Amanda was right and we both know it."

"Just because she's right doesn't mean you can't admit it. It's better to let your feelings out, Spencer." I said and smiled. "I just talked about why I didn't want to go back to your house now talk to me. I need to know. We might not have to lie." I said.

"No, we wouldn't have to lie to my family. We'd be lying to Amanda. That's worse." he said.

"You're not denying it."

He was silent.

I smiled. "Was it before or after the kiss?" I asked.

"What?" he asked.

"When did you admit it to yourself?" I said.

"I don't know. During, I guess." he said quietly.

"Really?" I asked.

He shrugged.

"That *is* why you kissed me back." I said. "Why didn't you tell me?"

"Again, we're back to the whole Amanda issue." Spencer said.

"Who cares about what Amanda thinks? She isn't in control of you." I said.

"She's my boss, Pen. Of course she's in control of me." Spencer said.

I didn't argue. I knew I'd just lose. I mean, he was right. He couldn't go against Amanda. If he did, he'd be in some major trouble.

"I'm sorry." I said and looked at him. He was staring at the road. I could tell that he knew I was looking at him though. "Is this why you wouldn't let me have another guard?"

"With me is the only way to guarantee that you're safe at all times." Spencer said.

I smiled. "That's nice. I'm glad that you care so much." I said and leaned the side of my head on the back of the seat.

Before I knew it, I was asleep.

I woke up to Spencer laying me gently into his bed. He pulled the blankets up to my neck and returned to his spot on the floor. I was too tired to say anything.

TWELVE

"Wake up, Pen." Spencer said, shaking my shoulder gently.

I looked up at him and rubbed my eyes. "Is it time to get up already?" I asked.

"Yeah." he said.

I got up and went to get a shower. I scrunched my hair and got changed.

I went back into Spencer's room to get my backpack when I noticed the date. How could I have forgotten about my birthday?

I noticed the time too. It was past nine. I started grabbing my things and trying to find Spencer to take me to school. I was going to be late already.

"Spencer! Where are you?" I shouted.

I went down the stairs and Spencer was down in the kitchen cooking. The smell of chocolate chip pancakes filled the house. I just wasn't paying attention to that. All I could see was a shirtless Spencer.

"I have to get to school, Spencer. I'm already late because my alarm didn't go off." I said.

"I turned it off. It's your birthday. You shouldn't have to go to school." Spencer said. His whole family was starting to enter the kitchen. I got a few happy birthday wishes, but nothing from Allison. I figured as much.

I took what I got and didn't argue with Spencer on the birthday subject. Everyone sat down to eat since Spencer was cooking. I sat a seat down from Allison and I didn't want to cause any trouble so I sat on the other side of the table.

Spencer brought over probably four plates at a time so he covered everyone in two trips. He sat next to me. I wasn't expecting him to pull through with his promise, but he did.

When he kissed me, it was like a hundred tiny fireworks exploding on my lips. It was short, sweet, and intoxicating. I kissed him back and tried to savor the connection as long as I could. When he pulled away, I could feel my cheeks flushing. My heart pounded harder in my chest and my knees felt like Jell-O. I was glad I was sitting or I would have fallen over.

His mother smiled and Allison frowned and looked to the table.

As we ate, things began to get more awkward. It was so quiet. I wasn't used to it.

"How long are you guys planning on staying here?" Grace asked after a moment.

I looked at Spencer.

"Probably until I find a new job and get back on my feet." Spencer said.

"Thea has a job, right?" she asked.

"No. I won't let her work." Spencer said.

"Why not?" Allison asked.

"She shouldn't have to work and balance school. I never had to." Spencer said.

"Your parents were also rich. For all we know, she killed hers." she said, her voice cold.

It struck a chord. My breath froze in my throat.

"Excuse me." I said and left the table for Spencer's bedroom. I could hear Spencer's footsteps behind me as tears streaked my cheeks. My chest got tight and I wiped my tears away. I sat on Spencer's bed and wiped off my cheeks. Spencer came and sat next to me.

"She's right. I did kill my mother." I said.

"No, you didn't, Pen. You had no control over how weak she was. It wasn't you." he said.

"It was *because* of me!" I shouted. I was already crying again. "She's dead because I was born." I wiped off my cheeks to no avail of getting them dry.

"It was not your fault. You couldn't have controlled when you were born. Things happen that aren't anyone's fault. They just happen. This is just one of those things. No one could have saved her." he said, taking my hand gently in his.

"I could have. Anyone could have if they were a sympath. Someone had to have been." I said.

"No one was until your father found out about that new gene, Pen." Spencer said.

I clamped my eyes shut as more tears streamed out of my eyes. I couldn't help the sob that escaped me.

Spencer pulled me into his lap and held me there until I stopped crying. I just rested my head on his shoulder and took deep breaths. I enjoyed the way Spencer's arms felt as they held me to him and let me let it all out on him.

"I told you that your sister hated me." I said.

"She's just like that. She's always been hostile with new people." Spencer said and his fingers gently caressed my back through my shirt. It was a very settling touch. It made me curl into his chest.

"Do I deserve it?" I asked.

"No, you don't. I'm going to have a long talk with her again later. She's acting like a child." Spencer said.

"No, she's not. She's being protective. I can understand." I said.

"She still has no reason to act like this. This should be my decision, not her's." he said.

I looked up at him.

"Are you all right?" he asked.

"Yes. I'll be fine. We should probably go back downstairs. I mean, we have to put on a show, right?" I said and gave a forced laugh.

"Yeah, we have to put up a show." he said.

"What if I want it to be more than just a show?" I asked quietly. I hadn't thought through the question so my cheeks flushed and I jumped off of Spencer's lap. "I'm sorry. I didn't mean to say that." I said.

"Yes, you did." he said and smiled. "We already established this, remember?"

"What does Amanda matter? Why would she even have to know?" I asked.

"If she found out we were lying to her, she would not be happy. I could even lose my job." he said.

"How exactly would she find out?" I asked.

"Amanda can figure things out better than you think. She can get a hold of security tapes and everything. There's no way to hide it." Spencer explained.

"We're supposed to be acting, remember? How would it be suspicious if she saw anything? We're supposed to be doing this!" I shouted.

"She'd figure it out. Trust me." he said.

He'd stood up. I got an idea so I went with it. I put my hands on the back of his neck and pulled him down to kiss me. I put my arms around his neck and he pulled me closer to him as he kissed me back. His arms looped around my waist. My heart sped up and I couldn't calm down. When he started to pull away, my hands tangled in his hair and pulled his mouth back to mine. My knees grew weak so I used him for support.

His hands spread across my lower back and pulled my hips to his. I opened my mouth and he took it as a direct invitation. He pushed his tongue just past my teeth and my whole body flared up in temperature. I pulled away to catch my breath and my forehead was still against his. I pulled my hand through my hair without moving my head.

His breathing was just as ragged as mine. He didn't move his hands from my waist. My hands settled on his chest.

A flash came from the doorway. Both of Spencer and I looked over quickly. Miranda was standing in the doorway holding a massive digital camera. She looked at the screen and smiled. She looked at us.

"I'm sorry. I didn't mean to interrupt. You two just made for such a great picture. I mean, the kiss was great, but that moment was just magical." she said and smiled.

Spencer smiled and chuckled. "Don't worry about it, Miranda."

She left the room and Spencer looked down at me. "That was ambush."

"It was not." I said and smiled. "You seemed to like it."

"That's beside the point." he said. "Just because you like it, doesn't mean you can have it."

I rolled my eyes. "Would you stop being so reluctant? I promise you that we won't get caught!"

"You make it sound like we're like thirteen-year-olds smoking behind my parents' house or something." Spencer said and stepped away from me. He ran both hands through his hair.

"So, according to Amanda, you're not allowed to be happy?" I said and crossed my arms across my chest.

"No. I'm allowed to be happy. I'm just not allowed to be happy with you." he explained. He was pacing and had his hands on the back of his neck. I sat on the bed. "This never should have happened. It will only cause trouble."

I shook my head. "This is why I didn't want to come back here. All I'm doing is causing trouble. You should have just let me there." I said.

Before I knew he moved, he was leaning over me with his hands on the mattress. His body was so close to mine that it caught me off guard.

"I would never do that, Penelope. You know that as well as I do. No one deserves to be hunted down like an animal like you are. I can't let them hurt you because that means that they win. I won't let them win." he said through his teeth.

"If they win, it will be over, Spencer. You won't have to compromise anything anymore. You can just be free." I said.

"It will never be over. As long as there is one member of the Elite left and is reproducing, they won't stop. Innocent people are dying because these people are trying to destroy you all. If I wanted to be free, I wouldn't be here. You know that. Everything is difficult, but once we track down this leader, it won't be difficult anymore. I am not letting you out of my sight until I am sure that you will be safe." he said.

"Family comes first, Spencer." I said simply.

"They aren't getting hurt. I swear." Spencer said. "Just listen to me, Penelope."

"Penelope?"

The voice had come from the doorway. We both looked to the source. Allison was standing there with her arms crossed over her chest. She didn't look angry. At most, she looked confused.

"Allison." Spencer said quietly.

"What's going on? I swear to God, I'll know if you lie to me, Spencer." she said.

Spencer looked at me and I just shook my head. This *would* happen to us. No one else would ever have this problem in their lives. It was all just too complicated.

"Who is Penelope?" Allison asked.

"I am." I said. It was only loud enough for Allison to hear. I couldn't speak any louder with the fear that clogged my throat.

Her eyes widened. "What? No. You're Thea." she insisted.

Spencer stood up, took her gently by the arm, and brought her into the room. He closed and locked the door behind them.

"She's Penelope." he said.

"No, she's not." Allison said.

"This isn't going to work if you don't just let us explain, Ally." Spencer said and she sat on the bed.

She nodded. "Okay. I won't interrupt." she promised.

"You can't say a single word of this to anyone. You don't know a Penelope." Spencer said and Allison nodded again.

Spencer started explaining the whole story about the Elite and the story about my father. When he told her about my sympathy healing, she got all wide-eyed and I was terrified that she was going to pass out so I took her hand in mine gently. She looked at me and I smiled at her.

Spencer completed the explanation with the story of how I was attacked and he was my guard and Allison looked to me again.

"I was right all along. Both of you *were* lying." she said.

"We had to. We didn't have a choice." Spencer said.

She shook her head. "This can't be happening. This has to be some crazy dream because I refuse to believe that I am crazy."

"You're not crazy." I said.

"Then, why did my older brother just tell me that his girlfriend is really part of some weird race and can heal people? Someone's either lying or I'm totally insane." she said and managed to smile the whole time.

I grabbed my compact mirror out of my purse and opened it up. I pushed on the mirror until it broke. I grabbed one of the little shards with one hand and Allison's forearm with the other. Spencer didn't stop me as I slid the sharp shard the entire way down her forearm. She yelped and cursed at me before pulling from my grasp. I dropped the bloody shard and grabbed her forearm. I really did want to take her pain away because I had caused it.

As the pain blistered down my forearm, I yanked away and bit my lip. Spencer rolled his eyes and started wrapping the wound right away. I was glad he was always prepared with first aid stuff.

Allison stared at her forearm. "What the . . ." She couldn't finish the sentence.

"I healed you." I said and took my wrapped arm from Spencer.

"No. It's not possible. That should have taken weeks to heal. There's not even a scar." she said.

I was already really tired from the energy I used to heal her. I felt like I was gonna pass out. I blinked and I couldn't get my eyelids back open. I fell backwards onto the bed and Allison yelped.

"What's wrong?" she asked.

Spencer moved me so I was against the pillows. I opened my eyes and groaned. My head pounded because of my sudden release of energy.

"She uses a lot of energy to heal someone. The only other time she's done it is when I was shot a couple days ago." he said.

"She took a bullet for you?" Allison asked.

"You remember when I used to tell you about the little girl that liked me when I was a senior, right?" Spencer asked.

She did a double-take. "This is that Penelope?"

"It turns out she still has a thing for me." he said and smiled at me.

"You're a jerk." I muttered.

Allison smiled. "This is so weird." she said.

Spencer smiled. "If anyone asks, you don't know anything, got it?"

"I got it." She hugged Spencer tightly. "I'm glad you told me the truth."

Spencer chuckled. "No problem, Sis."

When she left, Spencer stood beside the bed and looked down at me. "You didn't have to prove anything."

"Yes, I did." I said in a quiet tone. "Can I take a nap?"

"Go ahead." he said.

I grabbed his shirt and—with the little strength I had—pulled him to my level and kissed him once. He pulled back and shook his head.

"You are so reluctant." he said.

"I know. But, you don't care. You love it." I said and smiled.

He left the side of the bed and I was asleep before I knew where he'd gone.

When I woke up, my forearm was healed up so I tore the bandaging off of it and threw the gauze in the garbage. I walked down the stairs and Allison smiled at me. "Good morning, Sleepyhead." she said and Mr. Kendal raised a suspicious eyebrow. He didn't say anything though. It probably wasn't the best thing to comment on my appearance since I had just slept for a couple hours. I was probably a mess.

Spencer came into the room when he heard Allison speak to me. "You look better."

"I feel better, too." I said and managed to smile at him. I still really didn't want to be here. I just wanted to be back in my little apartment in my old little town. I was doing just fine alone. I had hated it, but now, I missed it.

"That's good." he said and took my hand in his. I didn't resist. We had to keep this up for just a little while longer. Oliver and Amanda had to have found a lead somewhere. I'd be home free soon enough.

I just had to learn to lay low. I'd be doing it for the rest of my life.

THIRTEEN

DECEMBER 1ST

S pencer and I hadn't discussed a relationship at all in the past few months. Colleen had started talking to me and Josh and I had gotten very close again. He didn't believe I was even a threat anymore. Weston was still keeping his distance from me which I actually appreciated. I couldn't bring him down with me, too. He had been completely happy.

Spencer's sisters had all gone back home. Brittany and Grace visited often with their husbands. Allison and Miranda had come home again on winter break. Allison and I had been texting nonstop since she left. We'd become amazing friends and I told her everything. Spencer had been right that she liked me as long as she knew I wasn't using him for his money.

After school, I waited for Allison. She came into the house and I jumped onto her, hugging her tightly. She laughed in her usual innocent way as she held me up against her.

The whole family came for dinner. We ate and everyone chatted to each other . . . except me. I didn't say anything to anyone. I had never expected to be here this long so I never tried to get close to the other members of the family.

After dinner, I pulled Spencer aside. The hallway was empty. I had to speak quietly so it wouldn't echo. It wasn't the smartest thing to talk when the family was so close, but we couldn't go too far or they would get suspicious.

"You told me that we wouldn't be here long." I said.

"I also told you that I miscalculated the amount of time it would take to find Jacob's superior. I'm sorry. I didn't think it would take this long. I already talked to my parents. They really don't mind us being here." Spencer promised me in a low voice.

"I bothers me, Spencer! I hate thinking someone has to take care of me. They only want to do it because they think we're out of our minds in love." I said and crossed my arms over my chest.

"Let them think that. We're still in a secure place and that is all we need." he said.

I shook my head. "Do you really want me to run away again?" I asked.

"Of course not." Spencer said.

"Then, we need to get out of here. No one likes me except you and Allison. The rest just pretend to like me." I said.

"My mom absolutely adores you and Brittany and Grace aren't around enough to like you."

"Your father definitely does not like me." I said angrily.

"What does that matter? My family in general loves you." he said.

"Please?" I asked, pouting my lip.

He cocked his head to the side. "That is not going to get you anywhere, Penelope Ann."

I smiled and pulled him down to kiss me. I pulled back. "That might." I said and kissed him again. We kissed enough that I didn't understand why we couldn't be together.

He pushed me away gently. "No." he said.

I sighed. "You're so stubborn. Amanda isn't going to do anything about it; especially, if she doesn't know." I said and pulled him down enough so I could feel his breath on my lips.

"She'll figure it out."

"She will not. We're good at hiding, remember? That's why I'm not dead yet." I smiled.

He rolled his eyes. "Just stop it, Pen. You know as well as I do that it will only be a distraction."

"Why would it be? Wouldn't it just be more motivation to protect me?" I asked.

He pondered for a moment. "Perhaps."

"Then, it's settled."

"No, it isn't." he said. He kissed me once. "You know that I wish we could."

"No, actually, I don't. I still kind of think this is all for show." I said.

He shook his head. "I wouldn't go against everything I believe is right for show, Pen. You know that."

"Stop saying that. I don't know anything." I said.

"Of course you do." he said.

"All I know is that you're acting like a stubborn jackass." I said and smiled at him.

"Forgive me for trying to keep you as safe as you can be."

"This would be motivation! We could stop lying to your family for once." I was practically begging. I really never got my way when I was with Spencer and begging was a last resort.

"We'll still have to lie. They think I'm still unemployed."

"Fake a job." I said.

"Then, we'll have to move out." Spencer said.

"You're finally getting it!" I said and laughed.

He frowned. "No. We are staying here."

I groaned. "You never let me do anything."

"That's a lie."

"It is not! We can't actually be together. We can't live where I want to. What kind of freedom is this?" I asked.

"It's not. We can't be together because it would compromise your safety. We can't live where you want because—again—it would ruin the stable safety we have. There isn't freedom. If there was, everything would be different." he said. His hand rested on my waist and his thumb caressed my hip gently.

I pushed against his chest and away from him. "Yes, it would be. We would never have met again because you weren't willing to make a fool out of yourself to make a little girl's dream come true." I said and walked away. I knew that would hit him below the belt. He'd told me that he regretted his decision to break his promise.

Spencer followed me, but I got back out to his family before he could say anything.

I was talking with Brittany when she started playing with my hair. It wasn't that weird because she did it all of the time. Spencer had warned me that she'd do it. I didn't care because I loved when people played with my hair.

"You should come into my shop one time so I could get you a trim. Your hair's getting really long and—no offense—but it's full of split ends." she said and smiled.

"I just don't like when people pay for things for me and Spencer's won't let me get a job. I couldn't pay for it. I'm broke." I explained pathetically.

"I get a haircut and color for half off every thirty days. I'll let you use it this month and I'll just get one next month." She looked at my nails. "You could use a manicure too." she said.

"I can't let you do that, Brittany." I said.

"Why don't you just think of it as your Christmas present." she said.

I didn't argue further. I knew I wouldn't get anywhere.

As the family talked about old Christmas times together, I remembered my last Christmas. I had sat in my living room walking a twenty-four hour marathon of *Degrassi: The Next Generation*. It's not like I had family to share it with. I didn't have the spare cash to do anything away from home. All I had was a part-time job at the pizzeria and a crappy apartment that held everything I never wanted. The only extra money I had was the five thousand or so dollars that I was saving for college.

I was sort of jealous that Spencer had gotten to spend Christmas with his family and I didn't. I was growing quite fond of all of them. They were so loving and mostly accepting. I hated knowing that I'd never have that again once this is all done.

I tried to look at the bright side. There had to be something good in my future. Maybe, I'd get married. That was unlikely though. I never actually believed that I'd get married. I didn't want to tie a man down to my crazy life.

Being alone couldn't be that bad. I had always liked being alone. That is, until it was the only choice I had. Now, it sort of scared me.

I took a deep breath and played with my hair quietly.

As Spencer and I were getting ready for bed, he went to get the mail. One of the envelopes was addressed to him so he tore it open. He pulled out a piece of paper and read it silently. A smile lined his lips as he pulled something else out of the envelope.

He walked over to me as I was putting my hair up. He held out something for me. "Amanda thought you might want this back. They found it when they were cleaning out your apartment."

I looked at whatever it was and found it was a check. It was for over five thousand dollars. I smiled. "It's my savings." I reached out and took the check.

"Amanda put the cash into her checking account so she could send the check instead of the hard cash." he said and smiled.

"I can't believe they found it." I said. I looked up at Spencer and handed it back to him. "You can have it. You've been so amazing and I just feel like I can't give back." I said.

"I'm not taking your money, Pen." he said.

"Yes, you are." I said and put the check into his jeans' pocket.

"Why are you so stubborn? I have plenty of money. I don't want yours. Use it for college or something." Spencer said and handed the check to me again.

"Please, just take it. Once this is over, I'm probably just going to go back to my apartment and do whatever I can to hold down a normal life. I don't want to put this into an account that I know won't ever become anything, but grocery money." I said.

"By the time this is all said and done, there will be plenty of money in that account for college. Amanda already has an account set up for you because she knows you couldn't pay from a descent college by yourself. She thinks you deserve it. She's been putting a couple hundred in every week." Spencer said.

My jaw dropped. "No. *No.* She's not paying for my college. I won't let her."

"You don't have a choice. The account is in her name. Once you decide on a college, she's going to start making the tuition payments."

"No, she isn't. I won't tell any of you what college I'm going to because I'm not going to college. If I was, I wouldn't tell you anyway because I don't want her to do that. I hate when people pay for things for me and you know it." I said. It made me feel like a beggar and I just wanted to pay them back. I didn't like owing anyone anything.

"She wants to do this for you, Pen. Just let her."

"No! I won't be that person, Spencer!" I shouted. "I can't. I can never afford to pay her back."

He looked at me and raised an eyebrow. "She doesn't want your money."

"I don't care! I'm not letting her do this!" I said sternly.

He didn't say anything to that.

"Please, don't let her." I said.

"I'll make no promises." Spencer said.

"And you call me stubborn." I muttered under my breath.

"I'm allowed to be stubborn." He smiled.

"I just feel bad that she's paying me and I'm not doing anything for her." I said and sat on the bed. "I feel like I should be working for her."

He shrugged. "She just wants you on the right track to living the rest of your life normally and happily." he said.

"There has to be something I can do to work for her." I said.

"No. We are supposed to just stay secure."

"What if I want to help?"

I did want to help. There were people just like me that were running for their lives. Not a single one of them had done anything wrong. We were all just born into this. They need help too. I shouldn't be the only one getting attention.

"She won't let you." he assured me. "She just wants you safe."

"I'm sure there's something I can do. It could just be something that I wouldn't possibly get hurt." I was determined to help Amanda.

"When working for the WPP, there's always that chance." he said.

"I'll be careful, Spencer." I promised.

He took my face in his hands. "The answer is still no. It's too big of a risk. We can't risk losing you."

I pulled out of his grip. "Just let me try. This guy tried to kill me. I have a score to settle."

"Exactly! He tried to *kill you*! He's not going to let you do anything, but die. If you get involved with this, he'll kill you. No one would think twice about it. You would just be another victim of a serial killer." he said.

"I can't just sit around and wait for him to kill me! If I'm going to die, I want it to be doing something useful." I exclaimed. I was really frustrated. It was the Witness Protection Program for crying out loud! If I worked there, I could help and actually have something to do with my life.

"Getting yourself killed would be the opposite of useful." he said.

His phone started ringing so he excused himself to the hallways to talk. He was out there for a good half hour. When he came back, he looked stressed.

"What's wrong?" I asked.

"Jacob struck again. A thirteen-year-old kid was severely injured, but Oliver got to him in time. A girl that knew she was part of the Elite was killed. She was eighteen and had her son with her. He's only five. He just doesn't have anywhere to go, but he's all right other than that. Mom wants to be his counselor. I told her that my boss from my other job wanted her to check him out." he explained.

The story pulled at my heart. It was hard to lose a parent. He was a lot younger than I was too. It had to be horrible on him.

"Amanda thinks he's going to need counseling. He saw it happen and he hasn't spoken to anyone about it. He doesn't even seem like it registered. They explained it to him, but he doesn't really react at all."

He was talking a lot, but I understand why. It was his way of letting it out. Spencer needed that because he always felt guilty for the death of someone that could have been saved if he had been there.

Spencer sat down next to me and I took his hand in mine. He tensed for a moment, but quickly relaxed. "It'll be okay, Spencer. I promise."

Spencer looked at me. Guilt, thick and hearty, clouded his eyes. "You can't guarantee that, Pen. It's getting harder to catch these guys."

"I'm sure you guys will. Have a little faith." I said and smiled.

"In the meantime, more people are going to die because they can't control what they are. It's just not right. We can't protect all of them." He sighed and his hand squeezed mine. "I wish we could."

"I'm sorry." I said. I was. If I could have changed the fact that we had all been born into this life, I would have.

He chuckled. "How is this your fault?" he asked.

"I wish I could help." I said.

He smiled and kissed me softly once. "Don't worry about it."

"I can't help it. You just seem so stressed out and I want to help you through this."

"You don't have to, Pen."

"I should." I argued.

He shook his head. "We need to go to bed. You have school in the morning." he said and took his spot on the floor.

"You won't even consider it." I said.

He didn't reply. I just rolled my eyes and turned off the lights.

FOURTEEN

DECEMBER 2ND

I couldn't sleep. I'd stared at the ceiling for two hours. It didn't help that I was really frustrated from the lack of sleep. It was already one in the morning and I hadn't gotten a wink of sleep. I rolled over in the bed and sighed.

"Are you all right?" Spencer asked from the floor.

"Why are you still awake?" I asked.

"Why are you?" he countered.

"I can't sleep." I admitted.

"Why?" he asked.

"I'm not quite sure." I said. "I'll fall asleep eventually."

"Just relax, Pen."

"That's kind of hard, you know. Life is really complicated at the moment. I have a lot to think about." I said and lay on my back.

"Well, don't think about it. We'll take it day-by-day. Just close your eyes and go to sleep." he coached.

"You first." I said.

"I'm not supposed to sleep until you do." he said.

"Go to sleep, Spencer." I ordered.

"You need more sleep than I do." he said.

I sighed and rolled my eyes. He had a rebuttal for everything.

As I stared at the ceiling, I spoke. "What happens if your family finds out about me?" My voice was quiet and very timid. I had been terrified to ask the question to Spencer. I didn't really want to know the answer.

"I'm not sure. I'm just doing whatever Amanda tells me to. I'm not getting any more information than what Amanda wants me to know. She knows I've been giving you updates and I'm not supposed to be so she's restricting me." Spencer explained.

"Do you think she'd move us?" I asked.

"I really have no idea." Spencer said honestly. I knew that Amanda had a certain way of doing things. She had a way of getting people right where she wants them and no further.

I swallowed. "I don't want to leave."

He laughed. "Yesterday you sure did."

"Now, I don't." It was true. It was nice here. I actually felt like I was part of a family. I wasn't just a creepy loner teenager that sat in her apartment with the windows boarded up. I didn't like being isolated.

"Why not?" he asked.

"I'm just sick of being alone. It's not like I have a family to go back to." I said and sniffled.

"Don't you dare go crying on me, Pen." Spencer said, sitting up.

"I won't. I just hate that I kind of don't ever want to go home." I said. My chest tightened up and I bit the inside of my lip, successfully pushing away the tears. I was so done crying. Obviously, it didn't help anything.

He shook his head. "That's not such a bad thing. I'm not trying to be mean or anything, but your life really—*seriously*—sucked. I mean, my family likes you. I tell you that all of the time. I promise you that they wouldn't let you live like that again. My mother wouldn't stand for it. Worse comes to worst, you'll be here."

"What if I do something and she turns out to hate me? I'll be screwed." I said sadly.

"You will not. She sucks at holding grudges." he said.

I played with the sheets in my fingers. "I just wish I could go back to my dad." I said.

My voice had broken so I took a deep breath and swallowed. Spencer sighed and stood up. He walked to the bed and sat beside me. I didn't look at him because I knew he'd say something and make me cry.

"Look at me, Pen." he said.

I shook my head.

"Come on. I know that you're upset." he said.

I still didn't reply.

He sat and waited.

"Please, just leave me alone." I was begging.

"Not a chance. You need to talk to someone. You always just push it away like it doesn't bother you, but everyone can tell it hurts you like crazy. You just hate to admit it because you think that everyone thinks you're such a hard, emotionless person. We all get upset sometimes. Holding it in isn't a good way to handle it." he said.

I bit my lip and swallowed as the sadness crawled up my throat. "You wouldn't understand it."

"I don't need to understand to let you vent. You need to talk about it. Just tell me about what it was like before he left. If it doesn't help by then, you don't have to keep talking. If it makes you feel better, you can tell me as much as you want." he said.

I began talking just because I thought I wouldn't keep talking. I eventually started crying and just talking about everything that happened with my dad even if it hurt. I couldn't seem to stop talking.

Afterward, Spencer held me until I finally fell asleep.

I woke up to my alarm blaring in my ear. I groaned and smacked it with my hand.

That's when I noticed that I was still in Spencer's arms. He'd fallen asleep with me asleep on his chest. He was still asleep. My cheek was resting on his chest and he was holding me to him. His back was resting on the pillows at the top of the bed.

My hand slid down his abs gently. They felt just as amazing as they looked. They were defined, but not bulging. It was as if he was made specifically for my specifications. He was absolutely perfect.

I moved to sit up and his grip tightened for a moment before he opened his eyes. He looked down at me, smiled, and blinked. Then, I stood up and swallowed.

"I'm sorry. I should have moved." I said and tried to gather my clothes.

"I would have moved you if I didn't want you there." Spencer said and smiled.

I took a deep breath and left the room. I couldn't look at him and actually process what he'd just said. There's no way that I'd heard him right.

I came back in after I was dressed and grabbed my bag for school. Spencer came in behind me. He kissed me gently and I pushed away from him instinctively.

"Are you drunk or something?" I asked.

"I don't drink often, Pen. Now isn't even a special occasion." I didn't see how he was so amused with this. He loved playing with my head.

"Then, why are you acting like this?"

"How am I acting?" His voice was sincerely confused.

"You're acting like we're actually together. We're not allowed to be, remember? You are the one that told me that. 'No, Pen. We could get in trouble!'" I quoted him.

"Who's going to get us into trouble?" he said and smiled. His arms snaked around my waist and he kissed me again. Even if I had wanted to, I couldn't stop. I just let him pull me close to his chest.

By the time he pulled away, I was panting. "What is wrong with you? Yesterday, this was a crime. What changed?" I asked.

He shook his head. "I just realized that there's no way Amanda will find out unless we're very, bluntly obvious." He touched my cheek softly. "What's the worst she could do? If I really would lose my job, my parents wouldn't know. Besides, I doubt that Amanda can afford to lose me."

I smiled. "Maybe." I said.

Spencer kissed my forehead.

I was sort of arguing with myself that he didn't really mean this. Something was different. I was just too caught up in it all.

"I have to get to school." I said and pulled out of his arms.

We left and got to school right on time.

Josh met up with me and hugged me tightly. I returned it and he told me about his date with Jayden the previous night. I wished I could tell someone about last night and this morning, but I couldn't.

I mean, it may strike them as a little weird that I was making out with my brother.

I could talk to Allison. She'd listen. I figured she would because she's told me about her very explicit love life. I could tell her about my innocent session with her older brother.

School seemed to roll on forever. I was just ready to go home and live in the shadows again.

When the final bell rang, I was out of the school and to Spencer's car in a matter of two minutes. He pulled away from the curb with a grim expression.

"What's wrong?" I asked.

Spencer swallowed. "Allison's pregnant."

I allowed my jaw to drop. "What?" I asked.

"She's due in June. She's already three months along." Spencer said.

"How long has she known?"

"She just had me pick up the test today." Spencer rubbed the back of his neck with his hand. "I don't know what she's gonna do. She's in the middle of college."

"I'm sure she'll figure it out." I said. I had a lot of worry myself.

"Ally's not even old enough to drink, let alone to be a mother." Spencer was panicking. He loved his sister and he knew that having a baby changed everything. Her life would never be the same. *She* would never be the same.

"Is the father still around?" I asked.

"No. Once he found out that Allison wanted a serious relationship, he dumped her." Spencer said.

"That jerk is the one that got her pregnant?" I asked, angry. Allison had told me about that no more than two months ago. Allison had been so torn up about it. I clenched my teeth. "I could kill that guy."

Spencer smiled. "If I ever see him, I'll let you have your chance."

I couldn't believe Allison was pregnant. I never would have thought that she'd be a mother. She never even told me that she had a suspicion.

I ran a hand through my hair. "I can't believe this." I said.

"Neither could I." Spencer said.

I shook my head. Memories of my father trying to give me the sex talk when I was eleven came flooding back. I swallowed them back.

Spencer looked at me. "What's wrong?"

"It's just the normal." I said and smiled. "I'm fine."

We were quiet. As we got out of the car, Spencer spoke. "Mom and Dad don't know about the baby yet. Allison is going to wait a little while to tell them."

"It's nice that she trusts you so much." I said.

He nodded in agreement.

We got inside and I couldn't find Allison. I eventually found her in her bedroom, hugging a pillow. She looked like she'd been crying. Allison looked up at me. "Spencer told you?"

"He figured you were going to anyway." I said.

She nodded. "Yes, I would have."

I sat on the bed with her. "How are you feeling?" I asked.

"Better than last week." she said. "I thought I had the flu. I guess I was wrong."

I sighed. "I'm sorry. I wish I could have guessed."

She shook her head. "What am I going to do? My mom is going to be so mad."

"I'm sure she'll understand. I mean, she's your mom. She won't disown you for having a baby." I said.

She swallowed. "I don't know. I guess that's what scares me. I don't know that she'll accept it. If she doesn't, I'm as good as street trash. My mom doesn't like having things that she opposes near her. She'd kick me out."

"No, she won't. Your mother would never be able to live with herself knowing she put her daughter and a baby onto the streets." I promised her and took her hand in mine.

She shook her head.

"That's what I'm afraid of. I don't want her to raise my baby, either, but I have nowhere else to go. I don't have money to pay for anywhere either." She pulled her knees to her chest. "I don't know what to do."

"You should tell your mom, for starters." I said.

She bit the inside of her lip. "I can't."

"Of course you can." I said with a light-hearted smile. "I can help."

She shook her head. "This isn't your problem to deal with. I'll take care of it." she said and started down the stairs.

I followed her. The moment she saw her mother sitting on the couch with Spencer, she burst into tears. She explained through her tears and her mother's jaw dropped.

Spencer looked at me as I tried to calm Allison quietly.

Brenda swallowed and stood up. "Excuse me for a moment." she said and left the room.

Allison sat on the couch and cried into Spencer. Spencer tried to calm her and tell her that everything would be okay. She just kept crying.

After she was done, she leaned onto my shoulder. "She hates me. I bet she's calling Dad right now and he'll hate me too." she said.

"They do not hate you, Ally." I said and stroked her hair gently.

"They do, Pen. They'll never look at me the same again." she said quietly.

Spencer's father came through the door shortly after. He looked at Allison and she clung close to me.

He walked in to Allison. "I need to talk to Allison, alone." he said.

"But—" I began to protest.

"Go." he said through his teeth.

Spencer took my hand and led me into the other room.

"Why are we leaving her alone? He's furious." I said.

"You need to let my dad talk to her. He won't hurt her. I doubt he'll even yell. Mom will be out there with him soon enough." Spencer said. He was just as stressed out as Allison and he was closer to her than I was. Hell, she was his baby sister. He hated this as much as she did.

"I hope they don't do anything drastic." I muttered quietly.

Spencer raised an eyebrow. "As in . . . ?"

"They might kick her out. She's terrified of that." I said.

He chuckled. "My mother will not kick her out. No matter what she does, my mother will not do that, especially with baby-on-board."

I smiled. "Good."

"You shouldn't worry so much about Allison. You're the one in danger here."

"Not right at this moment. That would be Ally. She's the one that's pregnant." I said.

"That doesn't put her in danger, yet." Spencer said with a boyish grin. "You never worry about yourself."

I raised an eyebrow. "That's not a bad thing. At least I'm not selfish." I said.

He took my hands in his. "It still worries me. When you're in a position like this, you should be a little selfish." he said.

"Don't worry about me right now. Worry about your sister."

"I guess I can't help, but worry about her already." he confessed softly.

I smiled and put my arms around his neck. "That's good, Spence. It's good to want the best for your sister."

He kissed me gently. I tried to hold the connection when he pulled away, but failed.

"I always have, Pen." He paused. "She just doesn't like to ask for help. She's very independent."

"I know, but, sometimes, even loners need someone to help them." I said.

"You know that best, huh?"

I returned his smile. "Yes, I do."

After about twenty minutes, Allison emerged from the living room. Her eyes were puffy and red from crying. I tried to talk to her, but she ignored me and kept walking. I tried to follow her, but Spencer grabbed my arm.

"She'll be fine." Spencer said. I looked at him.

"I need to be there for her." I said aggressively. I yanked my arm away from him. I went upstairs to Allison's room. I got in and Allison smiled at me grimly.

"I get to stay." She smiled slightly. "I have to finish college, too. When I told them I wanted to keep him, they were all for babysitting." She sighed. "They just don't want Rob involved."

Rob was the asshole that got her pregnant. I wouldn't have a problem with him if he hadn't just up and left her.

"I don't blame them. Rob's a jerk!" I shouted. My emotions had taken control of my voice and made it harsher than I had intended.

"He has a right to know his kid." she said in the same harsh tone.

"I guess so." Even if I disagreed, Ally didn't need my opinion right now.

"He helped make it. The least he can do is pay for the kid."

I nodded in agreement.

She grabbed her phone. "I need to call him."

"To be honest, I don't think he'll give in easily. He won't believe it." I said, sitting next to her.

She swallowed. "I'll just text him."

I didn't argue as she typed two words. "I'm pregnant." Send.

She took in a deep breath and let it out slow.

He didn't answer until we had sat in fifteen minutes of silence. "You're kidding."

"I wish I was." she replied.

"Is it mine?" he asked.

Allison bit her lip. "Yes." She started crying. "He's not going to want him."

"How could he not?"

"He didn't want kids." she said between sobs.

As the window broke in, I jumped in front of Allison. The person pushed me to the ground and I recognized his scent right away.

Jacob.

His hands pressed down my shoulders just as Allison screamed.

Jacob's lips came to my ear. "This time, you're not getting away, Babe." he said with his gun to my heart.

Fear clogged my throat. This was it. I was going to die at the hands of a criminal. I had only lived for eighteen years. It would have had to be enough time. I hadn't truly experienced anything special, but it had been *something*. If I had died the night of Gene's party, I wouldn't have been happy. Now, I was. If I died, I had had my thrill. I had been on the run from something that was guaranteed to kill me. I had made it this long.

My breath caught in my chest as I heard a gunshot, but didn't feel it. I felt Jacob jump off and pull the trigger. A searing, piercing pain burned in my arm. I shrieked.

Spencer's entire family was crowded at the door as Spencer shot again. Allison was pressing her hands to my arm and putting pressure on the shot wound. She was crying and telling me it would be all right.

I wasn't listening. I was watching Spencer. I barely felt the wound in my arm. I was too focused on what would happen to Spencer.

Jacob pulled the trigger again and hit Brittany directly in the shin. Her eyes widened and she screamed. She hit the ground and her husband was right by her side. Brenda dropped to her knees once she took a moment to figure out what happened.

Jacob very slimly escaped as Spencer shot once more. Spencer cursed and knelt beside me. He told Allison to go help with Brittany while he took care of me.

He got the bullet out and let it heal quickly.

I started to stand. "I need to help Brittany."

"No, Thea, you don't. You're not healed completely yet." he said. I knew what he really meant. He didn't want them to know I was a sympath.

I looked at him. "They are going to find out anyway." I whispered and went over to Brittany. Spencer sighed and followed. He knew he wouldn't stop me.

"Back up." Spencer commanded. Everyone did as told, except, her husband. It wouldn't interfere that he was holding her hand, though. I pressed my hands to the gun wound and allowed the energy to flow.

Everyone stared and got quiet when it transferred to me. The only thing I felt before I passed out was the bullet falling into my hand.

FIFTEEN

DECEMBER 3RD

There was that beeping again. There was that damn uncomfortable tubing in my nose.

I opened my eyes and swallowed. I felt stitches pull in my shin when I moved so I settled quickly.

Spencer's hand squeezed mine gently. He was obviously grateful for my quick recovery.

"You scared me." he said softly.

I looked up. Brittany was with him. She looked a bit nervous, but I couldn't see any anger.

"Did you tell them?" I asked. My voice was a bit breathless and raspy.

"They know everything, Pen." he said.

"We have to leave, don't we?" I asked in a feared tone.

"I don't know. Amanda hasn't shown up yet."

"Great." I muttered. Something deep in my gut was telling me that this wouldn't end well. It would go wrong before it went right.

"Why did you heal me? I mean, it's not like I've been amazing to you." Brittany asked all in one breath and rather quickly.

I shrugged. "You got hurt because he thought it would get to me. It's my fault." I tried to move, but my stitches stretched so I had to stop. "Why isn't this healed?"

"You're exhausted. It's no wonder."

We all looked to Amanda standing in the doorway. She looked angry . . . very angry.

Spencer released my hand and sat his on his thigh.

"I don't know why you think you can get hurt and try to heal someone on top of that. It exhausts your body. It drains all of your energy. It may take a few days to gain back the energy to heal your leg." Amanda explained.

"I wanted to help." I said innocently.

"She would have healed on her own. Humans tend to do that." she said pointedly.

"You act like I know how this stuff works! I barely know any of this!" I shouted. My heart rate quickened and the machine beeped. Amanda didn't even react to the change. She didn't even notice that my whole body was shaking with frustration.

"You've known for months!"

"Calm the hell down, Amanda." Spencer said. "You've kept both of our knowledge very limited about these things. She doesn't know any of the things you do."

"I didn't tell her because I didn't want her using it! It attracts attention. All it's going to do is cause more problems." Amanda argued.

"That isn't the point. The point is that she helped my sister because she wanted to do what she thought was right. I never would have asked her to do that. Neither would Brittany. She did it because she wanted to and didn't know it would do this!" Spencer shouted.

Amanda sighed and frowned. "Can I see you outside for a moment, Spencer?"

Spencer swallowed nervously and followed her out the door. I was already nervous for him when the door closed.

"You don't think she'll fire him, do you?" Brittany asked.

"I don't know." I said and held my breath. *I hope not.*

After fifteen minutes of silence, Spencer reemerged.

"We get to stay, but she's really pissed that we're together." he said.

"You didn't lose your job?" Brittany asked.

Spencer smiled. "Amanda can't afford to fire me." He paused a moment. "She's just working on securing the house." He looked at me grimly. "Unfortunately, high school is no longer an option. It's just too easy to access information."

This time, my smile dropped. "What?" I asked, disappointed.

Spencer's hand touched my leg as he sat down. "I know, Pen. I'm sorry. I can get you in to take the GED and get a good college for you once this is all over. High school is just too risky."

"How long will it take until this is all over?" I asked.

Spencer swallowed. "I wish I could answer that."

After another hour, they discharged me. The whole way out of the hospital, Spencer had his hand on his gun.

We got in his car and headed home over a little bridge. I didn't like water because I couldn't swim so I closed my eyes.

"What's wrong?" Spencer asked.

"I don't like bridges." I said.

"Why?"

"I can't swim." I admitted.

Spencer did a double-take. "What?" he shouted.

"I never had anyone to teach me. My dad was always at work." I said.

He sighed. "We'll have to teach you, then."

"How will you do that? It's winter." I said.

"They have indoor pools. I'll get us a membership. I'll teach you." he said.

"You don't have to, Spencer." I insisted. "I can get a teacher or something."

"No one can get that close to your body." he said quickly. "It's too easy to get close to you and too much of a chance that they could kill you and call it an accident."

I raised an eyebrow. "If I didn't know better, I'd call you paranoid."

He smiled. "You do know better, though."

"Well, of course." I said and he kissed me once.

Spencer went to inform the school of my dropout and I was forced to go along . . . in a wheelchair.

For the next few days, I couldn't walk because of the stitches.

When we got to the school, the principal took Spencer into the conference room to get the rest of the details. It was during the school day so when Josh passed, I wasn't surprised. I just tried to hide.

It didn't work.

He came into the office. "What happened?"

I hesitated. "I fell?" It sounded more like a question than an answer.

He didn't look convinced. "Thea," he paused, rephrasing. "Sweetie, you can talk to me."

"I know, Josh. I really just tried to help someone and it backfired." Ha! Not a lie!

Josh sighed. "Then, why the dropout?" he asked.

My eyes widened. "How did you know?"

He sat down beside me. "I heard Spencer when I went in to buy my parking pass. What's going on?"

I swallowed. "I'm not allowed to talk about it." It was another truthful statement.

He nodded. "Okay." His eyes got moist. "Just call me so we can all hang out sometime."

I kissed him goodbye before I started to cry. Spencer took me back home after he was done. I was upset and Spencer didn't nag me to tell him.

The rest of his family was hugging me and apologizing for everything I've been through. It was really nice, but really odd.

The only person that didn't show was Spencer's dad.

Spencer carried me up to our bedroom. "I'm sorry my dad's acting like this. He doesn't like that we lied at all. He knew that we were, but he's angry that it's actually true."

I nodded. "I understand." I paused. "I feel horrible about it. I don't like lying to people."

"I know, Sweetheart." Spencer said, kissing my forehead. "I don't like it either, but we don't have to anymore."

I smiled. "I can breathe again."

"I know what you mean." He sat beside me.

I leaned on his shoulder. "I'm glad Amanda didn't move us."

He put his arm around me affectionately. "I am, too."

I curled up in his arm and leaned on his chest. I watched out the window at the storm forming. The clouds were all gathered together tightly and a dark gray. We were going to get snow. It wasn't going to be a little bit of snow either.

"I'm sorry all of this happened, Pen." Spencer said.

I snuggled in closer. "I'm not." I said.

Spencer tensed. "Why not?"

I looked up at him. "If it hadn't happened, I'd still be alone. I wouldn't feel like I meant anything. Just being around you makes me feel important."

Spencer pulled me into his lap and propped his chin on my head. "You are important."

"I'm not near as important as you're all making me seem. I shouldn't have a guard."

"Pen, you are the only one of the first generation Elite that we could save. You are very important. Not just to the project, but to me as well." he said.

I smiled and I couldn't help the thick ball of emotion that caught in my belly. I kissed him softly before I could cry. He kissed me back and pulled me tightly to him.

I settled across his lap, being careful to avoid my stitches. My chest pressed tightly to his and I put my arms around his neck. His lips parted mine gently. I could feel his pulse on my bicep and I giggled when I felt it quicken slightly.

His hands moved down my curves, then my hips, my butt, and rested on the back of my knees. Somehow, even through my sweatpants, his touch sent a sensual shiver through my entire body. He smiled at that when I froze. He put his palms on my cheeks and rubbed his thumbs across my brow.

"What are you doing to me, Pen? I never felt like this about anyone before. You seem to have me under your spell." he said and planted a soft kiss to my forehead.

I seized his mouth in a hungry, ravaging kiss. He fell back onto the bed and I was on all fours over top of him. He chuckled and I pulled his head back up to kiss him again.

"Jesus Christ, Spencer." a voice belted from the door. I looked to see Spencer's dad watching us.

Spencer sat up and away from me so he could see his father.

Mr. Kendal stepped into the room. "I can see that you lied, again."

Spencer raised an eyebrow. "I did?"

"You said that relationship was only an act."

"It was." Spencer said simply. "But, it's not now."

Mr. Kendal shook his head. He looked at me. "You've turned my reliable son into a liar." he said and left the room.

Regret rose in my throat. It was my fault. He had only lied to protect me.

I stepped up and off of his lap and ran a hand through my knotted hair. I took a deep breath as Spencer spoke.

"Pen, that's not true." Spencer said and stood up.

"It's not true? Spencer, you only lie because of me. You lied to protect me and you've never lied to you family before you brought me here! You would never have lied if I hadn't fought against Jacob and just let him kill me." I said and started crying. "I'm just a nuisance to everyone. All I'm good for is keeping my race going! I'd be worthless otherwise!"

Spencer gripped my shoulders gently. "Pen, you need to stop. That's not true."

"It is so! I should have let him kill me! I'm turning your family against you! You should hate me!" I shouted. I was breathing too quickly.

Spencer clamped a hand over my mouth. "You need to calm down. I don't hate you. None of this is your fault."

I pulled his hand away. "Yes, it is, Spencer! Just send me away, please!" I was still crying so I doubted he could understand what I was saying. "Just take me somewhere where I can't drive you and your family apart. I can't live with that."

"No. You need to listen to me."

I shut up. I couldn't keep talking. I'd start repeating myself.

Spencer sighed and started talking very calmly. "You are so much more important than just a member of the Elite. You are so amazing. You aren't turning my family against me. I was lying to them before all of this about my job. You aren't a nuisance. I've told you that before."

"None of this would have happened if it hadn't have been for me." I said.

Spencer smiled. "Exactly. If you hadn't been assigned to me, I would never have found out how much you mean to me." His hand rested on my cheek. "You're so much more than what you think, Penelope."

I shook my head. "Why don't I feel like it, then?"

Spencer kissed me gently once. "I'm sorry. Everything is just so complicated right now. Once this is over, everything will be better." He moved his kiss to my forehead. "I promise."

"I don't know, Spencer." I looked at him. "What if I don't survive this? How will it get better then?"

Spencer's gaze locked with mine. "You will get through this. Anyone would have to take me down before they could touch you and I'm not going down without a fight."

"If you're gone, I still have no one. It's not like I could live with your parents forever." I swallowed. "I can't lose you. I just can't."

Spencer didn't seem to budge. "I'm not going anywhere."

I closed my eyes as more tears burned my eyes. I bit my lip against the sob climbing in my throat.

Spencer pulled me into his arms and I took deep breaths. I was so sick of crying. I'd never cried this much. It was just so much stress all at once. It just never let up.

SIXTEEN

DECEMBER 15TH

I woke and Spencer smiled at me. "You know that my sisters want to take you Christmas shopping, right?"

I groaned. "When are we leaving?" I asked.

"I think the plan is to be on the road in an hour." he answered.

Another groan emerged from my throat. "It's too early."

Spencer's finger traced a line up my arm. "It won't be so bad. Allison is going. No one will bother you."

"It's not that. I just don't want to go out this early. It's too early in the morning." I said.

"Well, you should probably get up before they leave without you." he said.

I got up, got dressed, and did my make-up quickly. I headed downstairs and I looked out the window to see snow falling down quickly. Spencer gave me a gun to strap underneath my dress. He was going to be coming right behind us, but he wasn't leaving for another couple of minutes.

"You're just in time, Penelope." Brittany said and smiled.

All the girls were going. Brittany, Grace, Miranda, Allison, and I were all ready to go and packed into the minivan. We left and the snow seemed to slow up a little bit.

Everything was going great until Grace tried to slow down and pressed on the brakes and the pedal just sank to the floor. Someone had snapped the cable.

My heart pounded for the small second before we slid. Grace couldn't even counterturn because there weren't any brakes. I hated myself for letting them get involved in this. I never should have done it.

The tree came through my window and stabbed into my shoulder. We started to go the other direction and the tree snapped off. When I heard a scream, I didn't think it was mine. Pain seared deep in my shoulder like a fire burning a tearing, melting muscle.

All of their lives were passing before my eyes. Allison was the only one that held in her scream. Miranda was just crying with her expression glazed over in fear. She was staring at Allison. Brittany hit her head on the window, but she was still conscious.

The entire car rolled and I gripped the seat in my fists. A piece of glass flew at me and sliced right into my abdomen. I gasped and screamed again. There were fragments flying everywhere. They were piercing my skin and digging deeply into my muscles and tendons, burning and cutting wherever they went.

We finally came to a stop when the car was stopped by a tree in the forest beside the road. My hand touched my shoulder and I felt the pain coming around the protruding branch. I couldn't even touch the branch. It hurt too badly and it was embedded too deeply.

I unhooked my seatbelt and got out of the car. I got so dizzy and my legs wobbled uncontrollably. Allison followed me and helped me stand.

"Oh my, God, Pen." she said, crying.

I finally just collapsed. My body hit the snow softly.

Allison knelt over me. "Damn it, Pen." she said and shouted to Grace. "Call Spencer. We don't have time to waste right now."

I was losing blood quickly and I thought I was going to pass out. My vision began to cloud. I knew that it wouldn't be long until I passed out. My eyelids got heavy and I had to fight with all I had to keep them open.

"No, Pen. Keep your eyes open. Look at me, Sweetie." Allison said, tapping my cheek.

"I can't." I said breathlessly.

"Yes, you can. Just look at me and wait for Spencer. He won't be long." she promised. Her panic was growing more apparent.

"Just come on, Spencer! It's really bad!" Grace shouted. Everyone was out of the car.

Brittany knelt beside me. My whole body was feeling the effects of the blood loss. I kept my composure. If I was going to die now, Jacob would win. This was something Spencer couldn't even protect me from. It would look like an accident and they had no way to tell who had rigged the brakes.

"I'm so sorry." I said and took a deep breath.

Allison shook her head. "This wasn't your fault, Sweetheart." she said.

I nodded. "I didn't leave when I wanted to. This was all my fault. Everything that has happened to you guys was because of me." I said and started coughing.

"Dear God." Spencer's voice rang.

I looked to see him. He looked absolutely horrified. He ordered Allison to call an ambulance.

"I'm not going to make it, Spence." I said and my throat tightened.

"Yes, you will. I'm not going to let you die." Spencer said and took off his shirt. He tied the sleeve tightly around my shoulder. He tore off the rest and pressed it into my stomach. A painful gasp whimpered out of me. I couldn't help, but start crying. Partly, it was because of the pain. Mostly, it was just because of the fact of being so sure that I was going to die.

Spencer kept pressure on the wound. I'd never been hurt this badly. I was so close to death. My urge to sleep was only growing more intense.

"Stay awake, Pen. Just look at me. Don't close your eyes." Spencer instructed just as Allison had.

"Just stop, Spencer. If I'm going to die, I'm going to die." It came out harsh and fearless, but I was terrified. I'd felt this way too many times in these past few months. I had been convinced that I was going to die. This time, it might actually come true.

Spencer worked the piece of glass from my stomach. I screamed loudly and tried to keep what little composure I had left.

Allison returned and I must have looked worse at the way she froze. Her face had gone pallid and her hand fell to her stomach. I was sure she was going to vomit.

My stomach was hurting worse than anything. Every time Spencer rearranged, it only made it worse. "That really hurts, Spencer." I moaned.

"I need to keep pressure on it, Pen." he said and touched my cheek softly. "I'm so sorry."

"I'm still wearing the gun." I said breathlessly.

The gun was strapped to the top of my thigh. I knew Spencer would just think it was awkward.

I looked up at Ally. She looked at Spencer.

"I'll do it." she said.

Ally got the gun off my leg and held my other hand afterward.

Everyone was just watching me. Allison was probably still trying to process it. Miranda looked like she was gonna pass out. That's probably why Grace was whispering to her and had her arm around her.

The ambulance sirens were getting closer, but I was getting weaker. I soon wouldn't be able to hold on to consciousness.

"They're almost here, Pen. It's just a little while longer." Spencer said and pulled up his shirt to see if the bleeding was slowing. He took a few deep breaths. I knew that he was trying to calm himself because he was panicking too.

"You don't have to be so brave all the time, Spencer." I said.

He shook his head. "Actually, I do."

The paramedics got there and were rushing to get to me. I wasn't sure if I was really going to die. I was hard to focus on thinking about it. They strapped an oxygen mask to my face. I couldn't help, but think that an oxygen mask was the last thing I needed at this point.

They broke out the needles to start blood and fluids and I had to swallow back my fear.

The only one they let in the ambulance with me was Spencer.

I knew I wasn't supposed to, but I passed out right before they gave me the IV.

When I woke up, I was relieved to just be able to feel all of my body parts. My shoulder really hurt and my throat was sore from a tube that had to have been in my throat during surgery. My stomach started hurting the more I woke up.

I groaned and took a deep breath. I could feel the stitches where the line of my panties would have been. At least you wouldn't be able to see that scar when I was wearing pants.

I opened my eyes to see Spencer sitting beside my bed. No one else was there. For some reason, I was grateful. I just needed to be with him. I needed him to be my stability. I wanted the security of it.

"Hi." I said. My voice was raspy.

Spencer kissed my forehead. "Hi." he said.

"I'm sorry." I said.

Spencer shook his head. "This is not your fault, Pen."

"Yes, it is. If I hadn't wanted to stay with your family, I wouldn't have put the rest of them at risk." I said in a guilt-laced voice.

"They're all more worried about you. We were so close to losing you."

"I know." I said.

Spencer sighed. "You lost more than four pints of blood. The surgeon told us that it was a very small chance that you'd live through the surgery."

I swallowed. I'd been so close to death. My eyes welled up. "I could have died." I said.

Spencer nodded. "It was a long five hours. He wouldn't even wake you up right away, either. I just wanted to punch the guy."

I laughed, but it hurt so I just drained out with a whine.

"I'm so sorry." Spencer said.

"Don't worry about it." I said.

"Josh and the others are here to see you. They popped up on the doorstep earlier and my mom sent them here." Spencer said.

I nodded. He left to send them in, but I told him to stay with me while they did.

Josh, Jayden, Colleen, and Weston all came in and smiled warmly. I probably looked horrible.

"Hi." Josh said.

I smiled. "Hey."

Josh sat next to me on the bed. A pained breath hissed out of me as my torso tilted. Josh stood up quickly and a very concerned expression passed over his innocent little face. Jayden took his hand and whispered that it was all right and he hadn't known it would hurt me.

"It's all right, Josh." I said.

Josh cleared his throat. "How are you feeling? I mean, Spencer was really worried. I didn't know what to expect."

I shrugged. "I'm not dead."

"Too damn close for comfort." Spencer muttered. No one else had heard him.

Josh smiled. "That's good."

Colleen walked to my bedside. "I would hug you and tell you that I've been totally freaking for the past three hours and that I missed my three o'clock nap for you, Darling. I guess just saying that I'm so, so glad you're okay will do, right?" she said and smiled her beautiful smile.

I laughed and pain shot through me, but I ignored it. "Thanks, Colleen. I've missed you."

"I missed you too, Thea." she said.

That one four letter word broke my heart into a million pieces. None of them, my closest friends, knew my real self. I mean, Weston knew from the beginning. I didn't count him even if he was the closest friend I had.

I nodded and my throat tightened.

Jayden smiled. "I'm afraid that I'm going to break you."

"I'm a little afraid that I'm going to break myself, Jayden." I said and managed a small laugh before I hissed in my breath and pain burst in my stomach.

Jayden swallowed. "I'm sorry, Sweetie." Jayden said and pressed a kiss to my cheek. I smiled.

"Don't worry. It's not your fault." I said.

Weston stepped up and cocked his little half grin. I swear that's how he got out of everything. It definitely gave him a sexy, sharp edge.

"Not to be mean, Bud, but you look horrible." he said.

"Well, I just came out of a five-hour surgery. You didn't think I'd be all made-up and everything, did you?" I joked.

Weston chuckled. "I just didn't expect you to look so rough."

"It's just because it hurts . . . a lot." I said and I swallowed.

"I'd assume it would. I mean, a tree went through your shoulder." Weston shook his head. "You just don't stay out of trouble."

I nodded. "It wasn't my finest moment."

Everyone left and then Spencer's family came in.

Allison had relief spread the whole way across her face. She was going to hug me, but Spencer stopped her. She looked guilty and apologized.

Everyone was just happy to see that I wasn't still spilling blood.

Soon after, it was just Spencer and I again. He pressed a soft kiss to my lips. "You are so strong, Pen. I don't know who could live through that, but you did it. You never gave up on me."

I kissed his jaw. It was mostly because I couldn't stretch to reach anything else.

"I'm sorry I was so angry earlier at the car. I just wanted it all to go away. Putting more weight on it didn't help that it hurt." I said, my guilt blossoming deep inside of me. He'd been trying to save me and I just pushed him away and told him to stop.

Spencer smiled. "Trust me, I didn't care that you were angry. I was just glad you were feeling something. You were just so close to the edge and I was just doing all I could to keep you here. I was absolutely terrified."

Eventually, the pain became so excruciating that Spencer had to get the nurse to bring me pain medication. She gave it to me through a needled syringe through my IV tube. I couldn't even look at the IV. It made me sick.

Spencer laughed when the nurse left. "You're afraid of needles?"

I nodded as I started feeling the effect of the medicine. I was getting really tired and feeling amazing for what I came in with.

"You can take on a serial killer, but you can't get a shot?" he asked, still laughing.

"Don't laugh at me, you brat." I said and laughed.

"I can't help it." He kissed me one last time and hesitated for a moment. "I love you, Pen."

My heart fluttered in my chest. "Spencer." I said, smiling. I couldn't believe he'd actually said that.

"I'm serious, Pen. I would not lie about something like this." Spencer said.

"Spencer, calm down. I love you too." I said and Spencer smiled as he kissed me gently.

"Go to sleep." he said.

"You don't have to tell me twice." I said and fell asleep quickly.

Guards were lined along the door on the outside to fight off any unwelcome guests. We did not need any more of those.

SEVENTEEN

DECEMBER 16ᵀᴴ

I woke to Amanda opening the room door. Oliver followed her with a bouquet of carnations. I smiled and tried to sit up.

"Don't even think about it, Kid." Amanda said as Oliver set the carnations on the bedside table.

I relaxed. Spencer was still asleep.

"How are you, Penelope?" Oliver asked.

I swallowed. "Better. At least I got the pain medicine. It seemed to help."

"Good. When Spencer called us, he said you were in really bad shape." Amanda said and smiled.

"I'm so glad you're okay. None of us were really that optimistic. Spencer was hysterical and he doesn't get that way unless it's pretty nasty."

"I know. I wasn't hopeful either. I told Spencer to just let me die." I said.

"That man was never going to just let you go." Oliver said.

I nodded. I looked over at Spencer. He looked like a little kid when he was sleeping. It was an innocent look. He was snuggled tightly into a little ball and the blanket was wrapped tightly around his body. I could see the exhaustion in his face. His breathing was light and quiet.

I thought about Ally. "We need to get out of the Kendals' house. I can't stand thinking that I am putting them in danger. If Jacob wants to come after *me*, he can. He just needs to leave *them* alone." I said.

Amanda nodded. "I'll see what I can do. I mean, we could get you out of the area now because you're not in school. We could change a couple of appearance based things and maybe a new name. We may even change things for Spencer, too. We'll need to get you somewhere where Jacob won't find you."

"What about my friends? Will they ever be able to know?" I asked.

"Maybe they can when all of this is over. Not yet. It's not even safe to keep contact with them right now. Jacob can tap into cell phone signals and track them. We've been trying to limit all contact with anyone to e-mails." Amanda explained.

I sighed. "I understand."

Spencer rolled over on the bed and sighed before opening his eyes. He looked around even though he still looked absolutely exhausted. "Well, good morning." Spencer muttered.

Amanda ignored him. She was pretty grouchy. You could just tell. She'd probably spent another sleepless night on tracking Jacob. "Penelope, you will be released later on today. Return to the Kendal home and we'll arrange for a move." Amanda said and left the room.

Oliver waited a moment and then followed Amanda.

Spencer looked at me. "What was that all about?"

"She just came to check on me."

"We're moving?" he asked.

"It was my idea. I can't keep putting your family in danger, Spencer. It was way too close yesterday. Any of them could have died." I said.

Spencer nodded. "I see where you're coming from. I was going to mention it when we saw Amanda next. They're just too close to all of the action."

"She wants to change everything again. She's even changing everything with you." I said and looked at Spencer.

"I'm sorry, Pen. It's going to be hard adjusting somewhere else again, but we don't have a choice." Spencer said. "We can't chance having another close call. There have been too many because I haven't been as close to you as I should have been."

"It is not your fault, Spencer. The brakes would have snapped if you were with me or not." I said.

"I should have been there to get you out right away."

"Spencer, that wouldn't have helped." I touched his cheek, stretching my stitches a bit. "I still would be here."

Spencer took my hand from his cheek and held it. "I wouldn't feel so guilty for not even being there, though."

"It's not your fault." I said. I tried to stretch to kiss him, but pain shot through me. I lay back down and cursed softly.

Spencer swallowed. "This is all my fault." he said and squeezed my hand apologetically. "You're in such bad shape because of me. I should have checked the car."

"Spencer, stop." I said.

"Pen, it's my fault. You know it as well as I do."

"No, I don't. Jacob just knows me too well. We were so close that he knows me better than anyone."

"How close were you two, really?" Spencer asked.

I swallowed. "Very."

"What are you so nervous for? It's not like you did anything wrong by being close to him." Spencer said.

"I was so much more than close to him." I said, fighting off the memory.

Spencer raised an eyebrow. "What are you talking about?"

I bit my lip. "I'm not so innocent. I wish I was."

Spencer looked surprised and released my hand. "You slept with him?"

I closed my eyes as tears burned my eyes. "I was drunk and I barely remember it. I never would have done it if I hadn't been so smashed."

"Why didn't you ever tell me this?" Spencer asked and put his forehead in his hands.

"I'm sorry that it's embarrassing to have gone off and gotten drunk just before having sex with a guy that is out to kill me." I said and took a deep breath. "I didn't want you to know that I'd been so stupid."

Spencer shook his head. "It wasn't stupid. It's not like you could have known."

"Sex at fifteen is pretty dumb, Spencer."

Spencer's jaw dropped. "You were fifteen?"

"It was the biggest mistake of my life." My chest tightened as I just thought about it. "I'm so sorry." I took a deep breath. "God, I let him get so close. I barely knew him and then, what do you know it, just like the whore I am, I woke up next to him."

Spencer shook his head. "You aren't a whore." He smiled. "Is that really the most embarrassing secret you have?"

I nodded.

"Mine's worse." Spencer said.

"You don't have to tell me, Spence." I said. I didn't want him to think that I had to know absolutely everything.

He looked at me. "I'm a virgin."

My jaw dropped. "You have got to be kidding."

He shook his head. "I've never had sex or anything too awful close. Marcy was closest."

I blinked several times, trying to process what he'd just said.

"That's impossible. You're a grown man, Spencer." I said.

"That doesn't mean a thing. I just haven't found the right woman yet." he said. "Sex doesn't make you a man."

I smiled. "That's nice, Spencer." I said.

He kissed me gently. "Thanks, Pen." He paused. "How are you feeling?"

"It still hurts, a little. I just want to go home. I hate hospitals." I said.

"I know. I do too, Sweetheart."

Three and a half hours later, they sent me home. Of course, this was the last time I'd be at this home for a while. Spencer checked the brakes multiple times before we left.

We got home and I ignored the pain as I packed up and said my goodbyes.

Spencer stopped at Amanda's to pick up a different car. Now, he had an old baby blue Ford pick-up truck. He tossed our bags in the bed and put a tarp over it because of the rain.

I have to admit, I cried a little when Amanda told us we were moving to the country part of Massachusetts, more than ten hours away.

Spencer and I were acting as a newlywed couple from Florida. Our names were Jonathon and Kimberly Smith. There was no way our names would stick out.

On the way out, we'd stopped and gotten my hair cut into a ragged looking cut that came to my shoulders. We'd also dyed it brunette. I was gonna miss my hair that came to my hips.

Spencer couldn't change his looks. He needed to keep them for identification purposes for out-of-state WPP members.

I started to cry when we started driving again. Spencer put his arm around me. "It's going to be okay. This will be over soon."

I shook my head. "This sucks."

"I know." he said.

"Did Amanda give you the rings?" I asked as I tried desperately to change the subject.

Spencer nodded. "They're in my bag. We'll stop and dig them out at the hotel."

"We're stopping?" I didn't really want to risk stopping. If there was any chance that Jacob was on our tail, stopping would only give him a head-start.

"Just so you can rest. You won't heal properly if you don't." Spencer said.

I swallowed. "I'm sorry about all of this. I wish we could just be done with this." I said.

"I do too." he said.

We stopped a good four hours later.

Spencer dug out the rings and I looked at mine. It was a simple silver band with a medium sized square diamond perched on the band. The other band was just thin silver. Spencer's was a black platinum ring.

We headed into the hotel room and Spencer took off his shirt and changed into sweatpants. I changed into a tank top and a pair of sweatpants.

I could tell that Spencer was nervous. There was only one bed and we'd never been forced to sleep in the same bed. We'd only done it a couple of times and all of it was by option.

"I can take the floor if you want." I offered.

He chuckled. "No. I'll be perfectly fine." he said.

"I won't try anything." I promised.

Spencer looked up at me. "I appreciate that." he said.

Very soon afterward, we went to bed. I moved to the furthest edge of my side. I didn't want to make him feel awkward.

He hooked his index finger in the back of my tank top, tugged gently, and whispered to me. "Come over here." he said.

"Are you sure?" I asked.

"I wouldn't have told you to if I hadn't meant it." he said.

I moved back so I lay in front of him. He kissed me softly. "I love you."

"I love you, too." I said. He lay on his back so I laid my head on his chest and he put his arm around me.

EIGHTEEN

I woke up and Spencer was still sleeping. It was only five o'clock, but I wasn't getting back to sleep. I got up, got a shower, did what little hair I had left, and made a quick breakfast before Spencer woke up.

Spencer looked at me. "Why are you up already?" he asked.

"I woke up and couldn't get back to sleep." I walked over and kissed him quickly.

"You didn't have to get up alone. You could have woken me up." he said.

"I didn't want to wake you." The stitches were getting on my nerves so I asked Spencer to cut them out. He got them out; then, we ate, changed, and left.

Spencer let me drive so I did for about three hours. I started to get tired so Spencer drove for the last four.

We arrive at a small home in the suburbs. We unpacked and settled into the two bedroom rancher.

I put my things in one room and Spencer put his in the other. I had insisted so he didn't feel weird or pressured or whatever.

When a knock came on the door, Spencer and I both went to answer it. It turned out to be a beautiful elderly couple coming to welcome us to the neighborhood.

"You're so beautiful. How do you keep your skin so young looking?" the woman asked. Her silver hair was short and curly. She was actually short in general.

"I'm only twenty-one." I said, going with my new age.

"My, my, you look younger than that." she said.

"I get that a lot." I said and smiled light-heartedly.

She saw our rings. "When did you get married?" she asked.

Spencer smiled. "A little over a month ago." he said.

The man smiled. He was mostly bald except for a white crown. His glasses were thick and large. "Congratulations, Kids."

Spencer put his arm around me. "Thank you, Sir."

I fell asleep soon after just from exhaustion.

Jacob entered an office that looked relatively nice. All the walls were painted a light brown and several photos were hanging up. A wooden rectangular desk was sitting in the room. The top was cluttered. The chair was turned backwards, successfully hiding the person sitting on it.

"What failure have you brought me this time, Maslin?" a husky, male voice said from the chair.

"It's not a failure. There was no way she could have survived the crash. She was bleeding far too heavily." Jacob said. His fists were jammed in his pockets and his leather jacket was unzipped and hanging off his shoulders.

"Did you stay to make sure that she was dead? You've had far too many failures to have anything less than certain." the voice said.

"No, but she couldn't have sur—" Jacob was cut off.

"You don't know that. She's a healer. That guard of her's could have saved her."

"I highly doubt that, Sir." Jacob said.

"I don't. Make sure she's dead, Maslin. Do whatever you have to. Go after Spencer if you have to. If she's not dead, going after Spencer will get her heated."

I woke up with a gasp. My breathing was heavy.

"What did you see?" Spencer asked, kneeling next to the couch.

"Jacob. He thinks I'm dead." I said.

"That's a good thing." Spencer said and smiled.

"No. The big guy was telling him to be absolutely sure. If I'm not dead, he's supposed to come after you." I said and looked at him.

"They aren't going to find us, Pen." Spencer said, stroking my hair off my forehead.

"You can't be sure."

"He would never get anywhere close to you even if they found us. I will fight until I've taken my last breath." He kissed my forehead gently.

"That's the problem. They are going to come after you. They'll take you up on the whole last breath thing." I said. Even toying with the idea of losing Spencer was heart-breaking. I knew that I shouldn't have gotten so attached to him because of the huge possibility that he'd die. I just couldn't stop how I felt.

"That's a risk I'm willing to take, Pen." Spencer's voice was totally serious.

"You already sacrifice so much for me—" I began. He silenced me by putting his finger to my lips.

"I want to do it, Penelope. Now, stop arguing." he said. He moved his finger and kissed my lips. "I'm not going down that easily when you're on the line."

"They aren't afraid to kill you, Spencer." Tears burned in my eyes. I could defend myself now because Spencer and I had continued with our fighting sessions and working out. However, I wasn't sure if I could fight while I was dealing with Spencer's death.

"I'm not afraid to shed a little blood." he said.

I hesitated a moment. "I'm scared, Spencer." I admitted.

Spencer nodded. "I know."

"How is it that you never seem scared?" I asked.

Spencer smiled. "I have to hide it."

I shook my head. "No, you don't. Everyone's scared sometimes. I mean, I'd be absolutely terrified if I were you. You are putting your life on the line for me every day. Jacob could kill you at any second and you're just so fearless."

"I'm not fearless." Spencer confessed softly.

"You act like it."

Spencer kissed me once. "I'm going to do laundry. Get some rest." He touched my cheek, pushing his fingers into the hair behind my ear. "I mean it. You're so stressed, Penelope. Just take some time to calm down. Relax for a little while. Let me know if you have any more dreams."

I nodded. "I'm sorry. I shouldn't have gotten so paranoid."

"You have every single right to be paranoid, Sweetheart." Spencer said.

I smiled. "Yeah, I do." I said and laughed.

Spencer left the room and I just sat there for a while. I eventually got up and found a book that I'd started and never finished. I sat on the bed and started reading quietly.

Very soon, I was asleep again.

I woke up just before dinner. I walked out to where Spencer was reading the newspaper on the couch.

"Do you want me to make dinner?" I asked as I ran a hand through my matted hair.

"You don't have to. If you want to, you can." Spencer said.

I nodded and looked in the fridge to find something to make. I settled on one of the few things Amanda had actually stocked.

When I was putting the frozen food in the oven, Spencer came up behind me and wrapped his arms around my waist. I closed the oven and leaned back onto his chest. He inhaled the scent at the curve between my shoulder and my neck.

"You're so amazing." Spencer said.

I smiled. I wouldn't argue. I'd lose.

"That's why everyone wants me dead, right?" I asked, smiling.

"They're just jealous. You're too much competition." Spencer said as a small laugh rumbled in his chest.

I laughed with him. "Maybe."

After dinner, we decided the most normal thing for a newlywed couple to do would be to go out for a couple of hours. We went to see the newest horror movie. Normally, horror movies don't scare me, but I was practically in Spencer's lap. I was terrified. Damn *Paranormal Activity 2*. I'd never even seen the first one.

Spencer squeezed my hand. I looked at him. "It's just a movie."

"I know." I said.

When another ghost came from the shadows, I jumped. Spencer laughed and put his arm around my shoulders. I leaned against him, feeling suddenly safe.

When the movie was over, I was the first one booking it out of the theater, dragging Spencer with me.

Spencer got into the driver's seat and smiled. "We should rent the first one." he said.

"No way." I said.

"Come on. It wasn't that bad." He was laughing.

"I was terrified, Spencer." I pointed out as we pulled out.

"It was a good movie." he said.

"Yeah, it was for you. I probably won't sleep for a month." I said.

"Homicidal ghosts are the least of your worries." Spencer said.

"It's just those homicidal people we need to watch out for." I said and laughed.

Spencer smiled. "Exactly."

We got home and I went right to bed.

I just couldn't sleep. I heard a floorboard creak and I couldn't help but think about Jacob. He could be in this house . . . tonight.

I just lay on my back and watched as the clock ticked away the minutes.

Spencer headed to bed so he checked on me on his way through, as usual. He opened the door and I jumped and gasped. I left out a sigh of relief. "Oh, it's just you." I said, steadying my breathing.

"Who else would it be?" he asked.

"Jacob." I said.

Spencer raised an eyebrow. "Amanda has security everywhere. Are you seriously scared?"

"Pathetically, yes, I am." I said and sighed. "Just go ahead to bed."

Spencer hesitated at the door. The only light was coming in from the hallway behind him, backlighting him. It seemed to only intensify how sexy he was. The front of his body was shadowed, giving him a mysterious vibe. I could notice his tousled hair and naked torso. It outlined the muscles of his arm that was propping him on the doorway.

"Do you want to come in with me? I have plenty of room. It might make you feel better." Spencer said.

"I don't want to make it uncomfortable for you."

Spencer shook his head. "It's not like we don't sleep in the same bed all the time anyway."

"I know it makes you feel weird."

"Don't worry about me. I'll live. Promise." he said as if he was being honest.

"I'm fine, Spencer. I'm just being paranoid. There is no way that Jacob can get in and find us."

"What if I told you it would make me feel better to be able to keep an eye on you?" he asked as he tried to sound convincing.

I rolled my eyes. "Why can't you just take no for an answer?" I asked.

"Because you never did." he said, smiling.

I shook my head as I started blushing. He knew that when he brought up when I was a kid, he'd win.

"Are you sure?" I asked.

Spencer came in and turned on the light so he could see where he was walking. He grabbed my hand and I got up to follow him so I wouldn't get dragged. The whole way to the bedroom, Spencer was very relaxed. Even as we both crawled into bed, he didn't get tense or stressed.

Spencer put his arm around me and I tried to relax. It was odd how he made me feel so safe and protected when he snuggled in close like this. His hand traced up my arm. "Just relax, Sweetheart."

I propped my head on the crook of his neck and he pulled me close to his chest. I fell asleep immediately.

NINETEEN

"**N**o way, Spencer. It's not like I need to learn." I said with refusal slick on my tone.

"You need to learn to swim, Pen. It's too easy of a way to kill you." he said.

"It's not like I told Jacob I couldn't swim." I said.

"Good, but you still need to learn." he said and stood. "You're not getting out of it."

We left an hour later and went to the nearest YMCA where Spencer had applied for memberships.

We went into the public pool and it was only a couple of kids and us. I felt so childish-looking. The one girl looked a lot like me with my new hair.

"I'll be right back." Spencer said and headed to the locker room. He was probably going to change.

I heard the children laughing and then one bumped into me and we both fell into the twelve-foot end. I gasped and panicked. Someone grabbed my ankle and yanked me down when I surfaced. I tried treading the water, but it didn't work. The kid wouldn't let go.

I gasped and it was the dumbest thing I could have done. I felt myself inhaling nothing but water.

The next thing I heard was someone splashing into the water. They grabbed me gently and pulled me up. My back lay against the cold tiles.

"Kim, can you hear me?" Spencer asked as he took my cheeks between his fingers.

Right. We're in public. We had to use our fake names.

I couldn't answer him. I couldn't even look at him. When he released my face, my head just fell to the side.

"I thought she was Jinni. I didn't know." One of the boys was absolutely hysterical.

"Come on, Pen. Breathe for me." Spencer whispered and pinched my nose before tilting my head back and pressing his lips to mine to give me the rescue breath.

Of all the things I could have worried about, I wanted to know where exactly the lifeguard was.

The compressions felt like a thousand pounds pressing on my chest. I couldn't even get in a breath. No matter how much I wanted to take in a deep, full breath, I couldn't. I was too weak.

"Come on!" Spencer shouted and repeated the process again two more times.

I started coughing and Spencer sighed in relief as he helped me sit up. So much water spat out.

Spencer waited patiently for me to stop coughing. He put his forehead to my temple.

"God, not again." he muttered. "Why do I keep messing up?"

"You didn't mess up." My voice was high-pitched and off. I started coughing again after I spoke.

"You almost drowned!" he shouted.

"That wasn't your fault. Can we just go home?" I asked. I didn't want to be here. My chest and throat were sore from panic and the quick influx of air.

"I'm taking you to the emergency room. All they have to do is check and then we can go home." Spencer said.

I didn't have the energy to argue. He carried me to the car.

As Spencer was driving home, it was almost dinnertime. He was completely silent and I knew he was beating himself up on the inside.

I took his hand in mine. "Calm down, Spencer. I'm fine. It wasn't your fault. I should have sat down or something."

"I shouldn't have left your side! I should have learned my lesson the last time you almost died." he said.

I rolled my eyes. "Stop it, Spence."

He pulled over to the side of the road and shut off the car. Spencer put his forehead into his palms.

"I'm sorry. I'm just stressed out." he said. He didn't look at me, but it was obvious that he was telling the truth because he even sounded stressed out.

I put my hand on his shoulder. "What's wrong?" I asked gently.

He shook his head. "My friend's sister was killed earlier this week and he just called me today. She was part of the Elite. She was only his half-sister, but she was very close to him. He's one of the guards for the Elite and tried to guard her as well as he could. He just wasn't there for a couple of minutes."

"This is Christian's sister, right?" I asked.

He nodded. Spencer had talked about Christian a couple times, but we'd never met.

"Oh, God, Spencer. I'm so sorry." I said and swallowed. "I didn't know."

"I didn't want you to. You don't need something else to worry about."

"Neither do you. You're so stressed out." I said, trying to offer some kind of comfort.

He sighed and ran his fingers through his hair. "I just can't believe she's gone. He always used to call her annoying and tell her not to bother him, but now she's just gone. She didn't even know." He was just looking at the empty space through the windshield.

"How old was she?" I asked.

"Twenty. Her abilities showed late. They were just starting to come out when she was killed." he said. He shook his head. "You don't want to hear all this."

I used my thumb to brush some of the hair off his forehead. He looked at me. "I'm so sorry. I love you and I'm always here to listen if you need me. Talk all you want." I said and pressed a soft kiss to the top of his head. I could only reach it because he had his elbows resting on his knees.

He smiled slightly. "Thanks, Pen." he said.

"Anytime." I said.

He started the car. I knew he was still really tense so I took his hand in mine and kissed his knuckles.

He seemed to loosen up a little once we got home.

"You're not going to that pool anymore." he said.

As if on cue, I started coughing.

"God, I'm so sorry, Pen." he said.

I shook my head. "It was *not* your fault." I kissed him once. "I'm going to get a shower. When I get out, you need to talk."

I got my shower quickly and came out to finish making dinner. I'd had roast beef in the crock pot slow cooking all day.

Spencer had followed my example and went to shower himself.

When he got out, I'd already had his plate on the table ready to eat. He sat and still looked really rough. "Thanks, Sweetheart." he said and kissed my forehead.

"Feeding you? I've been doing it for months." I said as a way to try to lighten the mood.

He smiled. "Not that." he said. "You just never let me give up."

I smiled. "Good." I said.

From then on, Spencer and I always slept in the same bed. He was the one the proposed the idea. That way, he'd be there if something happened, no matter how small the chances were.

TWENTY

JUNE 7TH

We've been playing the married couple for six months with no complications. School ended for all of my friends four days ago and I wanted to go see them, but I couldn't. It's too risky. It was too easy to track me or get them involved. I couldn't do that.

When my phone rang, I answered.

"Hello?"

"Thea, it's me." It was one of the only times Weston had ever called me Thea. He had to be with Colleen, Josh, and Jayden. Otherwise, it would have just been Pen.

"What?" I was panicking. He wasn't supposed to contact me. I'd changed my number and everything.

"Which house are you in? Josh and Colleen went digging and found your new address." he asked.

"Hold on one minute." I said.

Spencer looked at me in an odd way.

"Weston and everyone are here." I said.

Spencer sighed.

"I didn't give them any information." I said, innocent. "I haven't spoken to them in six months."

"I know. We just need to get rid of the rings and everything." he said, standing.

I told Weston the house number and he said we had five minutes.

Spencer took off his ring and put it on top of the fridge. I couldn't get mine off. My hands swell in the summer time and the ring wasn't budging around it.

Spencer laughed and came to help me. He tried to slide it off, but it didn't move.

"Don't worry about it." I said. I was just frustrated that someone had found us after all this time.

"We can't tip them off." Spencer said.

I raised an eyebrow. "So keep your eyes to yourself." I smiled.

He smiled. "No promises." he said and kissed me. It wasn't just a peck, either. It was a real kiss.

"Holy hell!" Josh shouted.

Both of us looked to him. Weston, Josh, Jayden, and Colleen were all at the window. All of them had their jaws dropped except Weston.

Spencer stopped breathing. His expression reminded me of a seven-year-old that got caught with one hand in the cookie jar.

"Should we come in?" Weston asked.

"Get in here and close that window." Spencer commanded roughly.

Josh grabbed Jayden's hand and came in with Weston and Colleen close behind.

Spencer grabbed his gun as I closed the window. All four of my friends gasped at the gun. Spencer looked out to see if they had been followed. He put the gun back in his belt.

Spencer decided there was no chance to lie. We didn't have time to come up with anything.

As Spencer explained, everyone looked more sympathetic than ever. He left out the part about the Elite and let it at that small fact that I'm in the WPP.

When he was finished, Colleen's eyes were still on the gun. "Can you like, move that away from me?" she asked.

Weston put his arm around her shoulders. "He won't hurt you."

"You all know nothing and if I find out any of you spilled, I'll get you behind bars." Spencer said.

Everyone nodded.

Colleen looked at me. "No one knew?"

"I did." Weston said.

"What?" Josh asked.

"I knew. That's why Pen and I were so close all the time. I knew her when we were kids. I recognized her when she got here." Weston explained.

Colleen nodded. She was uncomfortable. I could tell.

"Colleen." I said. She looked at me. "It's all right."

"I just drove ten hours to find out that my best friend isn't who she said she was and that Josh had been right from beginning. She is actually in the Witness Protection Program and her brother is actually her boyfriend and they're acting like they're married. I'm sorry I'm a little flustered." she said.

"I understand, Colleen. Nothing has to change, though." I said.

"It does have to change! You've only been acting this way! This isn't really you at all!" she shouted angrily.

"Don't yell, please. We have to be on the down low." I said quietly.

"I can't believe you were lying the whole time!" Josh shouted. Venom leaked from his tongue.

"I'm sorry." I said. I felt horrible for lying. I couldn't apologize enough.

"Calm down." Weston said to everyone.

"She lied to all of us, Weston! You may not have been lied to, but we were and we have a right to be angry!" Colleen said.

Weston shook his head. "Maybe we should go." He looked at me. "I'm sorry, Pen."

I shook my head. "It's not your fault." I said.

Weston and Jayden hugged me before we left. They were the only ones not mad at me. Jayden kissed me goodbye when I told him we wouldn't see each other for a long time.

Weston spoke to me. "Don't let them get to you. They'll get over it."

"I hope so." I said.

After they were gone, I looked at Spencer. "I'm so sorry, Spence."

He pulled me into his arms. "It wasn't you, Sweetheart."

I hugged him back. "I shouldn't have gotten in anything with them. I should have just stayed away. Maybe I should have isolated myself."

He shook his head. "Colleen would have wanted to be your friend even more then."

I chuckled. "That's so true."

"Weston was right, though. Colleen will be begging for forgiveness next time you see her." he said.

I shrugged. I could understand why she wouldn't forgive me. Colleen hated liars. She'd probably be even angrier at Weston. That just wasn't fair to him. It wasn't his fault he figured it out.

He cocked his head to the side and smiled. "You are starting to be just like Grace. She always thinks way too hard about things. Just ease up. She'll forgive you."

"She overreacted." I said. "I didn't ask for this."

"I know. Neither of us did." he said.

I phone started ringing off the hook. I answered it and Brenda started talking quickly.

"Whoa! Brenda, slow down." I said.

"Allison just had her baby. She's been asking to talk to you since she woke up." she said.

"Pen?" Allison said.

"Ally, oh, my God. I'm so sorry." I said apologetically. We hadn't been there when I'd promised I would be.

"No, Pen. It's not your fault. My water broke like six hours ago and got to the hospital just in time. We didn't have time to call anyone." She sounded exhausted.

"But, I should have called to check on you. Man, I'm horrible." I said and swallowed.

"What's wrong?" Spencer asked.

"Hold on one second, Ally." I said and looked at Spencer. "Ally just had her baby." I said.

"What?" Spencer shouted.

Spencer reached for the phone and put it on speaker. "Is there any way you guys could come see her? Rob's not here yet because he had to work and Momma just called him." Ally said.

"We'll be there as soon as we can. It will take almost twelve hours until we're there. We will be there, though." Spencer said.

"Take your time. I just really want to see you guys. It's been so long." She sounded sincere.

"I know. I have to go pack. We love you, Sweetie." I said.

"Love you guys, too." she said and hung up.

Spencer tossed me a full bag. "They're our escape bags. I have them pre-packed for emergency escapes. I think this suffices as an emergency." He was already out the door with his keys. I followed quickly.

We got into the truck and we were off. Spencer was so anxious. I could tell.

"Calm down. We're just going to see Ally. It's not like they're going to put it together that we're driving around." I said. I was trying to be comforting, but it didn't seem to help at all. It only seemed to make him more tense at the mention of someone actually putting it together.

"No, but I really don't want to see this Rob guy. I want to kill him. Allison was way too young for him." he said. He was obviously heated.

"You don't really have any room to talk there." I said. I was a little hurt. He had always been against the whole age thing until me.

Spencer sighed and noticed his mistake. "I'm so sorry, Pen. I totally forget sometimes. I mean, you seem so much older and you've experienced so much more than even I have." he said.

I knew what he meant by that. I wasn't a virgin and he was. "I didn't experience it any more than you did! I was drunk and I barely remember it anyway! That doesn't make me any older." I said.

"That's not what I meant." he said.

"Then, what did you mean?" I asked.

"You're just so much more mature for your age. This whole situation just shows that. You've been taking care of yourself for nearly two years now. You're just so brave, too. I mean, you're in the WPP and you've never really lost it. I'm not forced to be here and you are. You're in so much danger and a lot of times it doesn't seem to affect you." He swallowed and took a moment to get a breath.

"I'm sorry. I shouldn't have jumped to conclusions." I said.

He shook his head and leaned over to kiss my forehead. "Don't worry about it."

The further into the night we got, the more tired I got. Spencer had stopped and gotten us both a coffee. The caffeine wasn't really helping though.

"If you want to sleep, you can. We won't get there until around two. We'll have to go to my parents' house and stay there until morning." he said.

"That doesn't sound too bad." I said. "I miss everyone."

"I do, too. My dad probably won't be too happy about it." he said and sighed. "I'll have to call the house and let them know."

I took his phone from the cup holder. "I'll do it." I said and dialed the number under "Dad".

"Spencer, I'm so glad you called. Did your mother tell you about Allison?" he rambled when he answered.

"Actually, it's Penelope and yes, we heard that Ally had her baby." I said.

"Oh," he sounded disappointed. "What's going on? Where's Spencer?"

"He's driving. We just want to ask if we could stay at the house tonight. We aren't getting there until late and we just need it for one night." I said.

"One night?" he questioned.

"Yeah, it's just for tonight." I said.

"If it's just for tonight, I don't care." he said angrily.

"Thank you so much, Mr. Kendal." I said.

"Just let me talk to Spencer." he said rudely. I swallowed and handed the phone to Spencer. He took it gently.

"Yeah." he answered. After his father talked for a minutes, he spoke back. "Would you just stop? Penelope isn't lying to anyone anymore! We didn't have a choice before!" His father said something else. "Dad, this was life was death for Pen. If we had told you,

someone else could have found her and killed her!" Spencer shouted.
Spencer hung up the phone and clenched his teeth.

I touched his forearm lightly. "Don't worry about him. I'll let you use my college money to get a hotel."

"No. He can deal with us for one night." Spencer said.

I nodded.

"I'm sorry." he said. He was trying to relax. "I'm sorry he acts like this."

"It's not your fault."

"No, but he's my dad. He should know better. I'm his son for crying-out-loud! He should be glad that I've found someone that makes me happy." Spencer was getting angry so I took his hand.

"He'll come around, Spence. We've only been together for six months. Give him a while." I said. My thumb rubbed the top of his hand. "What does he say about me that gets you all fired up?"

"He thinks you're only with me because of money. He thinks that you don't really love me." he said.

I swallowed. "I'm sorry. I should never have kissed you." I said regretfully.

"Don't ever say that, Pen. I love you and I'm so glad you did it." he said and kissed my temple. "My dad just hates that we're all growing up. Plus, I lied to him and everyone else and he thinks it's our lifestyle now."

"It kind of is. I mean, we aren't married, our names are not Kimberly and Jonathon Smith, and we aren't from Florida. We are lying to everyone except your family." I said calmly.

He nodded. "Yes, but we don't have a choice. He's treating us like we do. I'm so sorry for that."

I shook my head and yawned.

"Go to sleep, Pen. You get tired on long car rides." he said.

"I want to drive sometime." I said.

"I can drive. I'll get my coffee later and I'll be fine." he said and kissed me.

"I don't want you to be alone."

"I'll be fine, Sweetheart." he insisted.

I eventually couldn't fight the need to sleep.

TWENTY-ONE

JUNE 8ᵀᴴ

I woke up at one-thirty. Spencer had emptied two more coffee cups. He looked exhausted.

"Do you need me to drive?" I asked.

"No. We're almost there." he said.

"Are you sure? You look tired." I said sincerely.

"I am, but we'll be there in a half hour. No use in stopping now." He looked to me. "I promise. I can sleep when we get there."

When we got there, I sent Spencer to bed and got our bags. Spencer's father came into the kitchen as I threw out Spencer's cups.

"Did you two just get here?" he asked. He'd been sleeping. You could tell. His hair was tousled and he just looked tired.

I nodded and yawned. "Spencer's been driving all night so I made him go to bed while I unpacked the luggage." I explained.

He nodded and returned to bed.

At about three o'clock, I headed up to bed. Spencer was sprawled out in the bed, shirtless and on his stomach. The blankets were up around his waist.

He moved when I closed the door. "Penelope?" he asked.

"Yeah, I'm here." I said and walked to the bed.

Spencer pulled me close and sighed contently.

When Spencer's alarm went off, he got up and started getting ready to leave for the hospital. He wasn't wasting any time, either. He was dressed by the time I even found the energy to get up.

I changed quickly and pulled my hair up. I didn't have time to shower so my hair probably looked horrible.

We drove over. I'm not saying we didn't break a few speed laws on the way.

When we got there, Allison had to tell them to let us up.

Spencer knocked on Allison's door. A dark-haired man answered. He looked a little younger than Spencer. He was probably twenty-two or twenty-three. I wouldn't say he was unattractive in the least. His body was muscle-bound in a way that had to require long man-hours at the gym.

"You must be Spencer." he said.

Spencer nodded and the man stepped aside to let us in.

When I saw Allison, I was surprised how good she looked for just having had a baby a day ago. She had just gotten a shower. Her hair was still wet. Her skin was still pink from the hot water.

In her arms, she was holding a bundle of blankets. She looked up and smiled at us. "It took you guys long enough." she said in the usual Allison way.

Spencer smiled. "Sorry, Ally." he said and walked over to kiss her forehead.

"I'm so sorry we never even checked on you." I said.

"Don't worry about it. I understand that it's too dangerous. Rob's been taking care of me." she said.

I looked back to the man. He had to be Rob.

He smiled at Allison.

"What's her name?" I asked.

Allison had already handed her to Spencer. "Charity Leann." she said and smiled as Spencer moved the blankets back to get a better look.

"She's beautiful." Spencer said.

I didn't move toward the baby. I'd never been comfortable near young children. I was terrified that I'd hurt them or something would happen and I couldn't help it.

I didn't feel very comfortable here with Rob either. Maybe I was biased, but I had a horrible feeling about him. I wasn't sure if it was just because of the way he had treated Allison or because of something else. I couldn't shake it either.

Somehow, I was afraid of him.

Spencer looked up at me with a smile spread on his lips. "What's wrong, Pen?" he asked.

"Oh," I said. "It's nothing."

He didn't look convinced. "Pen," he said.

"Stop, Spencer. It's nothing." I said sharply. I was a little on-edge from lack of sleep as well. It didn't help that I felt like this Rob guy would ruffle my feathers the second he got the chance.

You don't even know him, Penelope. Just stop.

I took a deep breath.

Spencer walked over to me. "Do you want to hold her?" he asked.

My breath caught in my chest. "No." I said.

He really looked concerned now. "Why not?" he asked.

"I just can't." I said.

"You can't or you won't?" he asked.

I shook my head. "I can't, Spencer." I said.

"You won't hurt her." he said.

I swallowed.

"Come on, Pen." he said and laid her gently in my arms. Just then, she started crying. It started out as a little whimper, but grew quickly in intensity.

Spencer took her back over to Allison who calmed her quickly.

Spencer put his arm around my waist. "It wasn't your fault." he said.

"She didn't start crying until you gave her to me." I said and swallowed.

He shook his head. He knew I was tense and it was bothering him that he didn't know why.

The rest of the family got there in a few minutes. I tried to have minimal contact with Charity.

Spencer and I left to get lunch a few hours later.

"You've been so weird today, Pen. What's wrong?" he asked when we were in the car.

"I'm just not comfortable with a baby that little, Spencer." I said.

"It was before that. You were so tense like you knew something was going to happen. Did someone say something?" he asked.

"No. I'm always tense around people I don't know. Rob's there and I don't really know him." I said.

"He isn't going to touch you." Spencer said.

"That isn't it. I just don't like not knowing him." I said.

We stopped in a dark alley.

"Where are we?" I asked, very confused.

"Get out." he said roughly.

"What? Why?" I asked, startled and confused.

"Just do it." he said.

Fear rose up from my belly. "What's going on?" I asked. My voice was weak.

"Don't make me get you out myself." Spencer didn't look at me. He just stared at the steering wheel.

I opened my door and stepped out of the car. Someone was behind me. They covered my mouth with their hand and held the gun to my temple.

"Don't scream or this is going to hurt a lot more than it has to." Jacob said.

My breathing quickened and my lip trembled. He pressed the gun harder to my temple.

"We need to get moving before Allison notices we're gone." Spencer said.

He'd set this up. He'd set *me* up. Spencer had betrayed me.

Jacob nodded and shoved me in the direction of a little car with heavily tinted windows. Jacob pushed me onto the hood and let go of my mouth. He cuffed my hands behind me and shackled my ankles. I was crying, but I didn't scream. Nothing would have come out if I had even tried. Jacob put a gag in my mouth so I couldn't even talk.

Spencer lifted me off my feet and sat me in the back seat of the car and sat next to me. Jacob sat in the driver's seat.

I looked at Spencer and more tears fell down my cheeks. My eyes completely spelled out "How could you?"

He chuckled. "You can't trust anyone, Penelope." he said.

I took deep, calming breaths. There was no use in trying to convince myself that I wasn't going to die. Jacob had hit me right where it hurt. I knew I shouldn't have trusted a single person. I should have run while I could have. This time, it was for me; no one else.

Jacob looked back us through the rear-view mirror.

The drive had to be an hour or so.

When we arrived, Spencer lifted me from the seat and carried me into the building. It was a brick building in the middle of nowhere. All the windows were broken and the walls were covered in spray-painted graffiti. We walked down a flight of stairs to the basement. I recognized this room. It was the office from my dream.

"We have her, Boss." Jacob said.

The chair turned around and Rob smiled at them. My breathing completely stopped. I knew it. I knew he was no good.

"It seems as though Spencer finally pulled through with his part of the deal." Rob said and stood up. He walked to me and touched my cheek. "If only you had listened to him when he told you about trusting people, you may not be here."

My throat contracted as fear burned in me. If Spencer was against me, who was fighting for me?

I swallowed.

"Calm down, Babe. You're not dead yet." Jacob said and smiled.

Spencer seemed unaffected by all of this. He didn't even say a word.

They sat me on the floor by a wall and chained me to two large steel loops sticking out of the wall. It was only my hands. They were spread so I could only bend them slightly. They didn't chain my ankles. Spencer removed my gag and I noticed that he wouldn't make eye-contact.

He's a liar. Spencer Kendal is just a good-for-nothing traitor. He turned you in. He's ready to help kill you. My thoughts were firing at me so loudly that I couldn't pull my mind away.

I started crying again when I realized that I was going to die. They weren't going to let me out of here alive. I didn't know what happened after death. I could only hope there was some sort of heaven. I mean, I'd always somewhat believed in Christianity, but I couldn't be sure that there was really this place of eternal joy that my soul would go to or if death really was just an end.

Jacob's hand made swift contact with my cheek, making my head spin and my cheek sting in response. My next sob froze as a lump in my throat.

"Stop your crying. We didn't hurt you yet." Jacob said.

Yet. They're going to kill me. Just not yet.

Spencer just watched as all of this happened. I was surprised. Some little part of me was hoping that he'd hop in and pulverize Jacob for hitting me.

My whole body was shaking with fear. I knew I was actually alone in this.

"You're so scared." Jacob laughed. "It's probably because Spencer's actually with us, huh? You didn't expect that, did you? We always had one foot in the door."

"Shut up." I said. My voice even sounded hurt.

He took my chin between his index finger and his thumb. "Don't tell me what to do. That won't get you anywhere."

Adrenaline began pumping in my veins. I bent my hand down and bit into his thumb. I tasted the blood before I released. The worst I probably did was put a crack his fingernail. He yanked away quickly and cursed at me.

I looked at Spencer. "How many other times have you lied to me?" I asked.

He smiled. "Let's just say, I'm a much better liar than you are." he said.

I fought against the chains forcefully. "I told you everything!" I shouted.

"You should have learned from the first time. You can't let people close. All it does is blow up in your face." he said.

Sadness drew my chest in tight. I staggered for breath.

"Stop playing with the girl. We're not here for that." Rob said.

"The little whore bit me!" Jacob yelled.

"Grow up, Jacob." Spencer said. "It couldn't have hurt that badly."

"Shut up, Kendal." Jacob said.

"For once Jacob said something useful." I muttered.

Spencer looked at me. Anger burned in his eyes.

Rob crossed his arms. "Show her who's boss, Spencer. The last thing we need is for her to get a mouth on her." he said.

Spencer hesitated. He still looked angry. It kind of scared me. I mean, all of his anger was directed at me.

"Don't tell me Kendal's too much of a goodie-two-shoe to hit a girl." Jacob said.

I actually chuckled at that. Jacob kicked me in the ribs. I couldn't get in another breath around the pain. He'd kicked me hard and I felt pain burn down deeper. It wasn't just the fact that he'd kicked me that hurt. It was that Spencer didn't do anything about it. He just watched me get hit and beat on.

"Knock it off. You may think it's funny to just pound on her, but it's getting really old already." Rob said.

"What did you do to Allison and Charity?" I asked breathlessly.

Rob chuckled. "I didn't touch them. Allison's known that we were all against you. One more friend would help us keep your guard down."

I bit the inside of my lip. "Why don't you just kill me already?" I asked.

Rob laughed and shook his head. "You haven't earned a quick death. We have plenty of time, Penny." he said.

Every part of me recognized that nickname. My father had called me that forever.

I pulled against the chains. They cut into my wrists. "What have you done with him?" I asked angrily.

"You just jump right to conclusions, don't you? You immediately think I'm the one that has your father." he said and laughed.

"What are you going to do to him?" I asked assertively.

"You'll just have to find out."

"He didn't do anything wrong!" I shouted.

"He created you, didn't he?" Spencer said.

My stomach burned. I still couldn't believe Spencer was doing this. I looked up at him.

"How could you do this to me, Spencer?" I asked without thinking.

He smiled. "You really think I loved you?" he asked.

"It sure seemed that way." I said.

He laughed. "I thought you could read me better than that." he said.

"You made up everything?"

"How else were you supposed to trust me?"

I swallowed. "You're whole family knew about this?"

"I couldn't have done it alone."

"You're a son of a bitch!" I shouted.

Jacob came after me again. The most I could do was turn away from the attacks. He kept hitting me. Rob had left the room and I know Spencer wouldn't stop him.

One of his shots was a kick that hit me right in the nose. I gasped as I felt the blood streaming onto my lips. He stepped right on my ankle. I screamed as I felt a bone break. Actually, 'break' is an understatement.

"What did Rob say about getting a mouth on her?" Jacob said to Spencer angrily.

Spencer just stared and I started crying again.

After a few minutes, my ankle hadn't healed at all. I thought it was because I hadn't slept much.

"Oh, God, ouch." I moaned quietly.

Jacob smiled. "You're not healing, are you?" he asked. I looked at him. "The cuffs are imbedded with sapphire, which, in large amounts, blocks your powers. It's just a little something we found out from torturing hundreds of you . . . *things.*"

I didn't respond. They'd thought of everything to keep me down. They weren't going to give up either. No matter how much I fought or screamed, my fate was the same.

Jacob began flipping a hunting knife in his hands. "Think about it, Babe. If you wouldn't heal like you do, you would be dead." He smiled. "That is how you're better off after-all. That way, you can't feel anything." He touched the blade to my chin and I took in a shallow, fearful breath. He pulled my chin up so I looked at him.

"If you're going to kill me, just do it." I said.

Jacob chuckled. "Oh, I'd love to, but you still have a long ways to go before you deserve to die." He slid that knife down to press into my collarbone. I felt it break the skin and I started shaking. "Do you know how much envy you caused in your—*our*—high school? Everyone wanted your body. You had no really visible scars." He pulled the knife to my shoulder, slicing my skin shallowly as he went. Blood dripped down onto my shirt. My breathing was heavy and labored. "You know what this knife is great for, Penelope?" I didn't answer verbally, but I shook my head. He smiled at that. "Gutting." he whispered.

I swallowed. I pushed as close to the wall as I could.

"That won't do you any good, Babe. Struggling will only hurt worse." he said.

My lip trembled.

"Now that I think of it, nothing will do you any good. When you scream, no one will hear you." He brought his lips to my ear. "No one would care."

I bit the inside of my lip.

Jacob stood up and kicked me in the hip. "Why aren't you saying anything?" he asked.

I looked to Spencer. He looked angry, but I knew it was still directed at me. I mean, he was looking right at me.

"He's not gonna help you. He's been working with us the entire time. All he'll do is help me against you." Jacob said.

The door slammed and Spencer was gone.

Jacob cursed. "He's probably going to rat me out."

I still didn't say anything. My collarbone was throbbing.

"What did I tell you about beating on the girl?" Rob shouted as he and Spencer came back. "Get over here, Maslin. Kendal, stop the bleeding. We can't let her lose too much blood yet."

Spencer brought over his knife and cut off my sleeve. Then, he noticed his underestimation of the size of the cut and cut my shirt the entire way down. He cut it off my shoulders and pressed it to my collarbone. I winced, but didn't respond to him verbally.

"Sorry." Spencer muttered.

I swallowed. Rob had left once he was done his scolding. Spencer managed to stop the bleeding quickly.

Jacob had fallen asleep and Spencer was the only one with me. He wouldn't even look at me and I didn't want to talk to him.

I got more and more anxious. The least they could do was just kill me. Waiting was worse.

My ankle throbbed painfully. No matter how hard I willed it to heal, it wouldn't. It was sort of scaring and frustrating me.

I tried to sleep, but I was unsuccessful. Everything hurt too badly from being so tense and I couldn't calm down. The anxiety was killing me.

"Just try to calm down." Spencer said.

"Leave me alone." I said through my teeth.

He looked at me. "Pen, I'm not going to hurt you." he said and touched my cheek.

I cringed away. "Yes, you will! You're just like them! You're worse!" I shouted. Fear rose up quickly and violently.

Spencer grabbed my ankle and felt it. It's not like it could get worse so I didn't fight him. He took my foot in his hand. "This is going to hurt, but it won't heal right otherwise."

"I won't live long enough to heal." I said.

"Yes, you will." he said and pulled to reset it. I gasped as pain pulled through me. I yanked away.

"Leave me alone!" I repeated with more aggression.

"Just let me help you." he said.

"You're trying to kill me! Why would I let you do anything?" I yelped.

He put his hand over my mouth. "Don't yell. You'll wake up Jacob." he said.

"I don't care." I said behind his hand.

"I think you do. I won't hit you, but he will. I won't hurt you." he said.

I didn't move and he moved his hand. "Just stay quiet and let me explain." he said.

When he started to speak, Jacob shifted. Spencer stopped talking. Whatever this was, he wasn't letting Jacob or Rob know.

I swallowed. My ankle hurt worse and the swelling was getting really bad.

Jacob stretched. "Guess I fell asleep." he muttered.

"It was your shift." Spencer said.

Jacob rolled his eyes. "Don't be lazy. You were making out with her for nine months. I only ever had one night." He was laughing.

"I was drunk!" I shouted.

"It doesn't matter, Babe. We still did it." he argued.

"I didn't know you were twenty-three then! I was only a kid! You took advantage of a child!" I said as the memories of that night came back.

"Shut your mouth or I won't let you be willing this time!" he yelled.

I didn't speak.

"Put one more hand on her and Rob's gonna kill you. He doesn't want her too far gone." Spencer said.

Jacob pulled his lip over his teeth. "I'm not even sure if you're with us or against us, Kendal."

Spencer raised an eyebrow. "Guess you'll just have to trust me."

Jacob ripped his gun from his belt. He aimed the barrel at Spencer. "I don't *have* to do anything."

Spencer didn't move. "You won't shoot me."

"How much do you want to bet on that, Kendal?" he asked.

Spencer smiled.

"Put the gun away, Maslin. How old are you?" Rob's voice said as he came into the room.

Jacob slid the gun back into his belt. "I can't ever do anything." he muttered.

Rob looked over at me. He took my chin between his thumb and index finger. "What's wrong, Penelope? You look a bit scared."

My breathing sped. I knew something was coming.

"If you tell me where the rest of your kind is hiding, I won't hurt you. You could even work for me." Rob said.

"I—" I paused. "I don't know. Even if I did, I wouldn't tell you." When I said it, I instantly regretted it.

Rob seemed mad, but didn't do anything really.

He reached slowly into his back pocket and took out a box of cigarettes and a lighter. He lit one and waited a moment.

"You do know that that goes in your mouth, right?" I asked. I couldn't think of anything other than that he was just being stupid.

He chuckled. "Of course I do. Kendal just made my job easier." he said and knelt down beside me. "Just to give you a hint, I don't smoke."

He reached down and pushed the cigarette into my stomach, just above my panty line. The heat burned deeply into my skin. I cried out loudly even though I promised myself I wouldn't. He lifted the cigarette away and smiled.

"Any change in heart?" he asked as his sinister smile widened.

"I don't know where they are." I cried. The burn on my stomach was bleeding. It had to be bad.

"That's a shame then." he said and relit the cigarette.

I tried to move away, but he pushed it into my stomach on the other side. My jaw tensed up as I fought the scream. He kept this one to my skin longer. I started crying before I would let myself scream.

Rob tossed the cigarette to the ground and stomped it out.

I calmed myself and forced myself to look at the burns. They were both bleeding a lot. It was running down my hips and sides and pooling beneath me.

Spencer looked over at me. His expression was highly apologetic, but looked away quickly.

It was like an hour before anyone spoke. Jacob was already asleep again.

"I'm running out to get something to eat." Rob said and nodded toward me as he tossed Spencer the keys. "Watch her."

As he left, Spencer came over to me. "Are you all right?" he asked. "You have blood on your face." he said and tried to wipe it off. It obviously didn't work by the way he shook his head. He used my sullied shirt to wipe off my stomach. It hurt when he wiped over it.

"I know." I said. "I have blood everywhere."

"Well, I'm getting you out of here." he said and fiddled to find the right keys to fit in the lock.

"Don't do it, Spencer. They'll come after you." I said. Obviously, he was actually working for me. I wished I could appreciate it, but I was too busy worrying about getting caught . . . or worse.

"I'll frame Jacob's sleep-walking." Spencer assured me and unlocked the shackles. "When I get you out, I'm going to take you to my parents'. They're waiting for you."

"So, you're not really trying to kill me?" I asked.

He kissed my forehead. "I could never." he said.

Jacob woke up when the shackles clanked to the floor. He raised his gun to Spencer's head. "I knew it." he said.

Spencer grabbed Jacob's wrist, threw him to the floor, and threw the gun down. It slid over toward me, but not right to me.

Jacob tackled Spencer and got him down and started to choke him. I was already panicking. I wasn't sure what to do. One false move and Spencer was gone.

"You want to be a traitor? You'll get a traitor's reward." Jacob said aggressively.

My heart raced. He could have very well killed Spencer. I was just sitting and doing nothing. I needed to find something to do to help him after everything he's done for me.

I crawled over and grabbed the gun. I aimed it as well as I could have with my hands shaking. It seemed like I used an immeasurable amount of strength to pull the trigger. When it did go down, I held my breath as I heard the shot burst in my ears. It all happened in slow motion. It seemed like minutes before Jacob collapsed on top of Spencer. Spencer gasped in a breath and pushed Jacob's limp body off of himself.

The gun tumbled from my hands and landed on the concrete floor. My chest tightened and regret burned in me. I'd just killed him. My lip trembled.

"Oh, my God." I said and everything started shaking.

Spencer got over to me. "Are you okay?" he asked. It sounded very fuzzy, as if I was on the other end of a phone in bad reception.

"I killed him." I said and started crying. It was like I was numb, but I knew I'd done something seriously wrong. There were horrible consequences for murder. He hadn't been threatening my life. I had no right to take his.

THE ELITE

"It's all right, Pen." Spencer said and pushed my hair off my forehead.

I looked over to Jacob. His eyes were closed and he actually didn't look pained. I guess I was expecting him to look like he was in agony before he died.

"I didn't want to kill him." I said.

"You had to." Spencer said. "We have to get moving. Can you walk?"

"I don't think so." I said as I became more aware of how badly my ankle hurt.

"Do you mind if I carry you, then?" he asked.

I shook my head stiffly. He lifted me to a cradle at this chest, avoiding my ankle. He started walking and got me to the pick-up truck and sat me in the passenger's seat. He started the car and I was silent. I couldn't shake the image of Jacob from my mind. I'd killed him.

Spencer touched my thigh. "It's all right, Pen." he said.

"No, it's not." I said. My voice hadn't cracked, but tears fell down my cheeks. "I killed him." I repeated.

"You had to, Pen. He would have come right back after you if you hadn't." he said.

"I didn't have to kill him! I could have shot him in the leg or something." I said as my voice broke.

"He came after me. You didn't know what else to do. If you hadn't killed him, he would have pulled something on both of us." he said and kissed my hand. "You did the right thing."

"It's never the right thing to kill someone." I said and tried to take deep breaths.

"You had to get out of there." he said.

I remembered Rob calling me Penny. "But, what about my dad?" I asked.

"He's dead, Pen. I'm sorry. They killed him a long time ago. He left you because he knew if they didn't know you were his daughter, they might not find you. He loved you like crazy, but Rob knew that he knew something about where you were. When he wouldn't give it up, he got frustrated." Spencer said.

"He's dead?" I asked, fresh tears coating my cheeks.

185

"I'm so sorry, Pen." Spencer took my hand gently and I leaned on his shoulder while I cried. Of course he was dead. Just when I actually thought he was there. I thought he'd actually just been taken. But, those idiots kill him.

We pulled up to a hospital. I looked at Spencer.

"Why are we here?" I asked.

"It's the safest place for you. I have a lot of guards here for you." he said.

"You're not staying?" I asked, panicking.

"I need to find Rob." he said.

"He'll kill you." I said.

"That's a risk I'm willing to take." he said and got out of the car. He carried me gently into the hospital and kissed my forehead. "I have to go." he said.

"No." I said.

"I have to, Pen. I love you." he said and he was gone.

I was discharged and told that guards would be watching me at all times.

Brenda came to pick me up. We headed back to the house and my anxiety was skyrocketing. Spencer could die at any moment and I was just sitting around waiting for him.

"I'm sorry about this, Mrs. Kendal. I'll be out of your hair as soon as I can be." I said.

"Don't you dare worry about that, Penelope. Just worry about keeping yourself safe. We love having you with us." she said and touched my shoulder.

"I don't like having to come here just because I'm trying to hide from people trying to kill me. I hate putting all of you in this position. I mean, Charity's father is the man trying to kill me." I said.

"That's been horrible on Allison. She keeps saying that she led him to you." Brenda said and turned into the driveway.

"She couldn't have possibly known." I said.

Brenda stopped the car. "Try telling her that."

We headed into the house and I heard Charity crying. I sat down my bags and walked to find Allison walking around the living room with her little baby in her arms, trying to calm her.

"Mom!" Allison shouted. She turned and saw me. "Oh, Penelope. I didn't even know you were here."

"I wasn't until just now." I said and smiled.

"Does she need a bottle?" Brenda asked from behind me.

"I think so. It was like four hours ago when she ate last." Allison said. Her eyes were puffy and red and she just looked tired. I didn't know if she just couldn't sleep or if Charity was keeping her up.

Once Allison got Charity's bottle to her, she became quiet and Allison smiled. "She normally isn't this fussy." Allison said to me.

"I'm sorry I wasn't here to know." I said.

She shook her head. "You were locked in a basement. It's not like you could have looked at Rob and said 'Um, I want to see your daughter so just let me go.'" Allison's voice broke. "I was so stupid. He was so interested in you and I didn't put together why. He got so mad when I wouldn't tell him much. That's exactly why he got me pregnant. He'd have more of a reason to be near you."

"You could never have known, Ally." I said and noticed she was crying. "He was sneaky."

"I should have been more careful. I shouldn't have even told him you were with Spencer. He wouldn't have known." She swallowed hard and took deep breaths.

"Allison, stop. It wasn't your fault. He took advantage of you. I'm so sorry about that because he wanted me." I put my arm around her. "This isn't your fault."

Allison looked at me. "I slept with a guy trying to kill my best friend."

I shrugged. "I slept with a guy trying to kill *me.*"

"It's not like this, though. You were drunk." she said and lifted Charity to her shoulder and patted her back.

I rolled my eyes. "You didn't know, Ally."

"Why aren't you mad at me?" she asked.

"You didn't do anything but help me though everything." I said.

"What about Spencer? Is he mad?" she asked.

"He actually gave me up to them." I explained what happened quickly. I didn't want her to think that her brother had actually tried to get me killed.

"You must have been terrified." she said.

"Yeah, I was." I swallowed. "I still am."

Allison sighed. "I'm worried about him, too. He's too selfless. He doesn't know when to think that he should stay safe."

"Tell me about it." I said. I looked at Charity, who was again sucking on her bottle.

"You can feed her if you want." Allison said and slid her bottle away from her still sucking mouth.

"Are you sure?" I asked.

"Of course." she said and laid her in my arms with her head on my elbow. She handed me the bottle and I put it into her mouth.

"See? Nothing to it." she said.

"She's absolutely gorgeous." I said. Her curly blond hair was longer than I expected it to be. She was even smaller than I thought she'd be.

Allison smiled. "She is, isn't she?"

"I never even thought about being a mom. I never expected to settle down with anyone." I said. I was still wearing the ring that was my wedding ring. I didn't want to take it off.

"I'm not trying to pressure you with Spencer, but he'd be an amazing father. You guys make a good team."

I nodded. "I really hope I stay with him for a very, very long time."

"Me too. I've never seen him so happy."

"Really?" I asked anxiously.

"Remember that I was Spencer's only outlet before you." she said.

Suddenly, someone was leaning on the wall in the room. "Penelope, Sweetie. You should get some sleep. You've had a long couple of days." Brenda said.

I gave back Charity, hugged Allison, and went to bed. My phone vibrated soon after. It was Spencer.

I'm okay. If I can, I'll call you tomorrow. I'll let you know that I'm okay. I love you.

I replied, *I love you too.*

I went to sleep easily.

TWENTY-TWO

JUNE 9TH

The first thing I saw in my dream was Rob's face. "You actually thought I'd let you get away with killing my partner? You're nothing but a traitor, Kendal."

Then, I saw Spencer. He was beaten and bleeding.

"Once you're gone, no one will be there to protect your precious girlfriend." Rob said and stabbed Spencer between his bottom two ribs.

Spencer gasped for breath and grabbed the knife.

"You'll be dead in no time." Rob said and laughed.

Spencer closed his eyes and his head lolled to one side.

I woke up screaming.

The guards were in my bedroom immediately. Brenda followed and sat on my bed.

"What happened?" she asked.

"I think Spencer's dead." I said and started crying.

"What? Did you see it?" she asked.

I nodded. Brenda looked at the guards.

"Excuse us a moment, please." she said.

They left and she looked at me. "Are you sure?"

I nodded again.

"Do you have a way of contacting him?" she asked.

I nodded again.

"Try." she said.

I called him and no one answered the phone. Rob's voice was on the answering machine. He was threatening that no one should look for Spencer. It was too late. My lip trembled.

Brenda bit her lip. "Do you think he's already gone?" she asked as tears filled her eyes.

"I don't see how else Rob would have his phone." Tightness in my chest squeezed my lungs and I gasped for breath as I sobbed. Brenda held me to her while we cried.

Amanda called me and when I answered, she was crying. "I have such bad news for you, Pen." she said.

"Spencer's dead." I said and swallowed.

"I'm so sorry." Amanda said.

"How are you guys sure he's dead?" I asked.

"We tracked Rob and found Spencer's blood on the floor with a knife. There was too much blood for Spencer to have survived." Amanda said.

When we hung up, my crying picked up.

Mr. Kendal came in soon after, noticing the absence of his wife. Brenda had gone out to get us something to drink, though.

"Where's Brenda?" he asked.

"She went to get water." I said and my voice broke. A single sob shook me as I put my forehead to my knees.

He looked uncomfortable, but sat next to me. "What happened, Penelope?" he asked.

I looked at him. "Spencer's dead." I said.

His face turned to shock. "What?"

"I'm so sorry. I should never have let him go." I sobbed.

He put his arm around me and hesitated, but hugged me. "You couldn't have stopped him." he said.

"I should have made him stay. I should have fought him to stay."

"You couldn't have stopped him." he repeated.

I couldn't stop myself from crying. Spencer couldn't be gone.

When Brenda got back, she saw her husband and burst into tears again, sending the bottled water tumbling to the floor.

I eventually cried myself to sleep. I dreamed about Spencer and the very last moments we had together.

I waited up the next day for Spencer's call . . . but it never came. Surprise, surprise.

Twenty-Three

I woke up and it hurt to open my eyes. They were swollen and sore. I rolled over and noticed that I'd been crying in my sleep. My cheeks were still wet as well as my pillow. I sat up and tried to gather my thoughts. All I could think about was how tight and tense everything felt.

It had only been three months since Spencer's death and they'd sent out search parties to, if there were such things as miracles, find him alive. I didn't have high hopes. I was guaranteeing that Spencer was dead.

I crawled out of bed and got clothes for a shower.

I was going to ask Brenda to use her blow dryer when I heard her talking with Mr. Kendal.

"The last I saw him, I didn't say a word to him. God, I never should have treated him like that over his relationship with Penelope." Mr. Kendal said.

"You couldn't have known this would happen." Brenda said.

"I knew it was a possibility." he said and took a deep breath. "I knew that there was a huge possibility that all of this was going to happen."

"We never thought it would happen to Spencer, though. It wasn't just you. I wish I could have been there when he dropped off Penelope. I would have begged him to stay. I should have when I talked to him." Brenda said.

"It's all because of those Elite kids. It's their fault that he's dead."
Mr. Kendal cursed loudly.

I'll admit it. His comment hurt a bit. I knew I'd been blaming
myself for Spencer's death and any unhappiness before that. It just
hurt a lot worse to hear it from someone else. I knew that I should
have just taken off the necklace tracker and ran off again when I had
the chance. Spencer may actually still be alive if I had.

I sucked in a breath and pinched my eyes closed, fighting the
tears.

"Don't say that, Jeff. The poor girl didn't do anything wrong."
Brenda said.

"She got our son killed!" Mr. Kendal, Jeff, shouted.

"You think she should have died? That's what would have
happened otherwise." Brenda said.

"It's not like she actually has any family to learn to live without
their daughter or their sister. We all have to learn to live without
Spencer. Not a single person would have realized she was gone." Jeff
said fiercely.

"Spencer would have. He saved her. I swear, if he wouldn't have
made it in time to save her, he would have been so devastated." I
could tell she was trying to keep herself calm. "She made Spencer
happy. Can't you just be happy that he didn't die miserable?"

"That's exactly it! He. Is. Dead." Jeff said. He was getting louder.
"If she'd never come along, he wouldn't be."

"Stop it, Jeffery! She'll hear you!" Brenda scolded.

"I hope to God that she does." he said and stormed out. He saw
me at the wall. Tears were streaming my cheeks and I was trembling.
He looked at me and kept walking.

Brenda came after him and saw me. "Jesus." she said. She tried
to talk to me, but I just ran upstairs. I fell up the steps and I just sat
there, crying.

I cried for a while, but eventually pulled myself together.

"We're right back to normal." I said and stroked my newly
bleached blond locks.

I nodded and grabbed the gun from Spencer's nightstand drawer.
I slid it into the hole between my belt and my jeans like I'd seen
Spencer do so many times before.

I knew that I had finally talked Amanda into letting me go after Rob. He'd killed Spencer and he needed to be killed.

I nodded again and walked downstairs. Brenda stared as I nearly made it to the door with no complication.

"Where are you going?" she asked.

I looked at her. "I need to find Rob. He killed Spencer and my dad. I can't let him get away with it." I said.

She stood in my pathway to the door. "Is this because of what Jeff said? He was only angry."

I shrugged. "He's right. I killed Spencer. He died in saving me and if I have to die trying to give Rob revenge, I will."

"You can't possibly want to die. I could get you an amazing counselor. You don't have to feel like you want to die." She was trying to persuade me. I didn't want to die, but I couldn't let Rob get away with this.

"Dying is a risk I'm willing to take." I said and walked out the door. Amanda was in the driveway waiting for me. I got into the car and didn't say a word at first.

"Penelope," Amanda said. "You do realize that you're most likely not going to come back from this, don't you?"

I swallowed. "Yes." I said.

"Spencer would have never let you do this." she muttered.

"I know that." I said. "That's why I'm doing it."

We got to the WPP building and I got my permit to carry a gun, a WPP employee badge, and a little tracking thing. It was going to track the cell phone that Rob now had of Spencer's.

"If he destroys that, we have a tracker in the gun Spencer had. Rob wouldn't throw out a gun like that. It was too good of an opportunity to just throw away." Amanda said.

I nodded. Amanda also gave me a credit card for food and other things.

She just didn't know that I wasn't giving up until I found him, dead or alive.

She looked at me. "You don't have to do this." she said.

"Sure I do." I said and smiled. "He gave up everything for me and he had a great life. My life sucks. The least I could do is give him that little bit." I said.

"Then, you should get on your way before he moves again." Amanda said.

I left quickly and started driving the truck.

I followed the map on the tracking device. It looked like a GPS and told me directions like one. I heard them through a wireless earpiece I had.

My fear became more and more dominant as I drove. What if I died and I never really had the chance to see Spencer again?

I was fairly sure that I'd be in hell anyway. Jacob would be burning right alongside me.

I took a deep breath and fought my fear. No matter what happened, it was for Spencer.

TWENTY-FOUR

SEPTEMBER 13TH

I arrived at the location of the phone at around two-thirty in the morning. I peeked around the corner and saw the phone. It was setting on a coffee table and Rob was sitting on the wooden chair.

"Tell me, Spencer. How is it that you think you can be a traitor and never pay for it?" Rob asked.

I looked and saw Spencer. He wasn't dead. He was very badly beaten and looked very exhausted, but he wasn't dead.

My excitement grew. I was shaking with it. I hadn't killed him.

Guilt grew in me. I'd done this to him. I had made him feel the pain he was feeling right now.

I aimed the gun up and Rob couldn't see it. He took another punch at Spencer when he moaned in pain. I couldn't help but notice the stab wound in his chest. Spencer was surely too weak to fight him off. Spencer hadn't seen me either. I tried to pull the trigger, but I couldn't.

"Pull the trigger and I'll kill him." Rob said, looking right at me. He had a gun to Spencer's forehead. Spencer rolled his eyes to look at me weakly.

I argued with myself for a split second. I knew it was very unlikely for Spencer to survive his injuries anyway. I just couldn't risk getting Spencer killed. I laid the gun on the concrete floor and he aimed his gun at me.

This wasn't going as planned.

"Good girl." Rob said and took a step toward me. "You just can't seem stay away from me, can you? You just love the thrill of knowing that you've gotten away from death, don't you?"

I didn't say a word. My hand was close to my side so I bumped the alarm button on the tracker. It would tell other agents that I needed help and give a location.

Rob was so close to me now. He towered over me. Then, Spencer was on top of him. He was holding him down. The gun had been flung across the room.

Rob wasn't letting Spencer win. He kept hitting him even when he was down and no longer fighting back. Spencer was covered in his own blood.

I had no choice but to pick up my gun and fire. The familiar image of Jacob dropping to the ground shot through my mind. Rob fell the same way just as agents flooded in. I ran to Spencer and he was unconscious.

Christian got over to us and looked at my hands. I was putting pressure on the stab wound in his chest. "I can heal him." I said.

"No, Penelope. He's human. He'll heal on his own. An ambulance is already on the way."

"They might be too late! At least, if I die, no one will be around to miss me. Spencer had a whole family to go back to." I said and started healing.

Christian pushed me backward violently. The other agents grabbed me.

"Get her out of here!" Christian shouted. Christian and Spencer must have been pretty high up in status in the WPP. They were always the one's giving orders.

I didn't fight them as they took me outside. There was no use. The ambulance pulled up. Just seeing it made my anxiety grow tremendously. The paramedics rushed in and brought out Spencer minutes later. I just watched and tried to control my breathing.

Christian came over to me after they drove off with Spencer. "Are you all right?" he asked and sat next to me.

I nodded once. My whole body was stiff. I was sitting with my knees to my chest, my chin behind them. My arms were on top of my knees.

Christian's black hair hung into his icy blue eyes. He looked really concerned. "Did Rob hurt you?"

I shook my head.

"Did I hurt you? I'm sorry, but you can't always help everyone." he said.

I shook my head. "No. I'm just worried about Spencer." I said and my voice broke. I cursed to myself.

"I'm sure he'll be just fine. We all thought he was dead all this time. Nothing can be worse than that." Christian said.

"Feeling guilty for it is much worse." I said and my throat contracted.

"How could you have done this?" he asked. He was just trying to get into my head. Everyone had a nasty habit of that lately.

"I heard Spencer's dad saying how he blamed me for it and I finally realized that, if I had run away when I could have, none of this would have happened to Spencer. I wish I had." I said and bit my lip against oncoming tears. "He said that I should have died because I don't have any family to really miss me."

"That's why you said that?" Christian asked.

I nodded.

"Don't ever say that, Penelope. So many people would miss you. I mean, whenever Vivian and I get a chance to talk, you're the only one she talks about. Spencer, oh, Jesus, if he lost you, I don't know what he'd do. All of the Kendals love you like you're their own family." Christian said. Vivian was the girl that he'd guarded.

"That doesn't matter." I said. "All of my family is dead. I could have killed Spencer who has a loving family that needs him."

"It wasn't your fault that you were born into this." Christian said.

Christian drove me to the hospital and I just sat, trying to stay calm. Christian had left to pick up the Kendals and I was alone with only my thoughts.

I considered leaving everything traceable on the chair and leaving so I never caused any of them any more pain.

I wanted to explain to Spencer before I left though. I couldn't leave and just let him think that I didn't love him.

But, maybe that would be better. It may be more painful, but if I actually told him that I was leaving, he may not let me.

I walked down to the other end of the hospital to get a cup of coffee. When I got back, all of the Kendals were there. Allison had left Charity with the babysitter.

"Where is he?" Jeff asked me.

"I think he's still in surgery." I said and swallowed hard.

Jeff shook his head and ground his teeth. I shook my head and started sipping on my coffee. Allison came and sat next to me.

"No one would let me help him." I said.

"But, you did. You saved him." she said.

"No, I didn't. I put him here. I should have run off." I said and took a deep breath.

"No, you shouldn't have." Allison said.

"I'm leaving once I find out that he's okay." I admitted.

"What? Why?" she asked.

"I was only with Spencer to protect myself and all I've been doing is getting him into trouble. Your dad was right. I should have died. No one would have missed me. Spencer has an actual life to come back to." I said and sighed.

"You can't leave. You love him, don't you?" Allison asked.

"That's exactly why I have to go. I can't hurt him anymore. He needs to be with someone that your parents can be happy with. He needs someone that can relate to him more than I can." I said.

"Where are you going?" Allison asked.

"Back to my apartment if it's still open." I said.

"What are you going to do?"

"Go back to high school, I guess. I'll go back to my old job." I said and remembered the little pizza shop. It was the only place that would hire me.

"You don't have to do that." Allison said. "We could find a little place and live together. Charity loves you. I have plenty of money to get us up and going."

"No. I love you to death, Ally, but I don't want Spencer to have a reason to come find me." I said.

Allison nodded. "We'll still talk, right?" she asked.

"Of course we will, Ally." I said and hugged her.

We all waited anxiously for hours. A couple people fell asleep, but I didn't. I fought the exhaustion. I wouldn't have slept anyway. I would be too restless. I had to have drunk at least three more coffees.

Jeff and I were the only two awake at one point. I started biting my nails and he just watched me. I hoped he wouldn't say anything to me. I didn't want to talk.

Eventually, the sun came up and everyone was forced to wake up. We just sat in silence.

At around eight the surgeon came out and told us that everything went well and that Spencer was in recovery. I grabbed my stuff and got up to leave.

"Where are you going?" Brenda asked.

I shrugged. "Home, I guess." I said and left.

I took the bus to every bus station until I got to the Kendal's home. I gathered the little clothes I had there and my savings that Spencer never took. I'd need it.

I got back to my apartment and the landlord just told me to start where I'd left off in rent. I paid the month's rent and unpacked my things.

I went to work to see if they'd take me back.

They sent me home after reminding me of my many duties.

I was in the shower when my phone started ringing. I wrapped a towel around myself and answered on speakerphone.

"Yeah?" I asked.

"Pen, Spencer has been asking for you for hours. What am I supposed to tell him?" Allison asked.

I swallowed. "Tell him the truth. Just don't tell him where I am." I said.

I'd tried to push all of this out of my mind for the rest of the day. I needed to get through this without hurting both of us in the process. I was already hurting enough for the both of us.

"He's going to want to come after you." Allison said.

"Don't let him. Tell him anything. Just for a while. He'll be able to get over it faster than you think." I said.

"I don't think so, Pen. He seems really upset about this. It just scares him to not know where you are." Allison sounded oddly serious.

I shook my head and one tear fell to the counter. "If you're asking me to come tell him, I can't. I can't do that. I'll just get all emotional and he won't let me leave."

"Just come and tell him what's going on. He'll understand. It will just make it easier for him." she said.

"I can't, Allison. I'm sorry." I said and hung up.

I finished my shower and changed into my work shirt and khakis.

I headed off to my first day of work. My phone was ringing off the hook so I put it on silent. I tied up my hair and got to work.

"It's good to have you back, Penelope." the manager said.

"Thanks." I said. I would have said that I was happy to be back, but someone once told me that I was a horrible liar.

I was rolling out pizza dough the rest of the day. I have to admit, I was a little embarrassed to still work here. I didn't have any other choice, though.

I decided that I was going to go looking for another job tomorrow. A bunch of people from my high school kept coming in and I didn't want to be humiliated that I had to live like this.

"Penelope Ann." Amanda's voice came from the door.

"Hi, Amanda. I'm kind of working. I can't talk." I said and started another round of dough.

"You can take off a little time for little old me." Amanda said.

"No, she can't, Lady." the manager said.

Amanda showed him her badge. "Of course she can." she said and walked behind the counter to grab me by the arm. She pulled me along so we were standing out the back door of the shop.

"What is this all about, Amanda?" I asked.

She crossed her arms. "You realize that you have Spencer in a state of panic, right?"

"I'm sorry about that." I said.

"Then, why are you not with him?" She sounded angry.

I looked at her and pulled at the sleeves of my green shirt. "I can't have the possibility of him getting hurt again because of me." I said and took a deep breath. "I can't do that to him. He's too selfless. Spencer's going to get himself killed because of me."

Amanda sighed and rolled her eyes. "He's only like that because he loves you."

"I know that. It's hard enough for me without everyone hammering me about it." I said and my voice broke. "I'm sorry. I just can't do it."

"Is this because of what Jeff said?"

"Partly, I guess. He's right. I shouldn't have lived." I said.

"Then, your father's death would have been in vain, Penelope. He died so you could live." Amanda said.

My throat tightened. "How did you know about that?"

"Spencer told me." she said.

I shook my head. "It doesn't matter." I brushed off my shirt. "That has nothing to do with Spencer."

"Maybe not, but I don't understand. You fought so hard to be with Spencer and now you're just up and leaving him? This isn't how it should end." Amanda said.

"This *is* how it's ending, so just let him know that I'm sorry that it sucks so much." I said and my voice broke.

"What will it take to get you to go with me to the hospital? You want a job, a new place to live? I can get you whatever you want." Amanda said. Her voice was desperate. She really cared about Spencer and I knew it. It wasn't the way I did. He was like a brother to her.

I didn't answer her.

She nodded. "So, this is how you're going to be?" she asked and pulled the handcuffs off her belt. She put the cuffs on my wrists behind my back. "Penelope Crowder, you're under arrest for the murders of Jacob Maslin and Robert Osman."

I cringed at the sound of that. I knew that she had to come up with a reason to take me away with her, but I hated to think about killing those two.

"Is this really necessary?" I asked.

"You refused to come so I have a reason to make you." Amanda said. She pushed me through the back door.

"It's about time, Penel—" The manager froze in his words. "What's going on?"

I didn't answer and Amanda pushed me out to her car. She loaded me into the backseat.

She got into the car and started driving immediately.

"Amanda, I don't want to see him." I said.

"I know that, but he wants to see you and he told me to get you there kicking and screaming if I had to." Amanda said.

I decided that once she let me out of the cuffs at the hospital, I'd make a break for it. I'd figure it out when I saw what I had to work with there.

We got to the hospital and Amanda surprised me when she started leading me into the hospital by my elbow with my hands still cuffed.

"You're not letting me out of these things?" I asked.

"I'm not that stupid, Pen." she said and led me through the hospital. This was worse than working at the pizzeria.

"God, this is humiliating." I said.

"It's your fault you didn't come by yourself." she said roughly.

We got to Spencer's room and Jeff was just outside the door. He had two coffee cups so I assumed he'd gone to get the coffee. The door was opened.

"What did you do now, Penelope?" he asked. His voice was rough and unfriendly.

"I didn't do anything." I said.

Amanda pushed me through behind Jeff.

Barely anyone was still there. Brenda, Jeff, Allison, and Charity were the only ones still in the room.

I looked at Spencer. He was looking right at me. He looked like himself again. He didn't look weak or hurt. He just looked like Spencer. The same Spencer that I'd loved in fifth grade. The same Spencer I'd fallen in love with at seventeen.

I swallowed hard.

"Where have you been?" he asked. His voice was a bit weak.

I didn't answer at first.

Spencer looked at his family. "Why don't you guys go do something for a while? I need to talk to Penelope."

Everyone agreed and Jeff stared me down.

Spencer chuckled and looked at Amanda. "You didn't have to handcuff her."

"She wasn't going to come any other way." Amanda said.

"You can go too. I just need to talk to her alone." Spencer said.

After Amanda left—and didn't take the cuffs with her—it was silent at first.

Spencer saw my uniform. "You went back to your old job?" he asked.

I nodded. "My apartment was still open, too." I said.

"That's what Allison told me. Why? Tell me that she actually lied to me." Spencer begged.

I swallowed and didn't reply.

"What's wrong with us? You seem so happy all of the time when we're together. Why does it suddenly have to end?" he asked.

My tears spilled on my cheeks. "You were so close to being dead because of me. You always put yourself on the line for me."

"I love you. What was I supposed to do? Let them all kill you?" he asked.

I nodded.

"Penelope, did someone say something to you?" Spencer asked.

I would have lied, but I couldn't. I nodded.

"What did they say?" he asked.

"I should have died. No one would have missed me. He said that I killed you. It was my fault that you were dead." I said and bit my lip.

"Who the hell said that?" he asked, obviously angry.

I shook my head. "It doesn't matter." I took a shaky breath. "It's true, you know. I should never have lived."

"Don't ever say that, Pen." Spencer said sternly.

"No one would have missed me. I don't have anyone to miss me other than you. If I would have been killed at Gene's party, no one would have noticed I was gone." I argued.

"That is not true and you know it." Spencer said.

"No, I don't, Spencer." I said. "I can't keep risking you like this. You're in this bed because of me." I tried to calm myself down.

"I would have noticed. I don't know what I would have done if I had lost you that night." Spencer said.

"You would have moved on." I said.

"You don't know what happened when I heard that that scumbag was coming after you." he said.

"Yes, I do." I said and I would have crossed my arms, but they were cuffed behind my back.

Spencer looked confused. "What?"

I remembered that I'd never told him. "Um . . . I had this kind of dream thing of the day that Jacob came after me. I was seeing it from your point of view. I could feel what you did." I said.

"When was this?" he asked.

"It was the day that I got into the fight." I said.

"That long? You never told me about this!" Spencer said angrily.

"I thought you would find it creepy." I said and shook my head. "I'm sorry, okay? I have to get back to work." I said.

Spencer bit the inside of his lip. "Is this really how it's going to end?"

I swallowed. "I'm sorry."

Spencer sighed. "I just want you happy. If this makes you happy, go with it."

I could tell it hurt him to say that. He looked hurt.

"Just think about how good your life was before me. Your whole family was so united and good. You were happy just doing what you wanted. Just think about that and it won't be so bad." I said and remembered how my life was before him. I was only working in a dinky pizzeria and looking for another job to support my little barely-able-to-support-one-person, mouse-filled apartment. I had been miserable.

"I highly doubt that will help." he said.

I took a shaky breath as my lip trembled. "I'm so sorry, Spence." I said and stood up. I kicked the bottom of the door and Amanda opened it. She un-cuffed me and drove me back to work. She made up some story to tell my boss. I went right back to work.

"You should really work on trying to not get in so much trouble, Crowder." The manager said.

"I'm sorry." I said and sniffled.

"What's wrong with you?" he asked.

I just shook my head. "It's just allergies, Sir." I said.

"Better be."

By the time I got home, it was pretty late. I'd had to walk home in the pouring rain. I was cold and tired and I just wanted to go to bed. I'd been up for two days in a row.

I showered and went right to bed . . . alone.

TWENTY-FIVE

SEPTEMBER 14TH

I woke up and went straight to job hunting. I came up with nothing sadly.

I called Weston and it turns out that all of my former-friends were all still in the area, taking a year off. I asked him to bring everyone here.

When a knock came on the door, I left everyone in.

I held out my hand to Colleen. "My name's Penelope. You're Colleen, right?" I asked.

She smiled and nodded. I knew she'd play along.

I turned to Josh. "And you're Josh." I said. He burst into laughter.

I told the entire story of the past year.

"Oh, yeah. I'm completely broke and have to work at this dumb pizza place for money to support this filthy apartment by myself. I live by myself because my dad was killed and I can't be with my guard anymore." I explained.

Josh, Colleen, and Jayden all had their mouths hanging open.

"You and Spencer broke up?" Weston asked.

I nodded.

"I shouldn't ask?"

I shook my head.

"You said you can do that healing thing?" Josh asked.

"Yes, I did." I answered.

"Do you mind showing us?" he asked.

"Who's willing to volunteer?" I asked.

Jayden looked around and stood up.

I nodded and walked out to the kitchen. I grabbed the sharpest knife I had and grabbed his forearm. I looked up at him. "Fair warning: this is gonna hurt for a couple seconds." I said.

Jayden smiled and shrugged.

I traced the knife down his forearm, elbow to wrist. He cringed and drew in his breath in a hiss. I grabbed his bloody forearm and healed it. I grabbed mine and dropped the knife.

Everyone's jaws dropped again.

"Weston?" I asked.

"Yeah?"

"Can you get me a dark towel from underneath my sink?" I asked.

He ran out and grabbed one. I pressed it to my arm and swallowed.

"Are you all right?" Jayden asked. "That's pretty deep. Maybe we should get you stitches."

"It will be healed in no time. Don't worry." I said.

Once I was all healed up, Josh spoke.

"You know, you could stay with me for a while. I'm not sure this place is inhabitable." Josh said.

"Really?" I asked and laughed. "I just cleaned." I said.

"Really. Pack up your stuff. You're coming home with me, Young Lady." he said, laughing.

"I really appreciate that." I said. I threw out the towel quickly.

"So pack! Now!" he shouted.

I went and grabbed my little bag and my savings. Jayden carried my bag for me and loaded it into Josh's trunk.

"I guess we're all going to Josh's after this?" Colleen asked.

I really made the apartment guy mad when I left a day after I returned.

We loaded into Josh's car. Of course Jayden sat up front with Josh. Weston and Colleen sat in the back and I sat beside them against the door.

We arrived at Josh's house and he called his parents to let them know I was staying there.

"The guest room is beside Josh's bedroom. I'll show you." Jayden said while Josh was on the phone. I followed him and unloaded my bags into the drawers. The room was amazing. It was pretty big and had two dressers and a closet. The bed was probably a queen size.

"This is bigger than my whole apartment." I said and laughed.

"Pretty close." Jayden said. He didn't sound amused like his usual self

I pulled my eyebrows together. "What's wrong?" I asked.

"Oh, it's nothing." Jayden said.

"It's something." I said.

Jayden swallowed. "It's just that, sometimes, Josh doesn't know what he wants and I'm just scared that he'll start rethinking us and try to come to you. I mean, I'm totally gay, but you're really hot."

I shook my head. "Josh loves you. Don't get to worrying." I said.

"Are you sure?" Jayden asked.

"Of course I am."

"Can you just talk to him for me? Maybe just hint at it?" he asked.

"Yeah, but I'm sure he'll say the same thing I did." I insisted.

"You can never know." he said, shrugging.

We went back down to the living room. I had to get ready for work so I left and everyone promised to stay until I got off.

"We aren't gonna have any cops today, are we?" the manager asked when I got there.

"No, Sir."

"Good. We don't need all the negative attention." he said and slapped a huge party order for six in the morning tomorrow on my counter.

"This is gonna take forever!" I shouted.

"Well, I hope you don't have plans." He left the kitchen and headed to the office. No one was on duty to help me.

I called Josh and let him know that I'd be late. He told me not to worry. I was going to worry though. I was working overtime and not getting paid any more. I should have taken Amanda's job offer.

I was only done half the order by the time my shift was supposed to end.

Now, I remember why I hated this life.

After another four hours, I headed home. Josh had sent everyone home. I apologized for being so late. He just told me to get a shower and not to worry about it. I headed up and did as told.

I went to my bedroom and tried to relax my sore shoulders. I rubbed over them roughly.

"Are you sore?" Josh asked from the doorway.

I nodded. "Being back to work has been a little rough." I said.

He sat on the bed next to me. "Let me help you." he said and worked his thumbs into my shoulders. It hurt, but definitely in a good way.

"That really feels good." I said.

He moved my damp hair to the side and kissed my neck. I jumped away from him. "What are you doing?" I shouted.

Josh looked like a little kid that had just been caught. "I'm sorry, Penelope. It's just . . ." he hesitated.

"It's just what?" I asked.

"Jayden and I have been dating a long time. I'm just not sure if he's what I want forever." Josh said. He gave me a once over. "And I can't complain about you."

"Josh! You're gay!" I shouted.

"Yeah, but maybe I just want to be sure. I wish I could just get a day pass to be with a girl and find out." He paused. "I'm sorry."

I swallowed. "Just one day?" I asked.

"Yeah, you know, an experiment." he said.

"You're going to have to tell Jayden sometime." I said.

"I swear I will." Josh said.

"You're absolutely sure about this?"

"Absolutely." He looked me down again.

He kissed me on my lips hard. I kissed him back even though I felt nothing. I let him have his fun. He kissed me and touched me everywhere. I let myself like the physical feeling, but there was nothing emotionally except for a brotherly love.

He lay in the bed next to me, both of us panting. His shirt had come off sometime during all of this. I mean, I could never complain about Josh's kissing skills. Obviously, he was more experienced than I was.

"Yep, I am definitely gay." he said, laughing.

I smiled. "Good, you and Jayden are amazing together."

He looked at me. "No offense, Sweetie, but I'm never kissing you again. It was not as good as I expected."

I laughed. "Thanks, Josh. That really elevated my self-esteem."

"Don't let it get you down. I'm gay." he said with a laugh.

"I know." I said.

"What ever happened with you and Spencer?"

I sighed. "He was in too much danger." I said.

"What do you mean?" he asked.

I explained everything quickly.

"Wow." he said. "But, I thought you loved him."

"I do. That's why I left him. If I didn't, he would have gotten hurt worse than I already have done to him." I said.

"But, he just wants you safe."

I rolled my eyes. Everyone said that.

"That's not the point. I don't want him hurt because of me." I said.

"Penelope, he's protective. That is not a bad thing. He's going to come right back once he can." Josh said.

"Guess it's good I'm here, huh?" I asked.

"You can't just run away from him. He's a cop. He'll find you." Josh said.

"I don't have a choice, Josh. I just want him safe. If I don't run from him, he's going to get himself hurt again. I just can't let that happen." I said.

"I know that, but maybe that's all over. Maybe you'll live safe, happy lives now."

"I don't think that will ever happen, Josh." I said.

He shrugged. "It could."

We talked for a little while longer and then, I sent him to bed.

TWENTY-SIX

I'd lived with Josh for two weeks now and he had yet to tell Jayden about our one unfaithful night. I always nagged Josh about it.

Allison had called me a week earlier and told me that Spencer had been discharged. She just figured I'd want to know that he's all right.

I found Josh that morning. He'd been avoiding me because I knew Jayden was coming over later that day.

"You're going to have to tell him." I said.

Josh sighed. "He's going to be so mad."

"Maybe for a little while, but now he won't be so paranoid that you're going to cheat on him again." I said.

Josh groaned. "I always hated cheaters. Now I am one. Ugh!" he shouted.

"At least now you're sure." I said.

"I cheated on my boyfriend with a girl which just makes it even worse! Penelope, what if he hates me? What if he thinks I'm going to do this whenever you're here?" Josh asked.

"He won't. Just explain to him." I said.

Josh's mom came downstairs. I'd already met his parents and they were pretty cool. I mean, they were really catholic, but they didn't reject Josh for being gay. They didn't seem to mind that he was with Jayden either which only made it easier.

"When's Jayden coming?" she asked Josh. She looked just like him. She was on the shorter side with shoulder-length, dark hair.

"I'm not sure." Josh said and rubbed his eyes. He was still losing sleep over this. He was terrified that Jayden would be so mad and leave him.

"Are you going to tell him today?" she asked. She knew about Josh and me since she walked in on us talking one night.

Josh swallowed and nodded. "I can't believe I did this to him. He didn't do anything wrong and I just went off with a *girl*!"

"Calm down, Sweetheart. I'm sure if you explain, he will understand." his mom said and sipped at her coffee.

"I'm not sure." He shook his head. "If he leaves me, I don't know what I'm going to do. He was the first guy I even found some kind of interest in. He's my best friend."

I put my arm around his shoulder. "Don't worry, Josh. He was so worried that you weren't really gay that I don't think he'll care that we kissed a little."

"Maybe, but I'm just so worried." he said.

"You don't know what's gonna happen if you don't try." I said.

A knock came on the door and Josh's breathing practically stopped. "Oh, God."

"I'll get it." I said and walked to the door. As I opened it, Jayden smiled warmly at me. His dirty-blond hair was tousled everywhere.

"Where's Josh?" he asked, obviously worried that Josh hadn't opened the door.

"He's in the kitchen." I said.

Jayden walked to the kitchen and Josh was nearly shaking. "What's wrong?" Jayden asked him.

Josh's lower lip trembled. "You're going to be so mad at me."

"What happened?" Jayden asked, growing a bit anxious himself.

Josh started explaining and crying all at the same time. I could barely understand a word, but obviously Jayden heard every word.

"Oh, my God." Jayden said through his teeth. I couldn't tell if he was angry or hurt or even both.

"I'm so sorry." Josh said.

Jayden shook his head. He looked at me. "Can you excuse us a moment?" Jayden asked.

"Yeah, I have to go to work anyway." I said.

Josh looked at me. "Do you need my car?" he asked.

"No, I'll walk." I said.

I went up to my bedroom and put my curly hair into a pony tail at my chin. It hung over my shoulder. I put on my work shirt and left. At least it was a nice day.

When I got to work, there was another party order that I had to do. I started rolling out the dough and everything and didn't bother complaining. It wasn't going to help. This always happened when I was the only one working, too. I was used to it . . . at least I used to be.

I was rolling out more dough when the door rang open I looked up and saw a familiar face. Why was Spencer here?

I looked at him. "Go home, Spencer." I said.

He stood with his hands in his jean pockets. He was actually smiling at me.

"You look tired." he said.

"Yeah, I am." I said and swallowed. My heart picked up speed quickly. "How did you find me?"

"I went to your old apartment and the guy said that you moved out so I got out of Amanda where you worked. I've been here once every day for three days." he said.

The manager walked out and looked at me. "I'm not paying you to sit around and chat, Penelope. Get back to work."

I nodded. "Yes, Sir."

Spencer ripped out his badge and held it out for the manager. "She can talk."

The manager rolled his eyes. "How many cops are you gonna have in here? You know that you can't work here with a criminal record."

"I don't have a criminal record!" I shouted. He was frustrating me so much.

He looked at Spencer. "Then, why are you here?"

"I need to talk to Penelope." Spencer said.

"About?"

Spencer looked at me. "That's confidential."

The manager looked at me. "Take all the time in the world. You're fired."

My jaw dropped. "I didn't do anything wrong."

"Obviously, the cops think you did, so just go." he said.

I took off the ugly apron and sat it on the counter. I walked out from behind the counter and stood with Spencer. "Happy?" I asked.

"Not at all." he said.

I raised an eyebrow. "What are you talking about?"

"I haven't been happy at all. I know you haven't either or you wouldn't have so much trouble sleeping." Spencer said.

I shook my head.

"Get out of here, both of you!" the manager shouted.

Spencer smiled. "He's very demanding."

"You're telling me." I said.

We walked out of the store.

"Can I just go home? I'm not in the mood to talk." I said.

"Well, I need to talk to you. I haven't even been allowed to leave the house for two weeks and Allison has refused to give me any contact to you." he said.

"This was my decision, Spencer."

"I know that. You just aren't as happy as you thought you'd be."

"I knew I wouldn't be happy." I said grimly.

"I hope you know that it's been hell for me." Spencer said. I could tell he was exhausted.

"And, I'm really sorry about that. But, I can't keep putting you in danger." I said.

"Who told you that? You still haven't told me." Spencer said.

"You can't get mad." I said.

"Fine. I won't be mad." he said.

"Your dad didn't really *tell* me. I overheard him talking about me with your mom." I said and took a deep breath. "They were right."

"My dad?" he asked, a bit shocked.

I nodded. "I'm sorry."

He took a deep breath. "I guess it doesn't matter."

"Yes, it does." I said.

"We can argue about this all day and you know that I'm going to win, Penelope."

"I'm not going back with you, Spencer. It's been hard for both of us, but I can't do this to you. I've been putting you in danger for too long and it was all because I was selfish." I said.

"Then, I'm being selfless and I don't care. I love you, Pen. You know that. We fought to be together and it paid off. You are so much more miserable without being with me." Spencer said and put his arms around my waist. "I know you hate that job and I know you hated that little apartment and being alone! Just listen to what I have to say."

I swallowed. "Fine, I'll listen."

He took a moment to get himself together. "Penelope, you know that I love you."

I nodded.

"You know that I've put my life on the line for you more than once."

Another nod.

"That isn't your fault. If I didn't want to do it, I wouldn't have. You're more important to me than anything that I could get if I didn't have you. You're my best friend and the most amazing person I've ever met. I know that you think you're so flawed, but I honestly couldn't care less about those little things. You know that I'm not the perfect person either, and I know you accept that. You've dealt with all of my family's disapproving thoughts and outbursts and you dealt with it because you love me. You told me to think about this life I had before you, and I did. I thought about all the luxuries and amazing life that anyone would have killed to have. You know what I realized?"

I shook my head.

"Nothing could have compared to the messed up, complicated time I've spent with you."

"Spencer." I said and my voice broke.

"Let me say one last thing." He paused. "Don't take this the wrong way."

"Okay, yeah." I said and nodded.

"I love you and I want you to be my first and my last." he said.

My breath caught in my chest. "Spencer, are you sure? I mean, that's huge."

He kissed my forehead. "I wouldn't have said it if I hadn't meant it, Pen."

"Aren't you looking for that special girl to share it with?" I asked as a million emotions flooded through me.

"I think I've already found her." he said, smiling. He bent and hesitated a moment before pressing his lips to mine. I kissed him back timidly.

"Why don't we go home; you're real home?" Spencer said.

"Spencer, I left for a reason." I said roughly.

"And you kissed me back for a reason. That's a better reason." Spencer said and laced his fingers through mine. I felt the cool metal on my skin. I looked down at his hand.

"You're still wearing the ring." I said, smiling.

"I put it back on the second I could." He looked down at my eyes. "It reminded me of you."

I felt myself blush. All of me filled with a warm, satisfied feeling. "You really missed me, huh?"

"Of course I did." he said. "You thought I wouldn't?"

"I knew you would, but I didn't think that much." I said.

"I don't want to miss you anymore." Spencer said. "Just come back for a few days. I'll show you that it's safe now."

"Let's not argue about this now." I said.

"Then, just come home. I have a place of my own that only five minutes from my parents'." he begged.

I looked at Spencer. "I need to stop at Josh's to pick up my stuff."

Spencer smiled. "Thank you so much, Pen." He put an arm around me. "Let's go." He opened the car door for me.

I led Spencer to Josh's house and I noticed that Jayden's car was still there, so, obviously, it hadn't gotten too bad.

"Be careful coming in. Josh and Jayden had a huge fight." I said.

Spencer raised an eyebrow. "What was that about?"

I bit my lip. "I'll tell you later."

We went in and Jayden was leaning against the counter. Josh had obviously calmed down. He was leaning on the opposite counter than Jayden. His eyes were red like he just stopped crying.

They both turned to look at me as I walked in.

"Is everything okay?" I asked.

Jayden nodded. "It will be." he said. He chuckled. "You know, in an odd way, you definitely helped us. You did what I asked, just, in a very different way. But, I still appreciate it."

"Don't worry about it." I said.

"Did someone come in with you?" Josh asked.

I smiled. "Actually, yes." I said.

Josh raised an eyebrow and smiled. "Who is it?"

I pulled Spencer over gently by his hand.

Josh's eyes widened and he laughed. "I should have been able to guess."

I explained that I was leaving and he congratulated me and told me that I needed to come see him again. I agreed and gathered my things. Spencer just sat and waited for me. When my bag was packed, he wouldn't let me carry it. He did it for me.

When we left, Spencer actually let me drive. He showed me the way to the new house. It was a two floor gray house with a large window on the second floor.

My jaw dropped. "How do you afford this?" I asked.

"I have a special agent's salary, Pen. This is cheap living for me." Spencer said.

I laughed. "Of course it is."

We went inside and Spencer set all my stuff in his bedroom. He came back down and I was exploring the kitchen. Every room was huge.

"Like it?" Spencer asked.

"It's huge." I said.

"Not really. Your apartment was just really small." Spencer said, smiling.

"I guess so." I said.

"By the way, Allison did her best to keep me away." he said.

"I know. You would have found me sooner if she hadn't." I said, laughing. I turned around and he put his arms around me so I could wrap mine around his neck. "I'm sorry. I know you don't understand why I left, but I'm sure you would have if you were in my position."

"Probably, but you're not going to keep me away." he said.

"You are totally setting yourself up to get killed by being with me, you know that?" I asked.

He leaned down and kissed me softly. He pulled back just enough to speak against my lips. "I don't care. If I have to have myself risk dying for us to be happy, I'll do it."

"Why?" I asked. I felt as if I would do that same for him, but I never thought that any man, let alone Spencer, could feel like that for me.

"Because I love you." he said. He ran his fingers through my hair and pulled out the pony-tail gently. It fell over my shoulder. "You need some sleep. I can tell you haven't slept very often."

"You haven't either." I said.

He shrugged. "I'm used to it." he said.

"Come and get some sleep." I said and pulled him with me.

I headed to the bathroom to change into sweatpants and go to bed. Spencer was already in bed. The lights were off and it was almost completely dark. I had to feel my way there. When I did, I just lay down and Spencer pulled me close. I settled into his body.

"I've missed this." I said quietly.

"Me too. It's been forever." he said.

"It has." I said and laced my fingers with his.

"I'm going to visit my mom tomorrow. Do you want to come?" he asked.

"If you want me to I can." I said.

"Of course I do."

"Do you think Brittany would do my hair if I asked?" I asked.

"Yeah, she still wants to pay you back for healing her." he said.

"She doesn't need to. I didn't do it to get repaid. She didn't deserve that." I said and swallowed hard. No one would have deserved to get shot just because they were in the wrong place at the wrong time.

"Neither did you, Pen. You didn't deserve any of this." he said.

"I didn't deserve you." I said.

He sighed. "That, you did. You've been so brave through everything and you tried your best to help us in every way that you could. You even saved my life."

"I didn't even think you were alive or I would have come sooner." I said.

"I never would have let you come after me." he said.

I chuckled, remembering Amanda saying the same thing. "I know."

"Amanda shouldn't have."

"I talked her into it. She didn't have a choice. I was either going to go with a gun or without one. She didn't want me out there, defenseless." I said.

"Can I ask you a question?" he asked.

"Of course you can."

"Did you kill Rob?" he asked.

I tensed up. I hated talking about this. I had taken two human lives. I hadn't just witnessed it. I had done it.

"Pen, it's okay. I know it's not fun, but it'll be okay." Spencer said and rubbed his palm down my upper arm.

"No, it won't. Both of them are *dead*. Their entire life is gone. I'm the one that stopped them from even, maybe, righting their wrongs." I said and took a deep breath.

"Pen, they killed hundreds of innocent people." Spencer said.

"It's still hard." I said and my voice broke. "I am so sick of always crying." I muttered.

"It's all right to cry. It helps you feel better." he said.

"I'll never feel better about killing those two." I said softly.

"I know, Sweetheart. I'm sorry you had to go through all of this. It shouldn't have happened." Spencer said.

"Can we not talk about it?" I asked.

"Okay. Go to sleep, Pen. I love you." he said calmly.

"I love you, too." I said.

His grip tightened just a little. He kissed my neck gently and I took in a deep breath. Soon, I was fast asleep.

TWENTY-SEVEN

SEPTEMBER 29ᵀᴴ

W e both woke up early and got ready to go over to Spencer's mom's house. Amanda had called Spencer late that night and told him to stop in with her afterward.

Spencer even let me drive. We arrived at his parents' house in a matter of minutes. Everyone was happy to see me, except Jeff.

"I'm so happy you're okay." Brenda said and hugged me. "I was so worried when you left."

Jeff exited the room quickly and quietly. I knew that he didn't want me here. He'd never want me anywhere near his family.

Spencer sighed. "Go talk to Brittany and I'll take care of my dad."

I agreed and Brittany started on my hair. She had finished trimming the split ends when the yelling started.

"Fine, If you're going to be with that trash, you need to leave, right now." Jeff yelled.

"Dad, be reasonable." Spencer said calmly.

"I warned you already! Get out and don't come back until she's gone!"

The door slammed loudly.

Brittany sighed. "He's so stubborn." she said.

Spencer came in as I stood up. He kissed my forehead. "Your hair looks good, Pen."

I looked at him. "I can go if you want me to. I'll head back to the house."

"No, it's fine. He'll get over it." he promised.

Ally came into the kitchen and smiled. "How about I steal you for a while? Mom's watching Charity."

I looked at Spencer. He shrugged. I smiled. "Yeah, let's go." I looked at Spencer again. "Are you coming?"

"I'm gonna stay and talk to my dad." He kissed me once. "I love you."

"Love you, too." I said.

We took Allison's new Ford Focus. She'd gotten it because her other car hadn't had a back seat for Charity.

"Spencer nagged you enough to come back?" Ally asked.

"There wasn't really any nagging. He begged a little, but he never nagged." I said.

We went to the movies and then went shopping. When we were in the mall, we ran into Amanda. She looked frantic.

"I'm so glad I found you!" she said.

"What did you need to talk to me and Spencer about?" I asked. I remembered her call to Spencer to stop by.

"Is he here?"

"No, he's not right now." I answered.

"You need to be with him."

"Why?" I was suddenly really confused. I thought we were through with this body guard stuff.

Amanda swallowed. "They're still after the Elite. We didn't find out until last night when another was killed."

"What? That's impossible. Rob's dead." I said. Ally tensed behind me so I put a hand on her arm.

"Just because Rob's dead doesn't change the way the rebels feel. They're still killing the Elite."

"No, Amanda. Rob was the mastermind."

"Well, they found a new one and they're being sloppy. They're bringing out the brutal killings from years ago. They aren't after you yet, but they will be."

"Have you told Spencer?" I asked as fear rose in my throat.

"Not yet."

I was panicking inside, but I was trying to hide it. They were still trying to kill me. They were still after all of us.

Until we all were dead, there wouldn't be a way out.